dying

light

Kory M. Shrum

TIMBERLANE
PRESS

ISBN-10:0-9912158-8-5

ISBN-13:978-0-9912158-8-1

Praise for the Jesse Sullivan Novels

"Kory Shrum's writing is smart, imaginative, and insanely addictive! I have begun to think of her books as my Kory Krack. I beg of you to pick them up. You will NOT regret it!" —Darynda Jones, NY Times Bestselling Author of the Charley Davidson Series

"Sexy, snarky, and supernaturally fantastic! This one has it all!" —Angela Roquet, acclaimed author of the *Lana Harvey, Reapers Inc. series*

"Twists, turns, and surprising endings–Jesse Sullivan marks a new era in urban fantasy." —Monica La Porta, Author of *The Ginecean Chronicles* and *The Immortal series*

"This book is filled with a cast of interesting characters … and a fat pug named Winston—all helping to solve the mystery around {Jesse Sullivan's} attack—and you have a fast-paced story, and a great start to the series!" —LG O'Conner, author of the *The Angelorum Twelve Chronicles*

"Jesse makes a living by dying in other people's place because she's a Necronite and comes back to life. The whole Necronite condition was both interesting and creepy. The author did a great job of explaining it and making it real for the reader."—*Urban Fantasy Investigations*

"{Kory M. Shrum} writes Urban Fantasy which I truly believe will become the next BITTEN on TV… a series and an author whom we have special dedicated shelves to."—*Cabin Goddess Reviews*

"Urban fantasy gold!...This is a well written urban fantasy with a murder mystery, dark humor and a pug named Winston."—Sharon Stogner of *I Smell Sheep* Reviews

"I LOVE Jesse as a character. She's not your normal protagonist...she's not perfect, she makes mistakes, she's prickly, funny, and is a smart ass. She's got a past, and part of the fun in reading this book is unraveling the mysteries of Jesse and the Necronites (a rare 2% of the population who can be death replacement agents).—Rebecca Poole, *Dreams2Media*

"This is not your typical zombie story. It is complex but well told. Jesse is a fascinating and relatable character. She has secrets, and she has engaging friends who help her along the way, but there is also an element of not knowing quite who to trust." — A.B. Shepherd, author of *Lifeboat* and *The Beacon*

"What a fun read. I loved the whole idea of this story and it was well-executed. If you love urban fantasy, you're going to love this book." —A. Brantley, *A Girl and Her Kindle*

"What a great, original concept. A completely new take on the supernatural." —*Must Have Fiction*

For Kim

The Jesse Sullivan Series

dying light

Chapter 1

Jesse

"Come on," I wail. "Jumping out of a burning building is not the craziest thing we've ever done!"

"If you hadn't panicked, the building wouldn't be on fire," Ally snaps back. She tucks the bundled laptop under her arm and starts yanking open desk drawers. Post-it notes of every color fly through the air, followed by pens, a stapler, paperclips and a Kleenex box.

I search the open office space for another door. Nada. Only one way in and out.

"I had to do something." I thought firebombing the bad guy was my one good idea on this mission to retrieve a laptop for Jeremiah. "If I hadn't, we'd still be stuck with *him*."

We both turn our gaze to the locked door twenty feet away. A row of unoccupied desks rests between us and where we entered. The office is spacious, with rows of silver tabletops running the length of the room. Spacious—but not spacious enough with a homicidal maniac just on the other side of the door.

Something large slams into the locked office door, rattling the walls. Ominous black smoke seeps through the cracks and the smell of campfire wafts in. That smell is surely going to cling to my hair until I wash it.

"Just because we've been reckless before doesn't excuse it now." Ally slams a desk drawer shut and yanks another open. Her disheveled blonde hair hides most of her face, revealing only terrified eyes. She gives up trying to find a weapon in the desk drawer and hurries to the window. Her gaze falls on the street below. "God, Jesse. *No*. We'll never survive a fall from this height."

I shrug and pucker my lips. "It's fine. I've fallen from higher. We'll be fine."

She blinks at me.

"You're forgetting about my shield thingy." I'm talking out of my ass here, but there is no way I'm letting him come in here and hurt her. He can trade punches with me all day if he wants, but not with Ally. I'll have to find a way to break the window, jump out, and shield her on the way down.

The door shakes for the fourth time and a thick crack appears to the left of the jamb. A thicker plume of black smoke rolls through the crack and floats to the ceiling. The white popcorn tiles disappear beneath the black fog.

I go to the window and look through the glass beside her. The glass is cold under my palms and my breath fogs on the surface despite the growing heat of the room. Down below, tiny cars cut corners around buildings. One could easily be mistaken for a child's toy.

Shit, it really *is* far down.

I meet Ally's eyes and shrug. "We don't have a lot of options."

Sweat forms at my hairline and in the folds where my coat sits snug against my body. Chicago shines brightly around us, each pinpoint of light from the buildings and streets illuminating the dark sky.

My gaze flits from building to building, from illuminated window to illuminated window, but I don't see salvation. We aren't close enough to another skyscraper to signal for help. No scaffolding or window-washer platform is available to carry us to the safety of solid ground or to the roof above, where we were supposed to meet Jeremiah.

The coms in our ears buzz incoherently for the billionth time. Ally sighs in irritation. As the coms stop crackling she mashes the speak button flat with her thumb. "For the thousandth time, we can't understand you. Something is wrong with our signal. If you can hear us, we are on the 34th floor of the Jensen building and we're trapped. Send help." A look of resolution solidifies on Ally's face. "Jason's going to kill us."

"No." I squeeze her arm. "So what if he's like a hell-bent terminator with unlimited healing ability." I snort, trying to hide my panic. "I've got this."

She cocks her head. "It's great you have firebombs and shields but we have to be careful. We don't know the repercussions of your powers yet."

"And getting ourselves locked in burning buildings with raging madmen is playing it *so* safe."

"You know what I mean." She steps away from the window and shifts the laptop in her arms. She yanks open more office drawers.

I arch an eyebrow. "A paper cut isn't going to hurt him."

"Paper cuts hurt." She forces a smile. "But we need something to slow him down. And you're not helping."

I throw my hands up and pick an aisle of desks. After uselessly searching two drawers, I lift one of the office chairs and immediately know this flimsy, ergonomic piece of crap won't be able to break a window. I throw it anyway. It bounces off the glass and comes back at me with a vengeance, clipping my knee.

"Fuckity fuck! Ow. *Ow.*"

Ally looks up from the drawer and scowls at me. "Injuring yourself before he even breaks into the room is not what I had in mind."

I give her a hard stare, rubbing my throbbing knee and stumbling to another desk.

I have half a mind to remind her that it wasn't *my* idea to come to Chicago. I was happy in Nashville. Sure, my boyfriend Lane—ex-boyfriend—wasn't talking to me, but everything else was okay. The first time Jason, the insta-healing terminator tried to rip my head off, Ally had a fit. Jeremiah capitalized on it, of course.

Come to Chicago where it's safer. We have more people and more power there. And Caldwell is up to something in the city. We could really use the extra hands.

I just wanted to stay in bed and mourn Brinkley,

the man who'd given his life trying to kill Caldwell. Everyone else keeps acting like I'm supposed to be working here.

The crack in the door widens and I see an angry eye fix on me. Jason screams as if the very sight of me enrages him.

Gabriel appears at a desk two rows up from the one I'm searching. He flickers in and out, unable to hold his form with another partis—a weirdo with powers like me—nearby. He's crystal clear when I'm alone, but when there's two or more partis, I'm lucky if Gabriel can materialize at all. This is real inconvenient given that I need him most when the others show up looking for a fight.

"Here." Gabriel points at a giant rock sitting on top of one of the desks. "Use this."

No, not a rock, I realize. I place my hands on the massive stone. It's an amethyst the size of a grapefruit. Beside it sits a little note: *Don't touch me. Please. You'll change my energy.*

I look up, but Gabriel's gone.

I lift the rock off the desktop. It sinks into my palms like dead weight, the purple spikes poking my flesh. "Sorry, but I need your energy to club this fucker."

I meet eyes with Jason again as he inches his fingers through the crack and starts swiping at the locking mechanism we latched behind us.

"Get over here," I shout to Ally.

Ally makes it halfway across the room before the door explodes. Splinters the size of my leg fly at my face. I duck behind the desk, clutching the gigantic stone to my chest.

I peek over the tabletop and see Jason standing in the flames. His body smolders. His blistered arm melts from burnt to scabby to pink. He spots me behind the desk and we lock eyes. His face twists into a murderous grin.

"Stop hiding," he calls out. "Let's do this."

In my peripheral vision, Ally darts to another desk, staying low.

Jason takes a step toward me. "Just think, this power could be yours if you'd challenge me already."

"Fighting is such a commitment." I stand slowly, but keep the desk between us. I'm hoping it buys me time if he does anything crazy like lunge for my throat. "You have to get close. You have to touch people. Sometimes, like you, they *smell*. No, thank you."

Jason's face goes perfectly smooth. Was it something I said?

A flash of black wings catches my eye. Gabriel's still here, even if he can't materialize. The scent of rain overtakes me as Gabriel dials up my power. My muscles contract and my body warms. My skin starts to itch around the collar of my shirt and across my belly. I feel like I have to pee.

I try not to squirm. "You know who else is in the city? Caldwell. Why don't you kill him instead?"

Jason's face twists up in fury again. "After I'm finished with you."

"Why does everyone keep saying that?" I would put my hands on my hip if not for the giant amethyst. "Don't you think I'm a badass?"

"You're smaller."

My temper flares. "You're trying to kill me because I'm *short*?"

Ally coughs on the smoke filling the room and I jerk my head toward the sound. Jason doesn't hesitate.

"Jesse!" Gabriel's voice booms in my head.

My soul rips open, power exploding from my center in all directions. It's like someone is yanking my intestines out of my belly button. I'm so overwhelmed but I can't stop the power from flooding out of me or even slow it down.

Fire and smoke whoosh away from me as if blown by a great wind. The air around me shimmers like pavement on a hot day. Blue flames roll over the surface of my body, suspended about three inches above my skin before erupting outward toward Jason, the office around us and anything else in its path. The only object that is safe is the amethyst cradled in my hands.

The walls and ceiling shudder under the force of my firebomb, raining dust and plaster down on our heads. One minute the windows shatter, and glass spills out into the night air. The next minute cold winter air is sucked into the room.

I open my eyes and find Jason sprawled on the floor, unconscious. My power blast knocked him out, burned his skin, but didn't kill him. Damn.

I come around the desk, or what is left of it, and peer closer. His flesh is already healing.

I try to use my breath to slow my heart rate. I need to calm down, but my head is throbbing.

"Ally?"

No answer.

"Ally!"

"Here." She pulls herself to standing in the middle of a cluster of desks that had obviously been pushed together in the blast.

She shakes glass out of her hair and checks the laptop in her arms for damage.

"Kill him," Gabriel says in my ear. The weight of the amethyst doubles in my hands. "*Kill* him."

The idea of killing Jason and taking his healing powers appeals to me. Instead of having to die in order to heal myself, I could simply stay alive, and after a few breaths, be as good as new again. Wasn't that a hell of a prospect? Less pain. Less wasted time. Less danger for myself and the people around me.

I lift the amethyst, my eyes fixed on his skull.

"Jesse."

I lift the rock a little higher as a strange calm washes over me. No, more than calm. Peace tinged with excitement. Oh god, I *want* to kill him. I don't think I've ever wanted to kill anyone.

"*Jesse.*"

Ally's face appears in front of mine. Eye to eye, she blocks my view of Jason. "Baby." She's whispering. "We need to get out of here."

Her voice. Something about Ally's voice seeps into my mind and untangles my thoughts. The cold hand inside me, the one delighting at the idea of peeling Jason open and stealing his ability to heal, grows warm. Its hold on me slackens as her brown eyes come into focus. I can't murder someone in front of Ally. What the hell am I thinking?

My muscles relax and I let the amethyst slip from my fingers to the floor.

"Come on." Ally squeezes my shoulders. "Maybe we can crawl down the hall a little bit and find the stairs."

"No we can't go that way—" I don't finish my thought. The smallest movement steals my attention and I turn just as Jason snatches up the amethyst and throws it at Ally.

"No!" I scream as the rock sails through the air. "Gabriel!"

My shield goes up around Ally. The shimmery purple light envelops her from head to toe. The rock ricochets off the force field, shoots through the broken window and out into the night. Jason screams and runs at me, head down as if he might tackle me like some football player.

"Fuck this." I sidestep Jason and grab hold of Ally. Her shield falters just long enough for me to wrap her in my arms and yank her forward. Before she can process what is about to happen, I shove her out the big window and don't let go.

Her shriek is muffled by the wind whipping around us, tearing at our hair and clothes.

I suppose this is a perfectly natural reaction to your friend shoving you out of a high-rise building.

"It's okay." I squeeze her against my chest. "The shield will hold."

"Right?" I ask Gabriel.

"What about you? What about you?" Ally screams.

"You will not survive the fall." He plummets with us, his wings folding back to embrace the drop. "You must shield yourself."

"Ally lives, not me. We have a deal."

"You must shield yourself also."

"I don't know how. You have to help me."

"Envision it." Gabriel's wings open, lifting him up into the air. "See it grow larger."

The field shines about an inch or so above Ally's skin, it touches parts of me, but it sure as hell doesn't cover anything important.

"Hurry," Gabriel says. "See it around you."

I close my eyes and see us falling in my head. The building rushes past us. The freezing air tears at our clothes and hair relentlessly. Lights shine from windows in a blur as we pass. I picture my shield bigger. I picture it around me and Ally, covering us both from head to toe.

"Good. Do not stop now," Gabriel says.

I peek my eyes open to see purple has crept over my arms and shoulder, the shield half devouring my body—until pain erupts through my legs, my back, and the whole world goes black.

Chapter 2

Jesse

"How do you feel?"

I pry one eye open, then another. Jeremiah's blue collared shirt and gray sweater vest comes into view. I blink several times and his face sharpens. He's trimmed his beard, and his glasses reflect the overhead lights, making it impossible to see his eyes.

"I feel..." I begin, swallowing against a scratchy lump in my throat.

My head throbs and my neck is stiff and I'm pretty sure a flamenco dancer did a number on my lower abdomen. "I feel like someone had to dig a donkey out of my ass."

"You shattered your pelvis," Jeremiah says. "Your death healed it."

"What about the cat?"

Jeremiah frowns. "I wasn't aware of any feline involvement in the mission."

"I'm talking about the one that must've shit in my mouth." I moan and try to sit up. A nurse rushes over to help me. I don't recognize her, but that's nothing new. Jeremiah has a huge operation, and his minions all start to look the same after a while. "Can I get some water?"

The nurse returns carrying a tiny plastic cup.

I throw it back in one swig. "Thanks. And now that I've wet my lips with this, do you think it'd be possible to get a Big Gulp?"

The nurse scurries away again. Okay, so I'm a bit of an asshole when I first wake up, but I'm in a lot of pain. It isn't easy dying and coming back to life, you know. I die. I decompose a little. I slip into a coma state and heal most of the damage until my organs can sustain me. Then I wake up stiff as hell while my cells try to push the extra calcium out.

"You didn't ask about Alice." Jeremiah drags a seat to the side of my bed. The room is an exact replica of a hospital room, but I know better. This floor of Tate Tower, Jeremiah's headquarters, closely resembles a hospital, down to the weird beds, horrible fluorescents, and unnerving stringent smell. It's where he brings everyone who gets hurt.

I force a grin and lay back on my pillows. "Of course she's fine. I'm the best."

He'd have to break both my arms to get me to mention my hallucination by name. I kind of have the sense that Jeremiah knows I'm not quite right, but letting him speculate and informing him of just how crazy I am are two different ball games.

He regards me with an assessing stare. I've gotten used to these over the past two months. I'm getting really good at giving him the blank face too. Or better yet, I make faces and see how long it takes for him to look away. He's never amused, but I am.

I'm still pinning my nose up into a pig snout for Jeremiah's pleasure when the nurse arrives with my water.

"Thanks," I snort and accept the drink. I get half of it down in the first go. God, it feels good. I swear, it's like death sucks all the water out of me.

This is only my second death since Brinkley died in October, two months ago. When Jeremiah insisted that we come to Chicago where we would be useful and safe, I thought he would use me for more replacements. After all, that's what I do. I die so others don't have to. I'm good at it. But just like the last time

I died, Jeremiah looks pissed.

"Why didn't you kill Jason?"

I meet his eyes over the rim of my Big Gulp water. "Uh, because I'm not a murderer?"

"Caldwell has killed at least three partis and absorbed their abilities. Acquiring a second ability would be useful."

"You're still talking about killing someone."

Jeremiah steeples his fingers. "You need to be stronger if you want to take him on. You have your shield and your pyrokinetics, excellent abilities. But think of what you could do with Jason's ability to heal."

"When I die, I heal anyway. Too bad he doesn't have super strength or the ability to fly. That'd be cool."

And who said I want to take Caldwell on? Where did Jeremiah get that idea? I want Caldwell dead. I'd bring maracas and a kazoo to his funeral. But actually taking someone's life is a whole other matter.

Jeremiah prattles on, unaware that I've stopped listening. "Your mission—"

"Listen." I cock my head to the side. "I don't care about the missions. I *only* care about keeping Ally safe. She's the one who insists we help you, so here I am.

She seems to believe that you're saving all the babies from war-torn childhoods or whatever. So I get why she thinks the work you do is important. But don't act like my handler or my boss, because you'll never be either."

"Your handler was a good man, but—"

"Don't." Heat rises in my face.

Gabriel appears at the end of my bed, his feathers ruffled. His gaze is murderous and fixed on Jeremiah. Good. I don't like the guy either, but melting Jeremiah in his seat is a bit of an overreaction, even for me.

I release a nice controlled breath. Some of the tension in my chest loosens and Gabriel's own feathers lay flat. I breathe again, in and out, and Jeremiah arches a curious eyebrow.

"You'll thank me for not boiling your eyeballs in their sockets. Or ruining this year's argyle." I flick my eyes down to his sweater vest. Jeremiah's lips press into a thin line.

The heat of my anger cools and I try to speak like a civilized person. "You didn't know Brinkley, and you'll never replace him. If you insist on trying, I'm out of here and I'll take Ally with me. Got it?"

I have no idea if I can actually get Ally to leave this

place. She believes that Jeremiah is trying to help people and save all the orphans Caldwell is leaving in his wake. Until I can prove otherwise, I have to hold on to her coattails and keep her out of trouble. No thanks to Jeremiah.

Even if I can't prove Jeremiah is secretly evil, maybe I can prove her new girlfriend Nikki is a traitor, liar, or cheater. Anything horrible would make Ally never want to set foot inside Tate Tower again. Who cares about helping people?

A girl can dream.

"Understood," Jeremiah relents. "I *am* your friend, Jesse."

I consider making the pig nose again. The door opens and Ally appears, smiling, cradling forty pounds of pug against her chest.

"Winston. Come here, squishy." I reach for him and his cinnamon-bun tail wags, slapping Ally's arm. She plops my fat pug on the bed, and he pounces on my legs. "You want to get under the covers? Get under these covers."

I throw the covers over his head. He turns circles between my legs, nibbling on my fingers playfully as I poke him through the bedding.

"This is a sterile room." Jeremiah presses one finger against his temple.

"Uh, therapy dog. I *died*. You can't deny me some pug love."

Jeremiah stands, scrapping his chair back from the bed. He doesn't say goodbye or another word to us. He just disappears out the door.

Ally sits on the only part of the bed that isn't lumpy with legs or pug. "Are you bickering again?"

"He's riding my ass about not killing Jason."

Ally frowns.

"Brinkley never asked me to kill anyone," I say. "And here Jeremiah comes in trying to tell me what to do, and acting like offing people is totally normal. It's *so* not normal."

Ally's eyebrows scrunch up and her mouth flattens into a grim line. "I understand his argument. Killing Jason would make you stronger."

"Yes," Gabriel adds. He stands at the foot of the bed, arms crossed over his chest and pouting. A wing draped over each shoulder.

"You stay out of this, Gabriel." There is a momentary hitch where I'm worried someone has heard me say his name. But it's only Ally here, so I relax. My shoulder blades ease away from my ears.

"What did he say?" Ally asks, her brown eyes searching mine. I suppose I could be worried that anyone, even Ally, knows that I have conversations with my hallucination. My ex-mentor Rachel spent years in a mental hospital for this very reason. But I wasn't afraid around Ally.

"I prefer you don't hide it. In fact, please don't hide anything from me," Ally had told me once. "We promised, no more secrets."

I am doing my best to keep that promise.

"Three votes for offing Jason," I say. "It seems I'm outnumbered."

I scratch Winston's belly.

"Again, I'm not saying it's a good idea, but just think about it, Jess. If you had Jason's power, you could heal without dying. Doesn't that sound so much better?"

Buttloads better, I think, shifting my weight to relieve the deep, throbbing ache in my pelvis.

"You're the ultimate pacifist." I lean back into the pillows. "I can't believe you want me to off a guy."

"I don't." She tucks her straight blonde hair behind her ears. "Every time I think of you fighting, it makes me sick. But I also don't want Caldwell to have any more power."

"I agree," Gabriel adds, folding his arms over his pristine suit jacket. The black lapel lies exactly where it should without a fleck of dust on it. The tie changes from an emerald green to a fire engine red.

"Shut up, Gabriel. You're sadists. Both of you."

Ally smiles. "Says the person who pushed me out of a 34-story window."

She has a point.

I reach out and squeeze her hand. "How's your work going? Was the laptop helpful?"

"I don't know what Jeremiah is going to do with the laptop, but yes, we were able to place two girls, sisters, last night."

"You get so much done while I'm dead." I try to get comfortable on the pillows but it isn't happening.

She smiles. "You grew an entire pelvis cradle. You're hardly lazy."

"So tell me about these sisters." I want to keep her talking. Ally's voice is calming and it's a pleasant thing to focus on when really I want to mash the morphine drip button a hundred times. Maybe Jeremiah turned it off on his way out, the spiteful bastard.

"Caldwell has a four-person team that's been working the Louisiana death replacement circuit pretty hard. Nikki thinks they're looking for someone down there. Anyway, these girls had a mother with NRD. She was killed and the girls didn't have any other family. God, Jess, they were so poor. They barely had a chance to rebuild after Hurricane Katrina and then their mom is killed."

Tears well up in her eyes and I want to look away. I hate to see Ally cry. I squeeze her hand a little tighter as my gaze slides down to her shoulder, hopefully giving me a thoughtful look.

"We were able to find a wonderful couple in Philadelphia that wanted to take them in—both of them, which is great. I was so worried we'd have to separate them."

"They have you to thank," I remind her. "Alice Gallagher, protector of war babies."

She frowns and pulls her hand away. "I know you think what we're doing here isn't important."

"I never said that. I just hate these people, and I hate that we have to work with them."

"I know." Ally sits back in her chair. "But they have more resources than we do in Nashville. They are actually doing things to minimize the damage. We can't just pretend people aren't dying and go about our lives like everything is okay. We have to do what we can to help until—"

She stops. She looks almost apologetic as if what she intends to say next really is the worst thing ever.

"Until I kill Caldwell. And the sooner the better because that's fewer babies to find homes for."

She takes my hand again and squeezes. "He's your father, but no one holds you responsible for his actions."

Is that supposed to make me feel better?

"But they do expect me to use my gifts against him." They expect me to do what they can't. "If I don't try to stop him—if I don't *kill* him—then I'm not doing my part."

She searches my face. "Maybe there's another way."

Chapter 3

Jesse

Once Jeremiah's medical team stops hovering and Ally says goodnight, I scoop Winston up and carry him to the elevator. By the time I reach the silver doors, my back is throbbing. I set Winston on his feet and he looks up at me as if I've just stolen a treat right out of his mouth.

"I'm sorry, but I can't carry you. I hurt. Everywhere." I gesture at all of me and he cocks his head as if trying to understand. "Come on."

The illuminated red numbers descend, counting down to the hospital ward on the 8th floor, where I stand with the pug.

I shift my weight, trying to relieve pressure from one aching joint to another. I'm clenching and unclenching my jaw when the doors finally open. Winston follows me inside the small, warm space and I press the button that will take us to the rooftop terrace.

The doors ding open and an icy blast of cold air hits me. I suck in a breath, taking that moment to recognize the thinness of my hospital scrubs. I should've brought a coat.

"Sweet gee-*zus*." I squeeze myself and nudge the reluctant pug out of the elevator with my foot. "Do your business quick, and then let's go cuddle where it's warm, okay?"

Winston waddles over to the large patch of grass growing against a brick wall. Most of the roof looks like a park. I guess that's what you do when you build cities. You level all the trees and lay sod on the tops of buildings. The only problem is that 65 floors above Lake Michigan is way colder than any park on the Magnificent Mile.

I go to the edge of the balcony and look out over the water. It's midnight blue and vast as an ocean. It could be the ocean for all I know, complete with seagulls, a lighthouse, and waves crashing against the embankment. Little boats cut waves on the horizon, probably a patrol, given the white searchlight splashing over the rocks. In the city itself, Christmas lights have cropped up on a few of the buildings, blinking like red, green, and silver stars.

The icy December wind pulls tears from my eyes, freezing them against my cheeks.

I hate being cold.

It makes me miss home more than anything. It figures that as soon as I start to think of Nashville as home, I have to leave. Or maybe it's the fact that Christmas is on the horizon, which always makes me a little lonely.

Ally is usually good about making me feel special during the holiday season, but this year we breezed right through Thanksgiving without much thanks and Christmas is on the horizon with no hint of eggnog, or presents, or mistletoe.

I guess this is what happens when you have shitty parents and no family. Is it too much to ask for a father that buys me an iPad instead of one that only wants to get together so he can drug me and bury me alive?

What's your Christmas wish, Jess? Ally would ask this if we weren't so distracted. And what would I say?

I wish my father was dead. I wish that the other Highlander-wannabes would stop thinking I'm an easier target and stop trying to kill me. I wish they'd just kill each other instead and leave me out of it. I wish

I could find Rachel and know that she's okay. I wish Gabriel would finally explain to me what it is he expects me to do with all these firebombs and shimmery shields. I wish I could talk to Lane—at least one more time.

"Jesse!" Gabriel screams. His voice jolts my heart, and my shield brightens around me.

I whirl to find Caldwell standing behind me.

"Hello, Jesse," he says. His hands are in his pockets and his suit-tie ensemble is a soft gray with a red tie, and white shirt beneath. No doubt it cost a fortune and was tailored to fit him. "It's good to see you again."

My pulse thrums so loud, I'm certain he can hear it. Hell, maybe he can see it with his fancy new Liza vision. He only had to kill the partis girl to gain that ability, but some people seem to think that's not such a big deal.

"Speak of the devil," I say, trying to assume an air of casualness. "I was just thinking about what a terrible father you are."

He takes a step toward me, a little smile twisting up the side of his mouth.

I straighten my back. I can't look *tall* exactly, but

not appearing as pissing-myself-in-absolute-terror is good enough.

I manage not to glance at Winston. I want him to come to me. *Run* to me. I'm hyperaware that Caldwell is between me and someone I love—which has never ended well. I have no reason to believe this time will be different.

"It's been very difficult getting you to myself," he says. "Your friends have done a great job of keeping you locked away from me."

"I guess they don't want you to kill me. You know, *again*." I shift my weight for relief. "Funny how friends care like that."

Caldwell's smile widens. He's showing too many perfect white teeth. "They're doing a great job killing you all on their own, aren't they?"

I keep my face unreadable, expressionless.

"How many deaths have you had since that night in Minooka?"

Two, I think, with no intention of telling him. Instead, I inch a little closer to the pug rooting around in the bushes. I move and the camera by the elevator follows.

Please send someone. Send someone before this gets ugly.

Gabriel is quiet. If he's somewhere deep in my head trying to send warnings about Caldwell's intentions, I don't hear him. Caldwell watches me with the intensity of a snake trained on its prey.

"To be fair," I begin, keeping the pug in my peripheral vision. "I'm doing most of the dying all by myself. They try to keep me safe, but you know me. I've always played a little rough."

He smiles another devilish smile. "You come by it honestly."

"Do I?" I inch closer to the bushes. I try for nonchalance, hands in my pockets. "What's got you dying these days? Don't tell me you only do it as a beauty routine. I'm surprised Maybelline hasn't called you yet."

The fact that Caldwell is my father, but doesn't appear to be more than ten years older than me, means he has to be dying, but why? With all his powers, what in the world can kill this guy? I'd pay good money to know the answer.

"We all have our secrets," he says. A gust of wind rolling in off of Lake Michigan blows his hair into his eyes. He brings a pale hand up to brush it away, his gaze never leaving mine. "I'll give you my secrets if you give me yours."

I snort. I can't help it. What doesn't he know about me? The richest, most powerful man in the world could have any secret he wants on a plate, if he likes.

I cross my arms over my chest. "You probably know more about me than I do."

He cocks his head. "In many ways, I suppose that's true. But I don't know what your intentions are."

"My intentions?" *To get to my freaking pug and get off this roof.* He has to know Winston is the reason I'm up here. Maybe he has no interest in the dog, but I'm not taking any chances.

"Has he started showing you your choices yet?" Caldwell asks.

I know I must look as confused as I feel. "My choice of—?"

"The worlds." He moves closer, placing one shiny, polished shoe in front of the other. "Has he shown you the worlds?"

"Jesse." Gabriel's voice rises in warning, echoing in the back of my mind. "Be careful."

I get the impression of black wings flapping and a feather brushing my cheek, but Gabriel doesn't materialize.

Be careful of what? The lies? I already know Caldwell can mindfuck anyone with lies. So what? He doesn't need to play with my head. But I can't sense the danger. Caldwell can read my face as well as my mind, apparently.

"Not yet." A tightness strains Caldwell's voice. I'm not as good at reading people, so a look of doubt or fear can easily be mistaken for constipation. "If he intends for you to be the apex, then why hasn't he shown you the worlds?"

The elevator doors ding open and men with guns rush out onto the terrace. More men climb over the lip of the wall surrounding us.

"Freeze!"

Caldwell disappears from where he stood in front of me and reappears beside Winston near the bushes lining the sod. He snatches the pug up in one fluid movement.

"No!" I run across the rooftop toward Caldwell and he takes a step back, but doesn't disappear. I turn my back on him, probably the stupidest thing ever, and put my hands palm out toward the gunmen. "No. He's got my dog. Don't shoot my freaking dog."

I whirl on Caldwell. He's smiling, the bastard.

"Give him back. Give him back or I'll kill you."

Caldwell bites back his smile. "Maybe it'll be easier if I give you a reason. Wouldn't you be more willing to face me?"

"I feel plenty willing." And it's not like I don't have a thousand reasons to kill the man.

Brinkley. Just thinking of him makes my chest ache. Brinkley was the one good man in my life, and Caldwell snapped his neck like he was nothing.

Caldwell's malicious grin softens. He adopts a look of sincerity that I don't trust for a minute, not with Winston squirming in his arms.

"We need to talk." Caldwell keeps his voice low. "There are things going on that you can't possibly understand. And you can't be naïve enough to believe Mr. Tate will tell you the truth. I need you to come to me so you and I can reach an understanding."

"Put Winston down and I'll come with you now."

"No."

I swear Caldwell's trying not to smile.

"Fucking bastard, give me my dog."

Winston squirms, his little squished nose and big eyes pitiful. The heat rises in my chest and the air starts to glimmer around me. Gabriel's power builds, making it feel like my flesh is pulling away from my bones.

"If you blast me, you'll kill your own dog," Caldwell reminds me. "Pull yourself together."

His chastisement infuriates me more. I struggle to breathe.

He grins again, triumphant. "No, I think I'll make you work for it. Walk out of here on your own accord. Show me you deserve to know the truth. You'll find it harder than you think to get away."

What kind of mind game is this? "What about my dog?"

"He'll be safe," Caldwell says and takes a step away from me. "Your sister will look after him."

My sister? My mouth falls open, heavy with questions, but Caldwell takes another step back and is gone.

Gone—and so is Winston.

Chapter 4

Ally

I'*m a liar. I'm a liar. I'm a liar.*

The words replay in my mind. Okay, I haven't lied directly, but I'm certainly vague about my actions. Jesse, Nikki, and Jeremiah all believe I'm working the child placement cases and *only* the child placement cases. The fact that I haven't corrected them, that I allow them to believe what they want about my work, is certainly a deception.

I lay curled up in the bed I share with Nikki, my back against the headboard, laptop resting on my knees. The bed feels a little colder without her, but I'm making the most of my time alone.

On top of a pillow, I flip open Brinkley's journal and unfold the white pages inserted in the middle. Hundreds of names are listed there, including *Jesse Priority 2, Nashville*, second from the top. Brinkley took this believing it was Caldwell's hit list. He must've been right. It's taken all of my free moments in the last two months to whittle the names down to just a dozen— everyone has either turned up dead or gone missing.

I maximize the web browser window and read the article title again:

Monroe Dupree, 53, Takes Own Life Twice.

My finger slides down the first page and stops at a name near the bottom: *Monroe Dupree, Priority 18, New Orleans.*

The article includes a sad photo of a black man standing in front of a dilapidated house. Is this the man Caldwell's team is hunting in Louisiana? Is he a partis like Jesse and that is why Caldwell is searching him out?

I'm not foolish enough to believe that Caldwell's men just happened to be canvassing the town this man lives in. There is no such thing as coincidence where Caldwell is concerned. But I'm not in a hurry to rush in and save him either.

Jesse tried to save another partis, Liza, from Caldwell and Liza nearly killed her. I won't make the same mistake. I want to know who all the partis are— how many potential threats are lying in wait out there—and hopefully gain a better understanding of the situation.

But I can't tell Nikki or Jeremiah. What if they want to take these people and force them into the fight? Based on the article's depiction of the man, Monroe couldn't handle that. He's suffering a severe depression after the death of his wife. He's unsuccessfully tried to kill himself twice, once by hanging, once by train. A person like that doesn't need to be dragged into war.

The door beeps signaling Nikki's entry. I scoop up the laptop, journal and papers and shove them under the bed with one violent shove. Then I throw myself into the pillow and close my eyes.

My heart is still hammering when I feel the press of a kiss on my cheek, then my neck, and then my collarbone. She conforms her body to mine, spooning me.

"Nicole Tamsin," I say in mock reproach. "Don't you know better than to wake a sleeping lady?"

I hope she can't hear my pounding heart or the unevenness of my breath as Nikki stretches beside me. She brings one hand to rest on my belly so that I'll roll over to face her. She has the cheekbones and pouty lips of a model. Her beautiful blue eyes crinkle at the corners as she smiles at me. Her hair is pulled up in its usual sleek ponytail, a streak of purple falling over one shoulder. She's beautiful, but her eyes look tired tonight.

"You were too gorgeous to resist." She kisses my nose. Her eyebrows shoot up. "And I'm surprised I was able to get away with touching you."

"Be fair. She's gotten better," I say. When Jesse could first cast force fields, her primary objective seemed to be keeping Nikki from touching me. Not the most useful way to practice one's power, and it certainly put a strain on our relationship. But lately, unless I am in direct danger, she seems to have relaxed her standards.

"I'm not complaining." Nikki purrs and pulls me close. She wraps me up in her arms, and I soften into the warmth of her. "I'll take whatever I can get."

I don't point out that Jesse probably doesn't know Nikki is here and therefore doesn't know she has to guard against her. "Jeremiah's kept you busy," I say.

Nikki frowns. "He doesn't think I can keep my head clear around you. Every mission he chooses is as far from you as possible."

"Would it be so different if you were here?" I ask.

Her nostrils flare. "You won't get pushed out of a

burning building, for starters."

"Jesse would never do anything to hurt me."

"She pushed you out of a 40th floor window!"

"34th," I correct her. "And she shielded me from the fall. You saw that part too, right?" Though I'm not sure how it looks on tape.

"Her shield collapsed the second she died. What if she'd died on the way down? What if she'd had a heart attack or was shot? Your brains would be all over Wacker Drive."

"That didn't happen."

"It *could* have." Her eyes are wide, fearful. "I don't like how easily she's willing to take your life in her hands. I *really* don't like how willing you are to let her."

My anger blooms red behind my eyes. "I trust her."

She swallows whatever she plans to say next. What could she say that wouldn't make me mad? *I don't trust her. She's reckless. She endangers you and I won't have it.* No. Nikki is too smart to walk into that trap.

"You're okay," she says and crushes me against her, kissing along my jawline. "That's all that matters."

She's warm and soft. My mind goes fuzzy around the edges and my limbs grow heavy. I fold into her, and try to relax. And while my body is thrilled she's returned, my mind won't sit still. I want her to explain why Jeremiah has such an interest in Jesse and why he seems invested in her actions. If anyone would know his motivations, it would be Nikki. But I don't press her for answers.

I have my own secrets after all, so it makes it difficult, given how much Nikki has grown on me.

Nikki doesn't know about Brinkley's journals. I've read them through twice now. While it answered a lot of questions I had about Caldwell, it left me with more concerns than ever. Maisie, for example. Does Caldwell really have a second daughter? If he does, she'd have to be sixteen now—if she's alive. Brinkley didn't seem to think so, but I'm not so sure. Caldwell might want to kill Jesse for her gifts, but if Maisie isn't partis too, she may not be a threat. How would Jesse react to the news of a second younger sibling?

Her thirteen year old brother is safe with his aunt and uncle in Illinois, growing up on a farm far away from all of this. But Maisie, if she's alive, must be in the thick of it. I suppose Caldwell could use his mind tricks to hide her.

I haven't shared any of this information with

Jeremiah or Nikki. I haven't told them about Gabriel or the fact that Jesse believes he is the source of her powers either.

She's kissing me on the neck again and an alarm sounds somewhere in the building. The snail-shaped intercom in Nikki's ear blinks to life, casting blue light across her cheek. She groans. "Just one night off. Is that too much to ask?"

She presses the button on her ear. "Tamsin here."

Her brow furrows.

"Yes, why?" she asks the person on the other end. Her eyebrows shoot up. "Understood."

I come up on my elbows. "What's happening?"

"Jesse's having a meltdown on the roof."

I throw back the covers and yank on my shoes. My coat is on the back of the chair until I tug it on.

Nikki catches up to me at the elevator and we ride up to the 65th floor. Everyone must be up there already.

32, 33, 34.

"Something happened." I'm certain of it.

"She needs to get better control of her emotions," Nikki says, checking the guns on either side of her hips. I shoot her a withering look, and she immediately takes her hands off her metal. "I'm just saying, she has a lot of firepower. She has to be more careful."

54, 55, 56.

"She doesn't lose control without a reason. She's reactive." I don't take my eyes off the ascending elevator numbers, willing them to go faster. "Something must've happened."

65.

The doors slide open, and all I can see is black Kevlar. Bodies covered in full armor block the elevator and the walkway leading out onto the terrace.

"Move," Nicole booms beside me. Since she's their commander, they obey her in one fluid movement. The only person here with more authority is Jeremiah, and I can see him up ahead. He's closest to Jesse, trying to talk her down.

"Jesse!" I yell. "Jesse, I'm right here."

I squeeze through the mass of limbs and make my way out onto the roof. The terrace is empty except for Jesse and Jeremiah who stand several feet away, his hands out in surrender. I make a motion for him to fall back.

"It's okay." I step in front of the soldiers, making myself the closest person to Jesse.

Nikki takes her place by Jeremiah's side, all eyes

trained on Jesse.

"Jess," I say again and this time she finally looks up at me. Her eyes are rimmed with tears and her cheeks are red from the wind and cold. She stands shivering in only scrubs. She must be freezing. I don't see Winston, so why is she here? "What happened?"

I come to a stop in front of her. I don't touch her yet.

"He took him." She screams and the hair on my arms rises. The electrical charge around her is active, and I shouldn't be so close, but if I move back it might upset her more.

I take a breath.

"Who, baby?" I keep my voice steady and soft. "I just got here. I don't know what happened."

"Caldwell *took* Winston."

The edge of my coat catches fire and I jump back. Nikki leaps forward, but I throw up a hand to stop her. "No. I'm *fine*." I yank off my coat and stomp out the flames. I love this coat, but it's not the end of the world. It looks like a dragon took a bite out of the bottom left lapel, but I'm not burned.

Her eyes are wide with fear. "Your coat—" She wipes at her eyes with her hands, and it's the moment

I'm waiting for. "I'm sorry."

I take her into my arms and hug her tight. "I know you didn't mean it. It's okay."

"He has Winston."

"We'll get him back."

"Gabriel—" She drops her voice and places her mouth by my ear. "Gabriel says Caldwell will kill him if I don't go."

"What do you mean if you don't go?"

"Caldwell said that if I don't come to him soon, he's going to kill Winston."

I can't imagine what in the world Caldwell will do with a slightly obese pug. What kind of ransom is that? Jesse seems to read my mind.

"He said my sister will be watching him. Of all the lies."

My jaw drops. "Maisie is alive?"

Jesse wrenches herself from my arms. "How do you know her name?"

"Not here," I beg, trying to desperately recover the ground I lost.

A slight shimmer comes alive around Jesse, and I recognize it as the gaseous precursor to the firebomb blast I've seen Jesse do dozens of times in the last two months.

"You said no more secrets!"

"Breathe," I tell her. "You need to calm down."

Jesse's body erupts in white hot flames. They dance two or three inches above her body, not touching her skin or clothes. I jump back, knowing it's a heartbeat before the pulse hurls the flames in all directions, Jesse herself serving as the pilot light.

Please Jess, no.

I see her lips part in surprise. Her shoulders roll back, and the first tinge of purple shines through around the edge of her flames. Thank god. She is calming down, calling the power back into herself. The outermost edge of flames flicker and die away.

Then she collapses.

She hits the scorched sod with a hard thud, and the flames extinguish on impact.

"Jesse?" I run over to her, placing my hands on her smoldering chest. The air around her smells electric, but as I put my fingers to her pulse, I find her heart beating fine. I pluck away the tranquilizer protruding from her neck. It comes loose in my hand, rolling along the ridge of my palm.

I look up and see Nikki lower the tranquilizer gun.

Chapter 5

Ally

"She was going to kill you," Nikki says through clenched teeth for the tenth time. "What did you expect me to do? Just *watch*?"

"She was calming down." I pace the hospital room, irritated beyond measure that I am here again so soon. "She was fine."

"Stop arguing." Jeremiah makes a final adjustment to Jesse's IV. "There were many lives on the roof, and we needed to sedate her. Surely you can understand that, Alice."

I glare at Jeremiah as I wring the metal bar at the foot of Jesse's bed. Nikki I have patience for. She is certainly patient enough with me. But Jeremiah has some explaining to do. "How did Caldwell get up there? I thought he had to see where he was going."

Jeremiah pushes his glasses higher up on his nose. "I can't possibly predict his every move."

"You mentioned a name on the roof?" Nikki hasn't tried to get close to me since we left the roof.

I meet Nikki's eyes and soften at the sight of her wide, concerned eyes. "Maisie. Caldwell has a second daughter."

"How could you possibly know that?" Jeremiah asks, placing his hands on his hips.

"Brinkley told me." I hope that I'm a better liar than Jesse. "Not long before he died, he told me about one of his first FBRD cases, which involved her."

Questions are written all over their faces, but I look away.

"Why didn't you tell us Caldwell has another daughter?"

"You didn't ask." I press my hands to Jesse's cheeks. They're growing warmer. Good.

"We're a team." Jeremiah falls back on his position as commander. "We can't keep things from each other."

Yet, I don't trust you, I think. I'm not saying Jeremiah is a bad man. I'm saying that he seems willing to pay any price to destroy Caldwell and I think some prices are too high.

"We invited you and Jesse here to be part of a

team. Teams work together. We share information, not hide it."

I know where my loyalty lies. "I wouldn't mention 'working together' when Jesse wakes up. She's going to want you to 'work together' to get her dog back."

"Out of the question," Jeremiah says. "I can't spare my resources on a rescue mission for a dog."

Nikki glances at him, mouth slightly ajar.

"What is it, Tamsin?" he asks, challenging her to open her mouth. He's never been foolish enough to offer Jesse such an invitation. It reminds me of how different he treats Jesse than everyone else. What I wouldn't give to know why.

"Sullivan is an important member of our team. With continued investment and support, she will help us achieve our objectives."

My heart warms at her words. She's willing to advocate for Jesse even though Jesse has never been nice to her. But that's just how Nikki is.

"Agreed," Jeremiah says, wearily.

"If you deny her request to retrieve Winston, we will likely see backlash from that refusal. She may leave our charge altogether," Nikki says. "This would be terrible timing given Caldwell's movements."

"She'll go get Winston with or without you," I say, hoping to add weight to Nikki's argument.

Caldwell's movements. I linger on Nikki's point. It was Jeremiah's strongest selling point in our coming to Chicago. *Caldwell has renovated almost twelve buildings in the city to have no windows or doors. It's strange. The city believes it is some kind of art installation, a giant joke to be explained later. I think it's a very bad sign.*

"You're asking me if the lives of my men are worth more than one pug," Jeremiah says.

Both Nikki and I tense for his possible reaction, but he doesn't say anything. His face turns red as if he is holding his breath. Then he turns and storms from the room.

"He's being unreasonable," I say, staring at the door, half-expecting him to return. "Did you see how he disregarded Winston?"

"Caldwell kills thousands of people a year." Nikki comes to stand beside me. "Are their lives worth less than Jesse's?"

To me, I think and I register the ugliness of such a thought. "I never said that."

"Is her life worth more than mine?" Nikki asks, softly, her fingertips brush my hand on Jesse's coverlet.

I open my mouth, shocked by the question. "What?"

"If I volunteer to lead a team into Caldwell's headquarters and I'm killed trying to rescue her dog, would you think that was worth it? Or if I died trying to save Jesse, would that make you happy?"

"No, of course not."

Nikki gives me a sad, sweet smile and kisses me on the cheek. The hint of irritation in her tone melts away, replaced with her usual kind patience. "I'm going to go take a shower before my shift in the control room starts. You're welcome to join me."

She manages a devilish grin and gives my hand another squeeze before leaving the room.

I exhale, but it doesn't loosen the tightness in my chest. The room suddenly feels too warm. My cheeks are ablaze. I tug at my collar and slip off my coat. The pungent smell of antiseptics makes my head swim.

Jesse sleeps in the white hospital bed, but not peacefully. Sweat beads around her hairline and her face scrunches then relaxes in turn. What wouldn't I give to chase all her demons away?

I want to stay here with her until she wakes, but I know if I don't join Nikki, she'll take it as a personal affront.

I watch Jesse for a long moment, weighing my desire to stay with the consequence of not going. Nikki was so quick to defend Jesse on my behalf. I want Nikki to know she matters too.

If I died trying to save Jesse, would that make you happy?

I give Jesse's hand a squeeze. "I'll be back before you wake."

Chapter 6

Jesse

The city is in ruins. Cement and mortar lay in heaps across a great road, tumbled over like a child's building blocks. Ash falls from the sky, landing on my hoodie and shoes. I look down to see the toe of my red sneaker smudged gray. I lift my hand and ash lands on the backs of my fingers like snowflakes, precariously balanced on the folds of my knuckles.

Gabriel comes to a stop beside me, a stark figure in the white haze. "It's fallout."

"Where are we?" My voice reverberates against the wreckage.

"Your world. Is this the one you choose?"

"What? No." I whirl around to face him. His eyes are the same demonic green, bright and iridescent as always. His dark suit jacket remains unmarred by the falling ash. "Who the hell would choose this?"

His eyes deepen from green to midnight blue. His

tie changes to match. "If you do not choose, this is the choice."

"What the hell does that mean?"

Light falls against my face as his wings open, and a brilliant red desert stretches out in all directions. The ruined city with its fallout rain has disappeared. Now there's only this desert and a great expanse of blue sky.

Poised in the sand in front of me is a globe, a perfect replica of Earth balanced on a thin wire that runs into the sand.

I look from the desert landscape, to the globe, to Gabriel's porcelain face. "What the hell is this all about?"

Gabriel walks around the globe and stands opposite me. Then he takes one slender finger and spins the globe. "Your world is protected by a magnetic field, not unlike the field that protects you."

A thin layer of purple light begins to glow around the globe, encasing it as it spins and spins.

"But this shield will weaken and fail." Gabriel jabs his finger against the globe and the Earth stops spinning. The purple light disappears. "When that happens, Earth will be destroyed by the first threat that comes along."

His green eyes meet mine, searching my face for comprehension. I don't understand and I'm pretty sure my slack jaw and arched eyebrows say as much.

Gabriel stoops down and grabs a handful of sand, clenching it in his fist. Once he stands, he positions his fist over the globe, opening his hand slightly to let the grains slip between his fingers in a thin, steady stream.

As the sand hits the painted blue surface, a weird thing happens. The globe begins to disintegrate. Whatever the grains of sand touch becomes sand itself, until the entire globe has fallen apart. The only sign it was ever there at all is the heap between our feet, with the thin rod still protruding from its center.

"Well, shit." I bend down and touch the heap. The warm granules slide under my fingertips. "This can't be good."

"No," Gabriel agrees, kneeling down so we are eye-level.

"So how do we save Earth?" I search his face for answers.

Gabriel extends his wings. "That is what you must decide."

Chapter 7

Ally

"What do you mean you're keeping her sedated? It's been nearly twelve hours."

The sedative would've been out of her system a mere hour after she was drugged. The sweat collecting on her brow, which I sponge off every so often with a damp cloth, is proof that her body is working hard to throw off the drugs.

"Jeremiah's orders." The nurse shrugs and moves to the next bed, to a young man with a broken arm.

"Why would he want to keep her sedated?" As soon as the question leaves my mouth I feel stupid. I know exactly why. A calm incapacitated Jesse is better than a living breathing one who would no doubt make high demands to save her pug.

I pull my phone from my pocket and consider texting Jeremiah. He won't answer. I consider texting Nikki next, but I can't ask her to side with me against him. She's been loyal to Jeremiah and his cause long before I came along. With a sigh, I slip my phone back into my pocket unused.

What can I do for Jesse right now? Nothing. Not without help.

I imagine Nikki in bed, her arms around me and her soft lips on my face. She cares about me and I like her back but there's this wide chasm between us. I don't know how to cross that gulf. Not as long as Caldwell is alive and the danger is real. The same work that brought us together, keeps us apart.

I can't think about that now. Yes, I could use her help, but I don't need it. I just need a plan. A plan for getting Jesse out of here before she wakes up, furious. And a plan that will keep her from doing anything rash—like waging a solo mission against Caldwell. I suppose one good benefit of her sedation will be the few moments I'll have to conjure such a plan.

The automatic door swishes open, and I prepare myself for Jeremiah or Nikki. Gloria limps into the room wearing a cast over her broken fibula.

"Gloria?" My heart hammers at the sight of her. Gloria doesn't live in Jeremiah's tower, having refused his offer for personal living quarters. She came here for a reason.

She stops just short of the bed. "They're keeping her sedated."

"The nurse just told me. What's going on?"

"We have to get her out of here." She plops her sketchbook on top of Jesse's legs. Jesse doesn't stir.

"This building is the safest place for her. Jeremiah is a bit of a control freak, but I believe his intentions are good. He wants to protect his people, that's all. He doesn't know Jesse like we do."

"It's more than that," Gloria flips a page and points at a detailed pencil sketch.

Jesse is standing in the aftermath of an apocalypse. A city has collapsed around her and the sky is gray with fallout. It takes me a minute to recognize the Chicago skyline despite all the rubble. But in the distance, the Sears tower stands untouched and half of Wrigley Field. Where Tate Tower should stand, shows only a stretch of vacant sky.

"We need to get away from this building." Gloria reaches up and yanks The Needle out of Jesse's arms.

"Hey!" I blot at the blood on Jesse's arm with the white sheet stretched over her. "Be gentle. You don't know that the building will be bombed right this second. When is that supposed to happen?"

She frowns. "We'll stay with her until she wakes up, and then we have to go."

"It could take an hour. The nurses will come back to sedate her, and then what will we do?"

"We'll guard the entrance, lock down the room."

An alarm sounds and Gloria rushes forward to smash the close button. It doesn't work. The sirens continue to wail throughout the building. Gloria gives up on the close button and tries to manually pull the door closed, but it won't budge.

"So much for locking down the room."

Footsteps pound against the linoleum, echoing someone's approach.

Gloria peeks her head into the hallway and swears.

"Tell Jesse what's going on. Tell her she has to wake up."

"She's unconscious."

"Maybe she can hear you." Gloria knocks back the first wave of respondents, two nurses who squeal. "No. You can't come in here. Stop trying or I'll be forced to hurt you."

As she talks down the nurses, I put my lips against Jesse's ear. I feel more than a little silly until I remember something about coma patients hearing the voices of loved ones.

"Jesse?"

Nothing. Maybe she can't hear over the sound of wailing sirens.

I speak louder. "Jesse, can you hear me? Wake up. It's an emergency. *Wake up!*"

Chapter 8

Jesse

"This is *weird*."

Gabriel and I are standing in one of Jeremiah's medical rooms. The big, open wall lined with beds is too bright and too warm. Ally is by my bedside, yelling into my ear, and Gloria is in the doorway, refusing to let a herd of doctors and nurses into the room. Every time they get too close she kicks at the herd with her gigantic cast. One nurse cries out when the plaster connects with her shin.

"What's all that racket?" I want to cover my ears. I can't. My body is stretched out in the hospital bed with Ally standing guard over it.

"Alice believes you are in danger." Gabriel's wings hunch, reminding me of an angry cat with an arched back. His fiendish green eyes survey the situation. "Alice is usually right."

I snort. "She'd love to hear you say that."

The commotion in the room doubles, and I turn toward the clotted doorway. Jeremiah stands toe-to-toe with Gloria who refuses to let him pass. Jeremiah's red in the face but his voice is steady.

"Captain Jackson." He even manages a hint of deference. "Please let us into the room."

"No."

He pushes his glasses up the bridge of his nose. "Jesse is in danger of hurting herself and innocent people."

An idea hits me. "My shield."

"Cast it yourself." Gabriel opens his wings.

I groan. "How?"

"You can command it, Jesse. Picture it. Call it forth."

I try to imagine what I would look like, laying there with a shield shining all around me. A tickle washes over my body and the shield appears, enveloping me.

I smile. "That was pretty easy."

"Oh thank god." Ally murmurs. Her shoulders slump and all the air whooshes out from between her lips. "Keep your shield up, baby."

I smile. "She called me baby. Did you hear that?"

Gabriel blinks at me.

Gloria steps aside and lets the flood of people enter the room. But now, none of them seem to know what to do with themselves. They stand in a disjointed huddle, glancing from my immobile form to Jeremiah as if waiting for instruction.

No one moves.

"What now?" I ask.

Gabriel turns those green eyes on me. "You are aware."

"I know I'm aware." I gesture at the room. "Hel-*lo?*"

He blinks at me.

"Look. We talked about this. I accept that you're either a real angel or that my head is totally busted from dying and you're an illusion. But either way, I'm going to need you to have good communication skills. We'll never get through this if you keep talking like a wookiee."

His eyes search my face and then he wets his lips. "You are waking up."

"Good job." I squeeze his biceps in my hands. "I understood you perfectly."

A hint of amusement crosses his face, the corner of his lips turning up.

"It's like a foreign language. You can't give me cryptic messages *and* blank faces. I don't know how to interpret that."

Gabriel grabs my hand, his fingers brushing mine.

"Uh, what are you doing?"

He tugs me closer. "I am using body language. I want to convey I am here with you."

I push him off of me. "Okay. Too much body language. And I know you're here with me. Just look at yourself."

He looks down as his waist.

"I didn't mean literally. Ugh, never mind."

"What will you do when you wake up?" he asks.

Jeremiah grabs hold of Ally, wrenching her away from my body.

"Transfer my shield to Ally."

"That is what they want," Gabriel warns.

I see what he means. The nurses stand poised ready to prick me with a needle. They're counting on me dropping my shield to cover Ally.

"Damnit," I swear. "What about the firebomb?"

He blinks at me with big eyes. "Alice."

"Let's fake them out. Make a show of it."

"A show of it?" He repeats each word carefully as

if they're made of fine china.

"Yes." I encourage him by throwing in jazz hands. "A little razzle dazzle."

His brow furrows.

"Okay, we need to work on your slang. Just make him *think* we are going to blow up the room. Got it?"

On cue, my body begins to thrum and shimmer with its pre-blast heat. The doctors and nurses all move back.

Gloria smiles. "You're pissing her off."

Jeremiah hesitates but his hold on Ally tightens.

"More razzle," I tell him.

The bed sheets catch fire, and the medical team flees. Sensing the fire, the sprinkler system springs to life. Cold water falls on my face and hands and I can feel it, not on my invisible body, but on the one lying in bed. Fat drops hit the back of my eyelids and it smells like the hosepipe I used to drink from as a kid.

"How can I feel the water?"

I don't need him to answer. When the nurse's took off with the drugs and needles, my subconscious saw fit to shield Ally instead of me. Gloria tucks her sketchpad under her shirt, pulling her flannel shirt over the pages to keep them dry.

The impromptu shower seems to help Jeremiah gain control of himself.

"You don't understand." He wipes at his glasses with his damp shirt. "This is what Caldwell wants. He wants to get you away from the safety of Tate Tower. He wants you to doubt us. If you go out there, Jason will find you. Caldwell will get exactly what he wants. I only want to help you."

"Keeping me drugged up is a great way to show it."

"Keeping her drugged up isn't the best way to show it," Ally echoes.

"Thank you." I point a gracious gesture at her, but she can't see me. I turn to Gabriel. "How long is it going to go on like this?"

"You'll wake soon," he says.

"Then we're going to get Winston."

"Listen to me, Jesse," Jeremiah says. He's speaking to my sleeping body with as much tenderness as you would afford a dying grandmother. "I'm sorry I sedated you. But I need to protect my people. You understand that, don't you? Do not take my action as anything but well-intentioned. I want to keep you safe. I want to keep Alice safe, and Captain Jackson and my people. Don't fault me for that."

Gloria snorts. I don't think I've ever heard her do that. I'm sure she's super insulted by the idea that some dude thinks he's supposed to protect her.

Jeremiah gives her a cold look. "Fine. Leave. All of you. We won't stop you. But I *am* trying to keep her safe, Alice. Tell her that."

Thoroughly soaked, Jeremiah walks to the doorway defeated.

Both Gloria and Ally visibly relax. Shoulders slump and everyone starts breathing again.

Ally rakes wet strands away from her own face and sighs. "Well, *that* could've gone better."

Gloria wipes the water off her face, revealing a tentative smile. "It could've also gone much, *much* worse."

Chapter 9

Jesse

My eyes flutter open to the sight of Ally wet and miserable. Her brows are pinched, water dripping off the end of her nose. It's still raining down on us from the sprinkler overhead.

"Hey, Jess. How do you feel?"

"Like I just had the most bizarre out of body experience." I adopt a Dorothy Gale Kansas drawl. "And you were there. And you were there."

Gloria gathers up her sketchbook and adjusts her wet clothes, pulling them away from her body where they clung to her skin. "We need to get out of here."

I try to sit up and my limbs are shaky. It's the same kind of feeling I get if I've had too much caffeine and not enough food. Jittery and a little sick. It must be the drugs, the power, stress or some combination. Ally reaches her hands under my arms and lifts me.

"I'm not sure Jesse's ready to make a break for it."

"You want to stay here with your girlfriend." I scratch my shoulder. A small bump presses against my fingertip like a bee sting. Where the hell did I get that? "Fine. Stay here with her and some dude that has no qualms about manhandling you just to get a rise out of me."

Her nostrils flare. "I know you're scared for Winston, but don't be mean to me."

I take a breath. "I'm *sorry*." It isn't my best apology. Certainly not Oscar worthy, but sometimes it's really hard work to get those two little words out of my mouth.

"You're forgiven. But I'm right. I know you want to go get Winston, but you can barely walk. You're of no use to anyone like this. Let's go with Gloria back to her place and regroup. We'll come up with a plan on how to save Winston there."

"We can't stay at my place long," Gloria says and yanks the covers off my legs. "Jason is due to make an appearance."

"Who cares about Jason?" I would love to have someone to beat up on right now. It'd be a great way to relieve some emotional tension.

Ally scowls. "He can heal a hatchet to the back,

and he wants to squeeze your brains out of your ears like a Go-Gurt."

"But what about Winston? When we got him, we promised to keep him safe."

"I know," Ally says, and all the sympathy returns to her softening brow and downturned lips. "I know. We'll get him back."

Gloria motions toward the door. "We should go while we can."

I'm suddenly super grateful that Gloria insisted on having her own place in the city outside of Tate Tower. She wasn't nearly as eager to integrate her life with Jeremiah's, no matter how much he offered her, and I wonder if that's because she knew this was coming.

Ally pulls me out of the bed and I place each shaky foot on the floor. After a couple of test steps, I feel strong enough not to lean on her.

Gabriel moves with us. "Don't let me fall on my face," I tell him.

The three of us hobble out of the hospital ward and down the hall to the elevators. The hallway looks darker than usual and suspiciously devoid of people. We stop outside the reflective doors and I can see myself in the metal. I look like hell. My hair is soaked and knotted on one side of my head. The other two don't look much better—all three of us could pass for drowned rats.

The doors open and we step in. Ally punches a button for my floor.

"We need help," Ally says and then she sees my glare. "I'm not saying we have to work with Jeremiah—or Nikki—I'm only saying that the three of us against Caldwell and his army, or just us against Jason, seems ridiculous."

"Gloria is worth ten thousand of those guys," I say in mock offense. No way I'm going to let her know how absolutely terrified I am of Caldwell. It's not what he'll do to me, even though we've been down that super fun road. It's what he'd do to the people I love. Already he's beat Ally half to death, murdered Brinkley, and kidnapped my dog. What's next?

He knows exactly what hurts me most, and he isn't the least bit hesitant to apply the pain.

"What about Rachel?" Ally asks. "If we could find Rachel, I would feel a little more secure. We could use her abilities to strengthen our defense."

"I've been looking."

Rachel disappeared the night Brinkley died, but

that was two months ago. I'm worried Caldwell has her captive or has already killed her. I can't imagine Caldwell would kill her and not taunt me about it, so I have to hope she's still out there, laying low.

Caldwell's conversation replays in my head as we step off the elevator and into my hallway. We need to stop by my room and get my things, and maybe Ally's room too—though I have no interest in running into her girlfriend or seeing them be all lovey and shit. Gag.

You'll find it harder to get out than you think. He'll be safe with your sister.

I stop dead. "Maisie?"

Ally stiffens beside me.

"You knew I had a sister. You said her name."

Ally's eyes roll up toward the ceiling. "Do we have to do this now?"

I stop in front of my room and press my thumb to the keypad. It blinks red, rejecting my print. I try the other thumb. It blinks red again.

"What the hell?"

"He locked you out of your room," Gloria says.

"No shit." I give her a look. "Any other wisdom you care to impart on us?"

I'm trying to remember what I have in my room

that I need. My phone and wallet are in my pocket. My computer is in there, my clothes, a picture of me and Lane—*Lane*. Don't get me started about Lane.

I want to punch a hole in the wall. I turn to Gabriel who's trailed us silently this whole time, his green eyes wide and alert. "No chance you can pick me up and drop me on the other side of this door?"

Gabriel shakes his head. "You must kill Caldwell first."

"Ugh. What good are you?"

"I am the midwife of the new world."

"Okay, that was a rhetorical question. We'll talk about those again later."

Ally and Gloria exchange a glance.

"Is everything okay?" Ally asks, her brow scrunching again.

"The angel's worthless." I finger the sore bump on my shoulder. "Either of you got any ideas?"

"Let's try my room," Ally says. "If Nikki's there, maybe we can get a few things."

I slump and fall against the wall dramatically. "Assuming she's allowed to open the door for us."

Ally cocks her head, unamused. "I want to tell her we're leaving at least. Maybe she'll come with us."

God, no.

"She probably knows we're leaving," Gloria says, running a hand over her head. Her hair is so short, it's practically dry now. Lucky.

"Yes." I try to capitalize on my window. "She totally knows. Can't we just go?"

Ally leads us back to the elevator and punches the down button. The apartment she shares with Nikki is one floor beneath mine. The silver doors ding open and we step inside the space for a second time. I'm a little surprised and hella suspicious of the lack of people. And I half expect the elevator to stop at any time, Jeremiah holding us hostage until we agree to be his Intel slaves again.

I step off the elevator and find another empty hallway, which amplifies my suspicion.

"I don't like this," I say.

Gloria and Ally stop.

"What's wrong?" Gloria asks. Her hand is itching toward her abdomen as if she intends to pull something out from under her coat. Does she have a gun in there?

"Where is everyone? Why is it so freaking quiet?"

Why would Jeremiah leave us alone like this?

Worse, I didn't feel alone *at all*. I turn to Gabriel. "Do you see anything I don't?

"Much. At times, it is like revealing the intricacies of the universe to an ant."

I frown. "I mean danger. Is there danger on this floor?"

"He's watching you."

Jeremiah? I ask in my head.

He nods.

Do a lap around the building. I want to know where his people are and what they're doing. Go ahead and check the street and roof too to be sure. I don't want to get outside and have Ally be all like, told you Jason was waiting.

Once he disappears, I turn to find Gloria and Ally staring at me with raised eyebrows.

"What?"

"You were staring down the hallway," Ally says.

"Sorry?" If Jeremiah is watching us through the cameras or whatever, I can't say more. "Let's check your room and get out of here."

Outside her sleeping quarters, Ally presses her thumb to the door and it blinks red. Access denied. She tries a second and third time, rolling her thumb a little to be sure it has good contact. Red. Blink, blink.

"Told you she wouldn't let us in. She's totally on his side anyway."

The door opens and Nikki glares at me. "I'm on her side too."

I open my mouth, and Ally tugs on my hand. *Please,* she begs with her eyes. *Please don't fight.*

The look on Nikki's face when Ally's hand takes mine is priceless. It makes it a lot easier to break into a smile and whip up a chipper tone.

"Hi, Nick," I say. "You look—tall."

She ignores me, focusing her attention on Ally. "Are you really leaving?"

Ally tries to wedge past her, but Nikki stops her with a hand. "Al—"

"Told you she's his lap dog."

Nikki's glare is sharp, but I'm not worried. I've never met anyone grumpier or more sardonic than *moi.* No, that's not true. Brinkley is—*was* grumpier than me.

My heart flops.

In my head, I replay the scene. Brinkley raising his gun to shoot Caldwell, but even as he pulls the trigger, Caldwell is already gone. Pale hands wrap around Brinkley's neck and—*snap.*

My chest compresses tighter and the voices in the

hallway sharpen back into focus.

"I understand I'm putting you in a horrible position." Ally leans against the door jamb, talking to Sasquatch. "I won't ask you to do anything to contradict his orders."

"Al," Nikki says, her shoulders slumping. "I'm supposed to convince you to come upstairs and talk. He only wants to talk."

"Hopefully about the stick up his ass. We really need to address it."

Nikki stands taller. "Why do you have to be—"

"So charming? Charismatic? Witty?"

"—such a bitch."

"Stop." Ally squeezes my hand so hard it hurts. "Don't fight. Please."

Nikki and I both go tight-lipped and red-faced. Neither one of us want to be the one to upset Ally first. I wish I could say I'm more mature than that, but Nikki and I have been at each other like this for months. I hate her. I hate that she's trying to weasel her way into Ally's life when it's so perfectly clear she is only doing it so she can manipulate her for Jeremiah's benefit.

So not happening.

Gabriel appears at my side. "The building is clear.

The remaining personnel are in the control room upstairs."

No secret plan to sedate us and lock us up?

"No." Gabriel doesn't have to use the mind speak since no one can see or hear him but me.

"Jess?" Ally is frowning at me again.

I turn and find they're all looking at me. The light from the hallway shines down on us, giving the impression that I'm a stage actor who's just missed my line. "What?"

"Nikki is volunteering to come with us." Ally's using her patient *I-hate-repeating-myself* tone. She knows I'm talking to Gabriel. She also knows that I don't want Nikki or anyone else to know that.

"No." I put my hand on my hip. "She wants to spy on us for Jeremiah."

"I want to help you." Nikki's face is still red, but she's fighting to keep her tone level. "You need me."

"No one here needs you, sweetheart."

"Jesse." Ally almost stamps her feet. "We do need her if you want to attack Caldwell head-on. We need all the help we can get."

Come see me alone, Caldwell had demanded. I hate to admit it, but now that I'm awake and the world is coming into focus without the blurry edge of drugs, I'm starting to see my situation a little differently.

I don't even want Ally and Gloria to come. I don't want the people I love anywhere near Caldwell. But do I think I can get Winston back without them? That's a soft maybe.

Is Caldwell going to try to kill me, I ask Gabriel.

"Yes."

Wow, way to sugarcoat it. *Like as soon as he sees me?*

"No. There is an order to abide."

Can I get Winston back alone?

"I do not know."

If I bring them, are they in danger of being killed? It's a stupid question. I know the answer even before Gabriel confirms it.

"Yes. He wants Alice dead."

"Jess?" Ally tugs on my hand.

"I think you guys should stay here. Maybe you shouldn't leave the tower."

"I know he asked you to go alone," Nikki says, ratting me out. "That's stupid and dangerous."

"No." Ally lets go of my hand and grabs her hips. "You are not going alone. Are you crazy?"

Gloria is the only one who doesn't chastise me.

"We all need to get out of this tower."

Nikki searches Ally's face for an answer.

"The tower is going to be bombed. Everyone should leave."

"Were you going to tell me?" Nikki asks, her eyes wide.

Ally frowns. "Of course. I wouldn't just leave without letting you know you're in danger. But you won't be in danger because you're coming with us right?"

"Can we at least have dry clothes," I moan. "It's like negative a hundred out there and my hair is wet."

A swarm of emotions plays over Nikki's face. She opens her mouth only to close it again. She stands aside and lets Ally into the room. Nikki closes the door, leaving only a crack.

"You're going to leave us," Gloria says.

I give her a nervous smile. "Am I?"

"You understand that Caldwell still wants to eliminate the competition." It's basically a really nice way of calling me stupid to my face.

"I know." I absentmindedly pick at the bump on my shoulder. "But I want Winston back, and I want you guys to be safe. I'll have Gabriel, my shield, and my firepower."

I think she's going to give me more shit about this, but she just nods, a bizarre kind of approval.

I peer into the dark room and see Ally shoving her things into bags. Nikki is murmuring soft words to her. I don't *want* to leave them. By the time I get back—if I come back—she might be engaged to this wench.

So not happening. The door opens wide again and Nikki steps out into the hall with her own bag packed and hanging from one shoulder.

"Okay, let's go," Nikki says.

"Issuing orders now?" I ask. "What about my dry clothes?"

"We'll stop by your room and let you change. But you have to be quick about it."

"Sure thing, Sasquatch."

"Can I dry my hair?" Ally steps out into the hall and lifts her bag up onto her shoulder.

"You're such a girl." Nikki smiles at her, taking one of her hands in her own. "I really like that about you."

Oh yeah. There's no way I'm putting up with this for long.

Chapter 10

Jesse

We reach the first floor and the elevators open to the sight of Jeremiah and a small team of guards. Given the immensity of the room, they aren't that intimidating. A huge domed ceiling hangs above, letting in the moonlight. A Christmas tree at least fifteen feet tall stands off to one side, its big red bows and cream decorations matching the soft swirls in the marble floor.

"I knew it. Shit's about to get real." I groan. The shield flares to life around Ally and knocks Nikki back a pace. God, if only I could make it bigger and push her halfway across the room. That'd be awesome. I wouldn't even mind that I stand exposed and vulnerable in the center of this grand foyer.

"I'm not here to fight." Jeremiah steps away from his detail with his palms out in surrender. I don't lower the shield. I glance at Gloria to make sure she's okay.

She's got her hand on her gun, but hasn't raised it yet.

"You're here to stop me." I step in front of everyone. *Keep an eye on her*, I tell Gabriel, aware that my back is exposed to Nikki.

"If you have to go, fine." His tone suggests it is everything *but* fine. "I only want to make sure you understand that I am on your side."

"You shot me in the neck, sedated me, let my dog get kidnapped, left me and Ally trapped in a burning building, tried to hold me hostage. Oh, I don't know why I must be so confused about whether or not you're on my side."

His jaw clenches. "If you need our help, you need only ask."

"I can't sit here in your fancy building while Caldwell has Winston. The fact that you expect me to do that is absurd. What really pisses me off is that you think you can just give Ally a good shake whenever you want something from me. If you ever do that again, you'll be lucky to keep both your hands."

My firebombing power flares. Ally is safe in the shield and Gloria is far enough away, assuming I don't actually explode. The flames dance up my body and I let them simmer, despite the creepy way my skin crawls. It's all I can do not to squirm like I have to pee.

"You know what they say about playing with fire, right?" Okay, I can be a little melodramatic. Shoot me. What's the point of having a fancy power if I can't make people back off?

He turns toward Gloria.

"I want to thank you for warning us about the bombing." Jeremiah meets Gloria's eyes. "You've saved lives."

"Damn right she did. And don't forget it."

I snap my fingers for dramatic effect, and the flames sputter out around me. I can smell the strange stench in the air, almost like burnt rubber. I wonder what the fire burns from the air?

"Now move so I can save my pug."

Jeremiah steps aside. His men do the same. "Call us if you need us."

I don't say anything more. I don't need to. That's the awesome thing about being me. Just go all fiery and walk out like, *what, bitches? What?*

We make it out of the building without further incident, Jeremiah and his men standing illuminated in the great foyer, watching us leave.

The freezing December air whips around my face,

tousling my damp hair. At least Ally was smart enough to ask for those dry clothes or I'd be completely miserable right now.

"This way." Gloria points us down North Michigan Avenue toward the subway.

I come up beside Ally and offer to carry one of the three bags she packed. She lets me take one.

"I need to talk to you," I say, adjusting the weight of the bag on my shoulders.

"I won't share anything you say with Jeremiah," Nikki says. "I promise."

"Pinkie promise?" I say, derisively.

Nikki's face falls flat.

"Seriously, can we have a minute alone?"

"Can it wait until we get to Gloria's?" Ally asks, pulling hair out of her mouth.

No, because I've already half decided that as soon as we reach Gloria's, I'm taking off, but I can't say that with Sasquatch listening.

I want Ally to know I'm leaving but not to worry about me. It will never fly, but maybe I can get her to understand if I explain it to her. I want to tell her what Gabriel said about the earth and the shield. After all, it's the first real clue we've received about what the angels might mean. Ally could figure out Gabriel's warning, I just know it. And I know she has her own secrets to share, like about this so-called sister of mine.

We descend the stairs to the subway. The pale fluorescents overhead flicker as we wiggle through the turnstile and then down another flight of stairs. At this time of night, the platform is nearly deserted. Gabriel catches up with us as we are stepping onto the car. His wings lay flat against his back as if in consideration of the few other passengers riding the train. I find it comical since they can't even see him, let alone get an angel feather to the eye.

Where'd you go?

"I was watching," he says. He floods my mind with images of Jeremiah returning to the control room. Jeremiah giving orders to tail and observe us. A man steps onto the adjacent train car at the next stop and glances at us through the small door connecting the cars. I know instantly he is one of Jeremiah's men, though I almost never see their faces with their black mesh full body armor.

"There's a—"

"I know." Gloria cuts me off. "Don't stare."

Of course she knows there's a tail. Gloria is like

the closest thing to a ninja I've ever met. She didn't need some froufrou angel to tell her shit.

We get off the train three stops later and climb the stairs to the street. The wind hits me again and I miss the slightly smelly streetcar. It really is the wind that makes Chicago so damn cold. It cuts me right to the bone.

"Here we are." Gloria stops in front of an unimpressive brick building. "Come on."

We file into the lobby, bringing up the rear behind Nikki and Ally. Instantly, I'm relieved that the wind stays outside. My iced cheeks begin to melt and I'm hoping my crunchy hair is next.

Gloria leads us to the stairs on the left side of the elevator.

The foyer of this apartment building isn't as glamorous as Tate Tower. It has more of a vintage 1920s feel to it with its dark wood walls, Victorian furniture, and large chandelier. The three of them take the stairs while I linger at the bottom, waiting to see the man from the train.

No faces show up in the front window outside the turnstile door, and when the lobby guard gives me a suspicious look, I smile and follow the others up the staircase.

I reach the landing of Gloria's floor and see the three of them standing outside her apartment door.

"We need to decide how to proceed," Ally is saying. She's already slipping into action mode, examining our problems and looking for a solution. I glance down at her bag in my hands.

"I want to keep you away from the tower," Gloria tells her as she slips a key into the lock. "In my sketch—"

"Wait, what *exactly* happens to the tower?" Nikki butts in.

"There's a picture that Gloria drew," Ally says, but I've stopped listening.

If I'm going to sneak off and meet Caldwell, now would be the best time. I drop Ally's bag on the stairway and slip down the staircase again. In the lobby, the guard gives me another suspicious glare, and I force a smile.

"I forgot something in the car," I lie and quickly cross the lobby out to the sidewalk.

Gabriel unfurls his wings beside me. God, if only he could block the wind. That'd be awesome.

"I don't know how to find him."

"Call him."

"Like on my cell phone?"

"No," Gabriel says.

Instantly, I know what he means. I search the street, looking for the tail that could show up any time, but don't see anyone. A couple of people are walking on the opposite side of the street toward some unknown destination, but they don't spare me a glance.

My teeth start to chatter and the tips of my fingers go numb. The remaining damp tendrils of hair ice on my head. Again. I close my eyes anyway and try to focus my mind.

Caldwell? I cast the thought out into the wide expanse of the city. If he's really watching my every move, he might hear me.

Caldwell, I think again. *Come and get me.*

Chapter 11
Ally

Gloria slips her key into the lock of her apartment and we step into the small living room. It's a studio with a hotplate in one corner on top of a cabinet and a water closet in the other. No doubt it is three times the cost of my apartment back in Nashville, even if it is only a fraction of the size.

I turn to Jesse, but she's gone.

It's only the three of us—me, Nikki, and Gloria.

"Where's Jesse?" I have to squeeze the words out of my throat over my pounding heart.

Gloria sits her bag on the bed and turns to me. "She might be with Caldwell."

"What?" Nikki and I yell in unison.

"You're kidding," Nikki says, dropping her bag on the floor of the apartment.

"Gloria!" I exclaim. "You knew and you just *let* her go?"

Gloria sinks into the chair. Her eyes are puffy with

exhaustion as she scratches the back of her head. "She chose this and it *is* her choice."

I turn and run from the room. After stumbling over my bag on the steps, I take the stairs two at a time. I fall against the wall as I wind my way down from the fifth floor to the first. I stumble into the lobby and see Jesse standing on the sidewalk, her hands in the pockets of her hoodie.

I rush across the lobby, straight for her. As I reach the door, Caldwell appears on the sidewalk beside her. He says something, but I can't hear their voices clearly through the thick glass.

"Jesse, no!"

She turns toward the sound of my voice. Stupidly, she turns her back to the one man who wants her dead more than anyone else in the world.

Our eyes meet, and the shield goes up around me. This makes me even more furious that at a time like this, she still chooses to protect me rather than herself.

I try to squeeze through the turnstile door but I can't with the shield around me.

"It's a trap," I yell. "He's manipulating you."

Caldwell reaches up and wraps his arms around her. Over her shoulder he gives me the most malicious grin.

Caldwell takes one step back, and then they're gone.

Jesse is gone.

Chapter 12

Ally

"How could you just let her go?" I whirl on Gloria who comes to a stop in the middle of the lobby, her cheeks flushed from her quick descent. Nikki reaches up and presses the earbud on her intercom.

"Caldwell has taken Sullivan. Keep an eye out and report to me if she's spotted."

"I didn't *let* her do anything," Gloria says, clenching her teeth. "And no matter what I did, we would still be here because people make choices. I have to work with what I'm given."

It's her self-restraint that gets me. It encourages me to reel in my anger though it's hot and fresh, picking at the sides of my face, throat, and chest. "I'm sorry." The words come out of my mouth, hard. I take a breath and try again. "I'm sorry. I know you would've done something if you could."

"Hopefully, they'll spot them and we'll know where to go," Nikki says.

I reach out and squeeze her hand. "Thank you."

"Is everything all right, Ms. Delaney?" the man behind the desk asks. It takes me a moment to realize he's talking to Gloria.

Delaney, as in her brother Micah Delaney. Now that I've read the journals, I understand Caldwell's A.M.P, the one who used his power of sight to trap Jesse and the rest of us, is—*was*—Gloria's brother. How hard it must've been for her to accept that her baby brother was working for the other side. What had it cost her to kill him herself?

"We're fine," Gloria tells him. She meets my eyes. "Can we go upstairs and talk?"

"Of course." All the fight leaves me. I'm still angry that Jesse let Caldwell take her. It is incredibly stupid and dangerous. But I can't take that anger out on Gloria. She's been through too much.

We take the elevator this time and enter Gloria's apartment with all the gravity of a funeral procession. As soon as Gloria shuts the door on her little space, I speak up.

"I don't understand, why would she *let* him take

her? She could have stopped him if she wanted."

Gloria takes a seat at her little two-person table. "Whether or not she will admit it to herself, she wants to be with him."

"Excuse me?" I can't wrap my mind around the idea that anyone would want to be alone with a sadist.

"She's changing," Gloria says.

I open my eyes wider at Gloria, and give a sideways glance at Nikki. *She can hear you,* I think.

Gloria shrugs. "This isn't anything Tamsin doesn't know."

Nikki gives me an apologetic smile. "Jeremiah has a theory. The longer the partis are exposed to their powers, and the more powers they acquire, the less stable they are. And on some instinctual level, they want to be together. Like a squirrel's instinct to bury nuts or a bird's instinct to fly south. The power is dictating their actions just as much as their own thoughts now."

Gloria flips open the sketchbook. "Just like the other partis are drawn to Jesse, she's drawn to him. It isn't smart, but it's instinct. I am not sure she can resist it, or even fully consider what a bad idea it is."

"Maybe he manipulated her mind," Nikki says, her

fingers still grazing the gun on her hip.

"He can confuse her, but not control her," Gloria says.

A snippet of Brinkley's journal comes back to me. *You can mindfuck us all day. But you can't fool her.*

"Or you," I tell her. Gloria doesn't spare me a glance. "I wonder why he hasn't tried that trick on me yet. You'd think he'd love the spectacle."

"Maybe you're different too." Gloria looks up from her sketchbook and meets my eyes.

I laugh. "I've no family history of NRD and I don't have the AB- blood type. Jesse was able to replace me, so that negates any remaining chance I have NRD."

"I don't understand why it was so essential that we left Tate Tower. We are better equipped, better staffed, better everything. If there was to be a bombing of some kind—"

Gloria hands Nikki the sketchbook and then locks herself up in the bathroom.

Nikki stares at the picture. "We need to evacuate to the South Side building then. Unless she's sketched that one too?"

I shrug. "I don't know. You'll have to ask."

Nikki gives up on trying to interpret the sketch and pulls me into her arms. She kisses my cheeks and runs her fingers through my hair. "Jesse is tough. She'll be okay."

"You're a saint," I say, wrapping my hands around her neck.

She laughs. "Hardly."

"Jesse is so mean to you, and yet you never bad mouth her to me."

"Because I know you love her." Nikki's voice constricts around the word *love*. "She's a smart ass, but she's also innocent. She doesn't deserve to be murdered. Jeremiah wouldn't let her be killed any more than he'd let anyone else be."

I look into her eyes. "It's more than that. Jeremiah's not protecting some child here. He wants something from Jesse."

A pained expression crosses her face. "I would tell you if I could."

"But you do know? At least admit you know. Don't try to make me think I'm crazy or imagining things."

"You're not crazy. But I can't tell you."

"You should go back to Tate Tower."

"No. Jeremiah gave me leave to be here, and I want to help you. I do, Al. Please let me help you. I understand why you don't trust him, but you can trust me."

"Okay, but let's make a deal," I say, because we do need her help to get Jesse back. *Again.* By filtering Jeremiah's assistance through Nikki, maybe we are keeping ourselves safer and Jeremiah at a distance without giving up resources. Or maybe that won't work at all. I don't know. "When you talk to Jeremiah, tell him I want to know the real reason for his generosity. I'll never be able to trust him unless I understand his motivation. Tell him that unless he's willing to tell us why he's in this, Jesse and I are never coming back."

Nikki's eyebrows shoot up. "Never?"

"Never. Tell him that."

Nikki frowns, clearly wanting to object. Then she tries to hide her sad smile by kissing me. "I'll tell him."

Gloria steps out of the bathroom and turns off the light behind her. "I ordered a pizza. Nicole, can you go down and wait for it?"

It isn't a subtle request by anyone's standards, but Gloria is trying.

Nikki gives me a sidelong look. "I was heading

down anyway."

She plants a kiss on my cheek and slips out of the room. As soon as the door closes, Gloria turns to me.

"What's going on?" I ask her.

"We might have to kill her," Gloria says, deadpan.

Shock rocks my body. "Oh my god, why?"

She doesn't answer me. Instead, she stares at the back of the door as if waiting for Nikki to pop back in.

"I hope you're kidding."

"Anything is possible." Gloria slips back into her seat at the table, her sketches spread out before her. "Sometimes the only option is to kill the one we love."

I sink into a chair at the table. "Surely you didn't send her down for a pizza just to let me know you intend to kill her."

"No. I thought you could use the time to work on the partis. Have you weeded them out yet?"

Guilt washes over me. Was I that obvious? I thought I handled the situation back in Tate Tower pretty well. When we were locked out of the rooms, I was near frantic. My laptop, papers, and Brinkley's journal were still tucked under the bed. What if Nikki had found them while I was away? Luckily, I was able to scoop everything up while Nikki packed her own bag.

"How many do you have left?" Gloria asks, prompting me again to spill it.

"I just crossed off two more. There are still twelve people I'm checking into."

Gloria nods, pulling her own laptop out of her bag. "Keep searching. We need to know everything we can about the others with powers. I think there are eight partis left, including Jesse and Caldwell."

I gather up my bag and open it. It's relief more than anything that I feel when I pull out the laptop and power it on. I always hated sneaking around. More often than not, I wondered who exactly I was protecting and if it was even worth it.

"I assume you don't want Nikki to know what I'm doing then."

Gloria flicks her eyes up to meet mine. "She is loyal to Jeremiah and Jeremiah does not want what we want."

My stomach churns. I trust Gloria's judgment, but I also hope that Nikki is on my side too, even if she and Jesse mix about as well as oil and water.

"Then maybe we shouldn't work for him," I tell her.

The lines between Gloria's brows smooth over. "The enemy of my enemy is my friend."

She has a point. Jeremiah is serving his purpose, I suppose. He provides support and a home base here in Chicago so we can be closer to Caldwell. He has resources we don't and he is doing some good. And Nikki *is* a good person, if nothing else.

"How did you know I was researching them?" I ask Gloria while waiting for the black screen to blink to life.

"I saw you."

I can only assume she means while viewing me. "And?"

"You should keep doing it. We may need that information very soon."

"Why?" I type in my password and I'm rewarded with the article on Monroe Dupree. His haunted face bores into mine.

Gloria's eyes fall on her sketchbook. Her fingers reach out and trace the edge of the yellow cover. "We've got company coming."

Chapter 13

Jesse

"So what's the plan?" I ask and push myself out of Caldwell's arms. "More mind rape? Or would you rather bury me in a box and let me suffocate repeatedly? *That* was fun."

"You have no reason to trust me," he says, running his hand through his hair.

"Nope."

"All that I ask is that you listen to what I have to say."

"Isn't that what the devil always says? Then you find yourself getting pitchforked from behind, 24/7 for eternity."

I take a turn about the room and realize I have no idea where we are. No windows and no doors. Shit. It's another kind of coffin.

"Walls can be knocked down," Gabriel reminds me, his voice faint in the back of my mind.

"This room isn't doorless to contain you," Caldwell says and crosses to the sofa on the far wall. "It's for my protection. No one can come in and out of here except me."

"So why am I in your safe room?" I'm trying to figure out where to put myself. "You plan to leave me here to starve to death? Because I will totally blow this room apart."

"I wanted somewhere private for us to talk."

"Where's Winston?"

"He's safe with your sister."

"Yeah, about *that*." I do another turn around the room but there's nothing to fixate on with the lack of windows, doors, or décor of any kind, save three pieces of furniture. Two rose-colored chairs and a sofa, which he drapes himself over, like a French courtesan. "Tell me about this so-called sister."

"Her name is Maisie. She'll be seventeen in February."

I go all weak in the knees.

"She's eight years younger than me. You must've had her right after you died."

"16 months after."

"And she's been with you ever since?"

"Breathe," Gabriel says. The scent of rain intensifies. "Breathe, Jesse."

"She was born in the camp and raised by foster parents until she was six. It took us that long to get her back. Georgia, her mother, insists we keep her close."

Her mother insists we keep her close. So while he saw fit to keep one daughter close he left the other one in the care of a pedophile. What. The. Fuck.

"Are you kidding me? And what about me?"

"You were already fifteen by the time I got out of the camps."

"That was when the worst of it started," I told him. "You could've come back for me. You could've saved me from all that shit."

The power rolls along my skin, and the more I look at his snide little face, the more I know I *want* to firebomb him. I want to watch the skin burn off his bones just like Eddie's.

"I couldn't have saved you from him," Caldwell says, steepling his fingers.

"Keep telling yourself that."

"He wants you angry. He wants you to make a mistake." The light brush of Gabriel's fingers pulls me out of myself. I turn, but the room is empty except for me and the jerk.

"Do you understand why he can't materialize when I'm here?"

If I lose my temper, I might make a mistake, and I will be dead, which is exactly what Caldwell wants. He wants to kill me and take my power.

"I have a feeling you're about to tell me."

"We are charged like magnets. There's too much commotion, too much charge and chaos in the space around us when we are close together," he says. He gestures to the room. "Electromagnetic interference, if you will."

"You could be feeding me a bunch of horse shit, for all I know."

He only smiles.

I see Brinkley in my head. Brinkley in his leather jacket. Brinkley with his James Dean smile and the look of sheer determination as he lifts his gun to shoot Caldwell. Brinkley would remind me not to get confused, not to let Caldwell too deep into my head.

"Brinkley and I had a long and complicated history that you know nothing about."

I fold my arms over my chest. "And that justified killing him?"

"I remove obstacles that lay in my path. I don't care what the obstacle is."

"So how do you intend to remove me?"

"Ah," Caldwell grins as if I've asked him the question he's been waiting for. "You're different."

"Dare I ask why? Or can I just expect a cryptic, noncommittal answer?"

"It would take days to explain why you're different and what that difference means for us."

I snort. "First you have to kidnap a dog and now you flatter me? I didn't realize you'd stoop so low."

My body aches to sit down in one of the rose-colored chairs, to move closer into the light instead of hanging on the periphery like this. But to sit down suggests complacency. I can't get comfortable in case he decides he wants to kill me here and now.

"You agreed to come and here you are. Take a seat."

I don't.

"So did you bring me here to starve? Or did you want privacy for the monologuing?"

"Gabriel won't tell you his plan, because he runs the risk of you shutting him out. He chose you of all the NRD prospects. He saw something in you that he desires," Caldwell's voice is smooth, the lilting tone of a mega church preacher.

"Why did your angel choose you?"

A fox grin spreads across his face. "Such a personal question. Perhaps he knew I would accept him and his will."

"Cute," I say. "Glad you guys are happy together."

His expression darkens. "The Earth's magnetic field is dying. Once it weakens completely, the Earth will be exposed, vulnerable, and incinerated in no time at all. A higher power has taken pity on us and offered us a choice. It will require a conscious act of sacrifice to recharge the field."

I sink into one of the armchairs.

"A partis will have to die, permanently, to recharge the field. That person is the apex and will also be the person who has all of the combined universal elements. All twelve partis powers collected in one body is all that's needed to create a new world order."

"So if I don't get killed by Jason or you, I have to die or the whole planet is incinerated?"

Caldwell's eyes meet mine. "Yes."

I fall against the cushion. I don't know what I expected him to say, but not yes.

"Yes?" I repeat. "The prize for surviving all the homicidal maniacs is *death*?"

"Everyone dies, Jesse," Caldwell says.

I throw up my hands. "This is the dumbest game ever."

Caldwell presses one slender finger to his temple. "To be the apex is a great honor. You get to make the new world in your image."

"You'd love that, wouldn't you?" I stand again and pace from one end of the room to the other. "Are you going to give us all kneepads or is a little rug burn part of your world domination plan?"

Halfway across the room a thought occurs to me. My sneakers squeak to a stop on the industrial carpet. "Wait, does the apex's death recharge the field or blow up the world? I'm getting some mixed signals here."

"It's whatever you want it to be," he says. "That choice is the privilege of the apex."

"I want this to end. I want my freaking dog, and I want you to stop killing the people I love." If Caldwell is determined to kill all the partis and absorb their powers, that means he wants to kill Rachel, Cindy, and anyone else with a gift.

Something flickers in Caldwell's eyes.

"What?" I demand.

"Where *is* Rachel?"

"Probably dead. Some psycho like you probably offed her."

"Would you kill her if it came down to the two of you?"

"No." I throw up my hands. "And she wouldn't kill me either, because we're friends. Do you know what friends are? They generally don't go around stabbing each other in the eyes with forks."

"Are you sure she wouldn't kill you, if she understood the situation?"

"Don't," I warn him. "Don't try to make me think everyone I love is planning to murder me. I already have enough to worry about."

"If it came down to the two of you, Rachel and Jesse, would you kill her if it meant saving the world?"

"Uh, hello? *Friends.*"

"Then you sentence the whole planet to death. The radiation alone would fry it. Think of it this way: would you die for Alice?"

I answer without hesitation. "Yes."

"Would you kill Rachel if it was the only way to keep Alice alive?"

This stops me. My heart lurches.

"You would have to kill her in order to be the apex and you must be the apex in order to save the world."

My stomach turns.

"But don't worry about making that difficult decision," Caldwell grins. "I'll kill all your friends for you."

"I can't let you kill them."

"Then you're sentencing us all to death."

"You said we all have to die anyway." My voice is cracking around the edges. It is harder to muster sarcasm and spite the longer I think about my situation. Best case scenario, my loved ones live and I die. Worst case, we all die. Where's the freaking bright side in that?

"All the partis have something in common," Caldwell says, after allowing me a long stretch of silence to consider the impending doom.

I flick my eyes up to meet his. "Our charming personalities?"

"We all *wanted* to die," he says. "You wanted to die that night in the barn."

I see the barn clearly in my mind—the flames, Eddie burning alive, the stars above me as my body lay saturated with the booze and pills I guzzled.

"The angels could have chosen any NRD-positive soul on the planet, but Gabriel chose you because you wanted to die and you had what he was looking for," Caldwell says again. "I made a similar plea in the camps. Rachel no doubt wanted to die every minute that Henry Chaplain had her tied to a bed."

Is it true? I ask Gabriel again. I listen but don't hear him in the back of my mind. *Did you really choose me because I was suicidal? But I want to live now.*

"This is the part I must make you understand, Jesse. Are you listening?"

I flick my eyes up to meet his.

"We are the north and south poles. We are the same bar magnet. It will come down to the two of us and the sooner you accept that, the better off we will all be."

"So you can be the apex and create your slave world?"

"Just world," he corrects. "I'll create a just world. If you let me."

I bite off a bitter laugh. "If I let you kill me, you mean."

"Your resistance is messing up the entire program. Everyone else involved has accepted their role. Why can't you?"

I throw up my hands. "Oh I don't know. Maybe because murdering my friends or exploding doesn't seem like the best life plan. Just give me Winston already. You've said your piece. We're all going to die. Got it. Now send me home." Ally is no doubt losing her shit by now.

He comes dangerously close and my shield flares to life around me. I've no idea why. If there was a threat, I missed it.

"I can't take you from the room without touching you," Caldwell reminds me.

"Don't let him touch you," Gabriel warns. I can hear the panic in his voice even if I can't see him clearly.

What's my alternative? Stay here forever? Hamster ball my way through the walls?

I force my shield down.

Gabriel screams and the next thing I know I'm falling, heavy in Caldwell's arms.

"Sorry," Caldwell says, positioning my limp body in his arms. "But we aren't done yet."

Chapter 14

Ally

"Jeremiah has checked every camera in the city, but neither Caldwell nor Jesse have made a single blip. He's extended his search to the rest of the world, given Caldwell's ability." Nikki looks up from her seat at the wobbly table and meets my eyes. Her face is illuminated, ghostly in the light from the computer screen. I will never understand why Gloria seems to prefer poorly lit living spaces.

I tuck my hair behind my ears. "Or wherever they are, there aren't any cameras."

Nikki snorts. "Does such a place exist?"

"With Caldwell, we never know." My voice is steady and sure, but inside, I feel sick. My muscles clench and unclench in turn, creating wave after wave of nausea. A sour burn has crept up the back of my throat and the pressure behind my eyes keeps building.

Jess, what've you done? Why do you have to be so rash?

I can wish all day long that she would take more time to consider her options before acting, but such a hope would be fruitless. I try to calm myself with reminders that we've been lucky so far, that now more than ever, Jesse has power. She can fight Caldwell, if she has to.

These little assurances aren't calming me. A voice in the back of my mind nags, reminding me that Caldwell rarely fights fire with fire. He fights with deception and confusion and illusion. He will break Jesse's mind first, before ever trying to fight her power with his.

In that way, I fear Jesse isn't as strong as Caldwell. Honestly, I don't think any of us are.

"Scratch that." Nikki's voice drags me from my thoughts. "I've got something."

I lean down over Nikki's shoulder and peer into the computer screen. My eyes settle on the opposite chair for a heartbeat, noting again Gloria's absence. She's been gone for nearly an hour, saying she needed to "get a few things." I wonder if it's a true excuse or if she has a trick up her sleeve.

"See here?" Nikki punches a few keys on the keyboard and the image gets larger. Caldwell is on a boat in a port somewhere. I can't tell more from the black and white video streaming into Nikki's laptop. The wooden dock stretching out to the ship is clear though, as well as the men loading the ship by hand and forklift.

"Where is this?" I ask.

"Finland," she says, punching a few more keys. A chat box pops up in the top right corner of the screen. Parish looks the same as he did the last time I saw him at Jeremiah's base in Nashville: plump, hairy, and half a burger in his mouth. He waves at the camera. "Parish says hi."

I wave back at the man in the little box. "Hey."

"This ship is headed to the North Pole."

"Why?" I can't suppress a surprised snort. "Is Caldwell planning to visit Santa?"

"I don't know." Nikki opens and collapses windows broadcasting video feeds. "I don't see Jesse, so either he dropped her somewhere or she could be on the ship. Parish is canvassing the pier and surrounding area."

"Or she's somewhere else?" My heart lurches again. I'm not sure why the idea of Jesse not with Caldwell frightens me more. I should be thrilled that he's in Finland, possibly thousands of miles from her. Yet, I think seeing her on a pier in Finland would calm some part of me that's imagining much worse.

Nikki takes my hand and gives it a squeeze. "I think this is good."

"How?"

She takes both my hands in hers. "If they'd had some giant firefight, we'd have seen it. You can't hide something like that. The fact that he's back to business an hour after taking her is good. He's not trying to kill her, right? So he hasn't tried to kill her, and he isn't doing it now. That's *good*. We still have time."

I squeeze her hands back and place a kiss on her knuckles. "I hope you're right."

"Of course I am." She grins and pulls on my hands until I'm forced to sink into her lap, her face close to mine. She kisses my cheek, then the corner of my lips.

"God, I hope she's okay. I don't know what I'll do if—"

"Shhhh." She covers my mouth with a kiss. "Think positive."

I wrap my arms around her neck and she presses her palms against my back.

She kisses my cheek. "If he'd taken you, I'd be

crazy right now."

Heat blooms in my face. "I don't expect you to be as worried about Jesse as I am."

She flicks her eyes up to meet mine. "I'm *saying* that I understand why you're so worried. I would be too."

I wrap my arms around her neck. "I'm worried about Winston too."

"We'll get them both back."

Three gunshots go off in the hallway and Nikki jumps up, dumping me onto my feet.

"Is that—" I ask, straightening beside her.

The door opens and Gloria bursts in with her gun drawn.

"Jason," she says and slams the door closed. "We need to go."

Nikki slams her laptop shut and shoves everything into her bag. I do a quick turn around the room, gathering up the few things that I removed from my bags. Gloria locks the front door and shoves the kitchen table in front of it. Nikki helps her pile the chairs on top without question.

"What's our exit?" My pounding heart makes it hard to speak.

Gloria points at the door beside the bathroom. "The closet."

"Closet?"

She isn't kidding. Just as someone begins slamming against the front door and rattling the table and chairs, Gloria throws open the broom closet.

"Gloria—" I begin, unsure.

She pushes aside several coats and grabs a crowbar off the top shelf. Wedging the crowbar into the corner of the closet, she pries away a piece of wood paneling to reveal a dark mouth of a tunnel.

"What in the world?"

"Go," Gloria says over the sound of the table rattling again.

Nikki steps into the dark first, pulling a pen light out of her pocket and shining it ahead. "It drops off."

Gloria tosses a bag into the darkness. "Just wait on the landing."

Nikki pulls me in after her and clicks off the pen light.

"I can't see anything." This isn't entirely true. I can see Gloria in the closet and the open door revealing the apartment's hallway.

Gloria lifts her hand. "Wait."

Gloria pulls the closet door shut and Nikki clicks on the pen light, illuminating the tight space. Gloria arranges the clothes to their original position, and begins to slide the paneling back into place.

"Turn off the light," she commands, and Nikki does without hesitating. I can feel her hands on my back, a warm assurance in the void.

The paneling snaps into place as a loud crash echoes in the apartment. The sound of tables and chairs tumbling to the floor is muffled by the big door. There aren't many places to search. It's only one room, the bathroom, and this storage closet.

The closet opens, the doorknob bouncing off the wall. Nikki's hand tenses on my back. No one moves or breathes for fear he can hear us through the panel.

The sound of hangers scraping along the metal pole makes me jump and goosebumps rise on my arm at the screeching.

"Goddammit," Jason yells, followed by the sound of a fist connecting with plaster. He doesn't hit the panel though, and I say a prayer of thanks for small mercies.

Another crash and then an echoing silence. No one moves or speaks in the cramped space until Gloria clicks on her own flashlight and points it past us. "Follow me." She speaks directly into my ear before she heads deeper into the passage. Her small, bobbing beam creates a lighted walkway.

Nikki stays close on my heels until we come to a stop. Gloria flashes the light at a small metal ladder.

Gloria climbs onto it first and begins to descend into the shaft. The first rung is cold in my grip and I only have a moment to situate myself before the light disappears. There is a moment of uncertainty and fear as I hang from the ladder in open space, unable to see anything.

The metal ladder bumps against my hip bone and a sharp pain cramps my side. I cling to the rungs harder, feeling one of the cold rungs pressed to my cheek.

Nikki clicks on her own penlight again and shines it on the ladder. "You okay?"

I nod.

"Just do it by touch." Her voice is gentle and calm. She doesn't let the urgency of the situation make her impatient, the way Jesse would.

Jesse. Please be okay.

Holding onto the bars, I stretch my right leg down

until I feel it graze the top of the next rung. Sinking my weight into it, I do this again and again.

"There you go," Nikki says and the light shifts as she climbs onto the ladder above me.

I descend, my heart pounding. I can't see anything, not even my hand inches in front of my face. Nikki's penlight is too weak to offer any support. I can see Gloria's light farther down, bobbing in time with her movements, but it's too far away to be of any use to me.

I try to focus on the task at hand, the simplicity of it. *Step. Sink. Grab.*

Again. Again.

But I'm plagued by the idea that at any moment I'm going to slip, fall into the unending blackness and be swallowed whole.

Nikki's foot comes down on my hand and I rip it out from under her shoe.

"Sorry, sorry."

"It's okay." I swallow down the panic. "I should be going faster."

"Take your time."

I begin again, seeking a rung with my foot, finding it, lowering myself down. It feels like we are in the black shaft forever. Gloria's light stops moving and settles at the bottom, and my heart leaps with joy.

It grows brighter and brighter, until once again, my feet are on solid ground.

"Let's take the elevator next time, shall we?" My breath billows white in front of my face.

Nikki jumps down and lands beside us. "That was fun."

Gloria goes to the far wall and pulls on a handle. Looking both ways, she holds up a hand, motioning for us to wait. After a few heartbeats, she lowers her hand. "Clear."

We file out of the narrow shaft into what resembles a storage room of some kind. Cinder-block walls, pallets with trash and recycle bins, and some unused equipment clutter the cold space.

Gloria leads us out of this room into the parking garage, her gold Cadillac in the first space by the room labeled "Recycle/Trash".

Gloria unlocks the door with her fob, and I climb into the passenger seat while Nikki jumps in the back.

"I have a feeling I know why it took you so long to find an apartment," Nikki says from the backseat. She's already opening her pack and inspecting the items she brought with her. She slips a communication device into her ear.

"I inspected the building schematics for all the possible apartments in the city until I found one with a secondary exit," Gloria confirms.

"You're amazing," I tell Gloria. "No wonder Brinkley had so much faith in you."

I regret the words as soon as they leave my mouth. Gloria's face pinches and her nostrils flare. "Yes, and look where it got him."

"Gloria—" I could say a million things: *It wasn't your fault. You did your best.* Gloria doesn't give me the chance. She drowns out my voice with a rev of the engine and she throws the car into reverse and backs out of the spot.

"Do you think Jason knows Jesse isn't with us?" Nikki asks, as she adjusts herself in the seat.

"No." Gloria meets her eyes in the rearview.

I pull my coat tighter around me. "Or he's attacking us, hoping it will draw her out."

I'm not sure it matters why Jason attacked us. And I'm not sure how it affects my plan to get Jesse and Winston back, except of course, it creates another obstacle. It shouldn't matter if there are a thousand obstacles, I remind myself. I just have to stay focused on getting them back.

"Step 1," I say, burrowing into my coat and punching the buttons on Gloria's dash for the heater. "Find Jesse."

"I know where she is." Gloria pulls out of the parking garage and onto a dark Chicago street.

Chapter 15

Jesse

A thick, wet tongue licks up the side of my face. Once, twice, and on the third swipe, the tongue slides right up my nose.

I jolt upright screaming. "Ugh, oh my god. What—?"

Forty pounds of pug slams into my chest, jumping and leaping trying to get at my face again. Snuffly snorts—pug's unique language—bring reality into sharp focus.

"Winston," I say. A wave of relief washes over me. "Winston, thank god. Come here, let me see you."

I roll the pug over onto his belly and run my fingers over the soft fur there. He squirms, desperately trying to flip himself over, reminding me of a turtle trapped on his back.

I flip him over. "Christ. At least you're okay."

I stand up to inspect my new prison. No doubt,

Caldwell dumped me here while he's considering how he wants to off my sorry ass. One turn around the room and I must admit that this is the strangest prison I've ever been in.

A full-sized bed sits in the corner with a thick downy comforter and too many pillows in shades of purple and pink. Posters line the wall illustrating boy bands who wear more eyeliner than I do. Soft music seeps from a stereo in the corner playing some weepy tune about never being loved for who they are.

A Hello Kitty alarm clock tells me the time from the corner and a teddy with a name tag that says Frederick sits on top of a black and white checkered beanbag.

"What the—?" I search the ceiling for the air vents that will surely send the death gas at any moment. "—hell is this?"

A door opens and a girl a little taller than me bounces into the room with earbuds dangling from one ear. A musical device sits clutched in one hand, a bowl of water in the other. She's scrolling through her playlist.

Winston bounds toward her, clamoring over a mess on the floor, papers and pens and shoes and vinyl records and books.

"Hey buddy." The girl stoops down to scratch him behind the ears. "Here's your water."

"What the *fuck*?"

She jerks her eyes up to meet mine.

"What are you giving my dog?"

"Chill. It's water." She closes the door behind her.

"Where am I?"

"My room."

Maisie. "You're my sister."

"So I've heard." She shrugs and arches her eyebrows "Though what Dad thinks will happen here, I've no clue."

Dad. My mind spins again and I try to still the room by reaching out and grabbing onto the closest solid object—a white dresser cluttered with makeup and folded clothes. Winston laps water loudly at the water bowl.

"You call him Dad."

"What do you call him?" I don't like her half-bored, half-angsty tone.

"Caldwell, son of Satan."

She frowns. "He said you didn't like him."

"It's hard to feel warm and fuzzy about a man who

buried you alive in a box after gassing you to death. Oh, and he abandoned me at eight, leaving me at the mercy of a rapist."

She arched her eyebrows again.

"But *you* wouldn't know anything about that, would you? Apparently, he's doing fine by you. You probably had presents at Christmas and cake on your birthday."

"If you say so." She scoops up Winston from the water bowl, wet face and all.

"So can I take my dog and go or is this like a trick?"

The kid smirks. "You can *try* to leave."

"Are you threatening me? I will throw you off a roof, kid."

She snorts. "Find a roof." She turns towards the door.

"Hey," I yell after her. "Don't walk away from me." *What a punk.*

From the doorway she turns back and gives me another sardonic stare. "Are you coming or what?"

She walks out of the bedroom without waiting for me to answer, so I run after her. She's halfway down a dim hall that lights up as she passes an opening to a huge circular space. It's more like a bubble than a room.

The walls are rounded and transparent. On one side stands Chicago, bright and illuminated. On the other, all I can see is the dark expanse of Lake Michigan.

"We're in The Needle?" I remember seeing The Needle when we first drove into Chicago. A tall, thin building with a rounded tip emerged from the waters of Lake Michigan, alone and isolated. Because of the rocks, no boat can approach it and the special glass prevents news crews and other airborne ships from seeing inside, but it must be one-way glass, because from here I can see the city fine. It is rumored that a rich eccentric dude built it as his private fortress. I didn't realize I knew the dude.

"You live here?" I search Maisie's face for deception.

She sighs. "For the last forty-eight days."

"Alone?"

"I am sixteen. I can cook and clean for myself."

"Who brings the food?" I've never died of starvation and I sure as hell don't want to now.

"My mom visits. And Dad."

"And we leave, *how?*" I ask. I've managed to do an entire lap around the room and have yet to see a single door.

"We don't. Dad is the only way in and out. I'm sure you know what I'm talking about."

"Unfortunately," I say. "But why the hell did he drop me off here with you?"

"How am I supposed to know? Do you think he tells me everything?"

"You call him Dad!"

Winston snuggles into her chest and a spike of jealousy hits me.

"Give me the pug." I grab Winston, but her hold on him tightens. Winston makes a small sound of protest, something like a choking squawk and Maisie lets go.

I win.

Cradling the fluff ball to my belly, I sink onto the sofa with him. He tries to squirm free but I hold him tighter. How ungrateful can he be? Does he have any idea the risks I took to get his curly-tailed butt back?

My eyes fix on a boat in the distance. Who the hell would be out on the water in these freezing temperatures? "Is there a way to go outside? Get fresh air?"

Maisie scrolls through her playlist again. "You'll die if you jump."

"So? It won't be the first time or the last, I'm sure."

"Even if you survive, Winston won't make it."

Shit. She's right, unless I can shield him. But I don't know how the shield works against water. Would I run along the top like a hamster ball? And if I break our fall but die like I did with Ally. Winston couldn't handle the freezing temperatures. He'd be dead from hypothermia before I regenerated.

I meet her eyes. "Back up. Why have you been here for a month?"

"Forty-eight days," Maisie corrects.

"Whatever. Is this like a grounding or something? Did you make out with someone cute?"

Maisie looks away. "Yeah, something like that."

"Shit. Harsh punishment."

Maisie's face softens. All the hard ass reluctance melts away. Her eyes round, her bottom lip sticks out a little farther. "You've no idea."

My chest clenches. Shit. Why does she look so sad? I know better than to ask. I have no interest in being sucked into anyone's problems. And really, I half-believe this is a trick. Caldwell is going to use this girl against me somehow, I know it. Better to keep my distance.

Yet, I find myself letting go of Winston and nudging him in the direction of the girl. She opens her arms to accept him immediately and he licks her face before flopping against her chest. I watch her love him for a long time.

She catches me staring and rolls her eyes. "What?"

"Nothing. You remind me of someone."

"Who?" Maisie asks, looking interested in something I've said for the first time.

Me. "Just a girl I used to know."

Chapter 16

Jesse

"**M**om!"

I jolt awake at the sound of Maisie's piercing exclamation. My heart is pounding and my mouth is sticky.

"Hi, baby," a woman's voice says.

A blonde woman steps into the light of the dim room. I must've slept most of the night away. Dawn creeps on the horizon. The water is bluer than when I closed my eyes and on the horizon itself, I can see a thick line of purple blooming red, like blood seeping into the water.

I stretch and take note of Winston sleeping on the couch. Maisie finally lets go of her mom.

The moment I get a good look at her, my shield goes up. "Oh *hell* no."

It's Caldwell's second—the polished princess in a

pantsuit who stands at his side for all public appearances. I think the press calls her his "primary advisor". The last time I saw her, I had my ribs broken by one of Caldwell's goons and she basically told me to walk it off. "What the fuck do you want?"

"Please don't swear in front of my daughter," she says, straightening. "I know you're an adult and can do what you please, but Maisie is still a minor."

Okay. This is the weirdest fucking thing I've heard all day.

"It's not like I've never heard the word, Mom," Maisie says.

I get a sense of silken wings darting, but Gabriel can't materialize. His voice is little more than a whisper in the back of my mind. "Calm yourself."

I can't. I see this woman and all I can think about is being Caldwell's captive. Maisie caught me off guard, being all teenager-y, but this woman—no. She's a stark reminder that Caldwell is a monster who wants to kill me. I need to get the hell out of here.

"Where is he?" Blue flame starts to lick up the side of my arms.

The blonde steps in front of Maisie, shielding her.

"I'm right here." Caldwell steps out of the

shadows and comes to stand beside Georgia. "Don't hurt my family."

He's grinning like he's on the verge of laughing hysterically, like this is one giant freaking joke to him.

The blue flames spike, growing in diameter, pushing everyone to the outermost edges of the room. "Are you *trying* to piss me off?"

"You're my family too." His eyes are luminous in the firelight, flames dancing in those shadowed orbs. "That's why I brought you here, Jesse. I want us to all be together."

"Stop fucking with me."

"I only wanted you to meet Maisie. I'll take you back to your friends now." He takes a step toward me like he has no problem grabbing a girl that's on fire.

"Don't touch me."

His grin doubles. He laughs like I'm being absurd. "I'm the only way out of here."

"Find another way to let me go or I'll burn this place to the ground."

"Your sister—"

"She's not my sister. If you wanted me to have a sister, you should've raised me with her instead of leaving me in that hellhole."

"Please." Georgia steps forward, placing herself more fully in front of Maisie. "Please don't hurt my daughter."

"Georgia," Caldwell snaps. His face warps from glee to fury in a second. "There's no need to beg. She won't hurt Maisie. Will you, Jesse?"

He's right. I can't firebomb a kid any more than I could firebomb Winston, who sits trembling at her feet. His fear dowses my anger. The flames flicker and die away.

What do I do? Gabriel doesn't answer me. Maybe Caldwell is right. Maybe the partis really do block each other's signals.

The flames are gone but I keep my shield up.

Caldwell comes closer, his grin back. "Don't wear yourself out."

"You'd like that wouldn't you?"

His smile is brilliant. *Yes*, the smile says. *Go ahead and weaken yourself for me.*

A long, thick silence stretches between us, tension still palpable in the air.

"Be careful with that one." Gabriel's voice makes me jump. A look of curiosity crosses Caldwell's face.

Caldwell? Tell me something I don't know.

"Maisie. She isn't like the others."

My eyes fall on the girl wrapped in her mother's arms. What are you talking about?

Silence.

"So?" Caldwell asks. "Will you allow me to carry you out of here?"

For a moment I can only blink at him. It can't be this easy. He can't simply have wanted to arrange a pep talk and reunion and then he's going to drop me off with my friends only to start trying to kill me tomorrow. Also, the longer I'm here, the more I learn about him. Maybe I can figure out how to kill him once and for all.

I might not be able to fight him *now*. If we blow up this needle, Winston will definitely get caught in the crossfire. I can't bring myself to endanger him like that. I also don't trust Caldwell to take me home. I'll wake up somewhere worse and I know it.

If he wants to play the batshit crazy card, so can I.

"No, we have so much catching up to do. I think I'll stick around for dinner." I mirror his grin, daring him to challenge me. "What're we having?"

Chapter 17

Ally

Gloria's erratic driving doesn't seem nearly as bizarre in Chicago as it did back home. I thought Nashville drivers were bad, but fifteen minutes on I-80 has reeducated me in a way I never expected. Even at this late hour, the traffic is unruly.

Gloria cuts across three lanes of traffic, while I white-knuckle her sketchbook. I finger the pages, intent on opening it.

"Don't." Gloria turns the wheel hard, rocking me in my seat.

"Is there something worse than Tate Tower exploding?" I ask.

She doesn't answer, her eyes remaining fixed on the dim highway stretching out before us.

"About that." Nikki leans up between the two front seats. "We don't have any context. It could happen anytime, right?"

I turn so I can see her face. "A.M.P.s can narrow

an event they view to a specific day."

Gloria glances at the sketchbook in my lap as if seeing something through the closed cover. "It happens the day after tomorrow."

Neither of us question her.

I look down at the cover too, scraping a nail along the metal rings binding the pages together. "We have a little time. Until then, we have to focus on getting Jesse back."

I can't hold the first two times Jesse was taken against her. She was kidnapped—but this time is different. She went willingly and it is hard not to be angry at her recklessness.

I'm sure Caldwell made some threat, but still. What are we going to do now?

I rock in my seat as Gloria slides off the highway onto an exit ramp. Two turns later and we pull up outside another apartment building. It's similar to Gloria's last Chicago apartment except darker and less inviting.

I resist the urge to lock the car door. "You've slept here right?"

Gloria gets out of the car. "We'll be safe here for now."

That's enough to get me to throw open the door and exit the gold Cadillac. Gravel slides beneath my boots and I hear a cat yowling from somewhere between the two brick buildings. I close the door and peek around the corner to see an alley with dumpsters and a herd of feral cats. Their little yellow eyes glow in the dark.

"Safe," I repeat. "The cats think so anyway."

Nikki places a hand on my back. "She's holding the door for you."

I glance over and see Gloria is in fact holding a door open for me.

"Oh sorry." I lift my bag up on my shoulder and shuffle across the dim lot, casting one last look at the sagging brick buildings before I dart inside with Nikki bringing up the rear.

The hallway is long and the same squash yellow as Gloria's kitchen back in Nashville. The wallpaper is some kind of fleur-de-lis design in repetitious patterns from top to bottom. Gloria hobbles up one floor, her cast scuffing the stained, industrial carpet on the stairs. She comes to a stop beside a door that was once white. Three brass numbers hang beneath a peep hole.

222.

The hallway smells like curry and someone is playing a TV way too loud. Upstairs, a baby is crying.

The deadbolt is reluctant to give into Gloria's key turning, so Gloria bumps her hip against the door. The bolt clanks open.

We step inside and Nikki locks the door behind her. The room is cold and smells stale. I maneuver around an armchair and go to the window, pulling it open a couple of inches to let the fresh air in.

"It's freezing outside." Nikki drops her bag on a gray loveseat.

Goosebumps rise on my arms. "We just need to get things circulating."

The lights click on, three weak 40-watt bulbs casting halos of illumination around the room.

"You're not a fan of luxury, are you?" Nikki's eyes slide over the secondhand furniture, the shag carpet the same color as the hallways, and the general cramped nature of the room. The cabinets of the kitchen nook are an old wood laminate and my guess is that there isn't any food here.

Gloria slides into a seat at the oak kitchen table. "I have all of my needs met."

I'm wrong about the food. I find a handful of cans

in the cabinet above the stove and several 2-liters of soda in the fridge.

Gloria removes her laptop from her pack and opens it on the tabletop. "You two can share the pullout bed."

"Where will you sleep?" I ask.

"I won't."

"Gloria," I begin, intent on scolding her. She's even worse at taking care of herself than Jesse.

Gloria sighs. "If I need to sleep, I'll take the chair."

Gloria is at least twenty years older than me. Probably twenty-five. She doesn't need to be sleeping upright in a chair in her own place. I can sleep on the floor, shag carpet or no and Nikki can sleep in the chair. Of course, I already know that will be a losing battle. Nikki won't let me sleep on the floor.

Nikki leans over my shoulder, peering into the open cabinets. "Boxed mac and cheese and canned chili." She kisses my temple. "We'll have chili mac."

My stomach rumbles. "Better get on with it."

Gloria doesn't look up from her computer, already deep in her task. "There's some cookware in the drawer under the stove."

I leave Nikki alone in the kitchen to do her thing

and sit at the table beside Gloria.

"So does this place have a back door too?"

"Yes." She leans out of her chair and pulls open the curtain, revealing a bridge stretching over a canal. She points at the shadows beneath the bridge. "I have a boat under there."

"Good to know."

"We can jump from this window if we need to."

"Are you trying to break your other leg and mine too?"

"Parachute jump."

I blink at her. She stands and demonstrates. "Put your legs together like this and bend into the knees. It distributes the impact evenly. Most of the time."

"How can you do that with your cast?"

"I'll manage."

"Or destroy your knee." I raise my voice so Nikki can hear me over the clank of pans. "Do you know how to parachute jump?"

Nikki who's got a pot of water on the stove, ripping open the box of macaroni, pauses. "Unfortunately." She fishes out the packet of powdered cheese and dumps the noodles into the water. Sometimes I'm amazed at how useful Nikki is, how functional. If Jesse were here, she'd be pacing the room or lying across the sofa whining dramatically.

I wish she was here. What is she doing right now? Is she frightened? Does she have Winston? Is she in pain?

I scoot my chair closer to Gloria. "You said you know where Jesse is."

Blue shadows dance across her face, projected by the computer in front of her.

"She's here." Gloria turns the laptop toward me.

Here is in the middle of Lake Michigan, about half a mile from shore.

"Oh my god." I grab the screen and adjust the angle. "They killed her and dumped her body in the lake?"

I imagine Jesse wrapped in chains and thrown into the icy water to die over and over and over again.

"No." Gloria pulls her computer away. "She's in The Needle."

It was described as a modern marvel on our city tour. Jesse had absolutely hated being on that bus with all the Asian tourists taking pictures of the buildings.

Why do they have to take pictures of everything? It's just a Coca-Cola can.

I enjoyed learning a little more about the city. It was a nice activity, incredibly normal, and for one afternoon it was just us. We got coffee and when I got too cold, Jesse wrapped her arms around me and tucked me into her coat, insisting I warm my hands in her pockets.

She was very sweet that day.

"So Caldwell owns the building?" Nikki grins at me triumphantly. "You owe me $5."

"I'll pay you later."

Gloria frowns.

"I bet it was Oprah's." I shrug. "She seems like the type to want an impenetrable fortress suspended over water. Don't you think? Caldwell has so many other properties in town, I just assumed he wouldn't need another."

"It was a good guess," Nikki says.

I lean over and peer at the screen. "How are you following her?"

"I implanted a tracker when we were still at Tate Tower, when I yanked out her IV."

She's very good. I hadn't even seen her do it.

I lean back in my seat. "What inspired you to tag her?"

Gloria frowns and suddenly looks very old. The skin under her eyes is puffy and unflattering. More lines than I've ever noticed before bisect her forehead and surround her mouth.

"When he took her before, we wasted too much time looking for her. As soon as I knew he'd contacted her on the roof, I wanted to prepare for this."

Nikki opens and closes several cabinets, making a whole lot of noise.

"What are you looking for?" I ask, turning in my seat.

"A strainer."

"I don't have one." Gloria's full attention has returned to the screen.

Nikki closes the cabinet door. "That's okay. I'll make do. You have a can opener though, right? If not, I might have a multitool in my bag."

"Drawer to the right of the stove."

I reach out and touch Gloria's hand, forcing her to look away from the computer and meet my eyes. "How are we going to get her out of The Needle? The tour guide said it was surrounded by rocks that would destroy any boat and no helicopter can land there."

"I'm working on that part."

"No doubt Caldwell can get in and out fine. Smart," Nikki says from the kitchen, peeling back the lid on a can.

I sigh and pick at a chip in the chair's wood with my fingernail. "Would it be too much to ask that our villain be a little more stupid?"

Nikki turns on the fan above the stove. For a moment, the grating whirl of the blades is all I can hear.

"I've called my back up." Gloria leans toward me, keeping her voice low. "They'll join us as soon as they can."

"Who?"

Gloria closes the laptop and gives Nikki a sidelong look. "You'll see."

Chapter 18

Jesse

This is the worst kind of torture I've ever experienced—close and constant contact with an emo teen.

Just when I think Caldwell can't get any more depraved, he pulls *this*.

I sit on the beanbag chair, watching Maisie lounge in her bed with her laptop in her lap. Huge earphones cover half her head, her eyes wide and focused on whatever internet crap she's engrossed in. Meanwhile, I'm sitting here with a pug in my lap surrounded by those eyeliner boys staring at me from the walls. Every few minutes, like clockwork, Maisie lets out a passive aggressive sigh to end all passive aggressive sighs.

Minutes tick into hours, and finally I can't take anymore.

"Sweet mother of god. You're killing me."

As soon as my leg muscles twitch, giving the signal of my intention to get up, the pug leaps. He lands on a pile of magazines. The glossy covers slide off of one another and create a cascading pyramid on the floor.

"What's your problem?" she asks, slipping the large headphones off of her head.

"I can't just sit here and watch you read articles about Jonathan Kiss-a-lots or Grant Great-hair or whatever the hell you're doing. It's making me crazy."

"Sorry." She throws up her hands. "I don't have an abundant social life here. I don't know anyone who flies, do you?"

I resist the urge to look for Gabriel, who's been strangely absent despite the fact it's just me and the kid. "*Did* you have friends?"

Her face goes as ice cold and unreadable as any sculpture in the Art Institute. "Yes. I *have* friends."

"I'm surprised." I shrug. "Caldwell doesn't seem like the type to encourage outside connections."

She blinks at me.

"Listen, I'm going a little stir crazy here. Don't you ever sneak out or anything? Don't you teens smoke or do drugs? Are you sure there's not some way to get a little fresh air?"

"Eww, gross. And no. There's not," she says with the same flat expression. "Unless you want to jump onto the rocks and get brained."

"I could use my shield," I say. "I can jump with Winston. Just point me to the window."

"You're not listening."

"*You're* not listening. I can't stay here."

She shrugs and puts her headphones back on. I fall back onto the beanbag and Winston curls up on my belly using me as a pillow. Within three minutes, he's snoring.

Gabriel, I think, hoping he'll show up.

Gabriel flickers into focus. He's standing like a giant in the middle of the girl's room.

Where do you keep going?

"I can't materialize here," he says as if that tells me anything. "I stay close."

How's Ally and Gloria? I couldn't care less about Sasquatch.

"Jason attacked. Gloria protected the group."

"What?"

Maisie rips her headphones off again. "What?"

"This is a private conversation with—me and myself," I tell her. "Put your headphones on."

"You can't tell me what to do."

"In most civilizations, younger siblings are

subservient to the older ones." I consider igniting my hand to prove my point. I decide against it, knowing that it could go really badly if this place doesn't have a fire extinguisher. Those boyband posters look very flammable.

"Whatever." Maisie rolls her eyes and yanks the headphones back on, punching her keyboard more furiously than before.

I watch her for a moment and I decide she probably muted the volume, waiting to see what I'd say. I storm out of the room. By the time I reach the center of the bulbous needle, Gabriel appears. To my surprise, he's pretty substantial. Not the so-real-I-can-touch-you Gabriel that I usually have my conversations with, but much clearer than before.

"I need to get back. They're defenseless without me. Okay, not really. Gloria's badass and Ally is super smart, but I should be with them, not here."

"They may succeed. He isn't invincible. None of you are."

"Do you see any way out of here? It can't really be sealed up, can it?"

I pace the great room, looking at the Chicago skyline. Ally is out there somewhere. Safe, I hope.

"There are no doors and the windows do not open. It would take immense force to break the glass."

"Like a firebomb?"

"Yes."

"Ok, if I firebomb the glass, can I survive the fall?"

"Winston would not survive the fall."

"What if I cradle him against my chest? He might be small enough to fit inside my shield."

"If your shield does not hold, he would die of hypothermia. You cannot leave with him. If you are willing to leave him behind, you may leave."

"No." I throw up my hands, irritated that Gabriel has nothing to tell me but what I've already figured out myself. "I didn't come here and suffer through all this—" I jab a finger in the direction of Maisie's bedroom. "—this *emotion*, just to abandon my pug now. *I* don't abandon people, unlike someone we know."

"Then you must wait and hope they come for you."

I frown. "No, I didn't come so Ally could do another risky rescue mission. I don't want her trying to save me." As soon as I say it, I realize my mistake. Of course, she's going to try. She'll always try.

"Fuck." I fall onto the sofa. "How did I overlook that?"

I pull at my face with my hands.

I look up at Gabriel. "Can you shield her, even if I'm so far away?"

No answer.

I clench and unclench my fist. I want to throw something. I decide the couch is too big so I snatch off the pillows and hurl one after the other at Gabriel. They sail right through him of course.

"Shielding her is the least you can do to make up for being such a giant asshole!"

Gabriel's feathers stiffen, rising up like fur. "What did I do to upset you?"

"You lied to me."

"I have never lied."

I want to slap him. "You sure as hell left out a lot. When did you plan to tell me I was going to die? Huh? When exactly were you going to say 'oh hey, by the way, you're going to have to blow up or the whole world is going to die, including the woman you love'?"

I stagger. "What did I just say?"

"You said 'you sure as hell left out a lot. When did you plan to tell me I was going—"

"Yes, I know what I said. Thank you." I look at Gabriel in such a way that I hope I can melt his face.

The woman you love.

I mean of course I love Ally. I tell her I love her all the time.

I wail and pull at my face.

Gabriel crosses the room and peers down at me where I lay collapsed on the couch. "Your heartbeat is elevated. Are you distressed?"

"I hate you. Go away."

He blinks his big cat eyes at me. "I do not sense that you actually want me to leave."

I cover my face with my hands. "Please stop talking."

Gabriel listens to this command at least.

For a long time, I sit on the leather sofa, face covered, listening to my breath.

"Is there anything else terrible you should tell me?" I lower my hands to make sure Gabriel is still there. He is, hands in the pockets of his black dress pants. "Is Ally going to be skinned alive in front of me or something? Am I going to go all dark and murder her? I want full disclosure now."

Gabriel turns away from me and looks out over

the water. "You are in control, Jesse. Not me. You will have whatever you want."

"I don't want to die."

"Is that all?" he asks, his back still turned to me.

I guess not. But how did I expect this to end? I was so sure insanity would get me first—and it still might at the rate I'm going, talking to angels, jumping out of burning buildings, and allowing psychopaths to cart me off into the night.

But this is a little different. I have this hope that I'll get lucky. Yeah, the odds are shitty that I'll sort out all of this mess with Caldwell and the partis, yet I hoped that I would and even better, that there would be an end to all this fighting. A *happy* ending.

The happiest ending I can hope for now is that if I explode, it doesn't hurt so much.

I pull my cell out of my pocket. No signal.

It couldn't have anything to do with being suspended over a huge freshwater lake, could it? I scroll through my contacts and see Brinkley's name on the screen.

My thumb hovers over the send button.

Oh B. What I wouldn't give to call you now and have you tell me what to do.

My chest aches the longer I stare at his name. In my mind, Caldwell appears behind him, grabs hold of his neck and—snap. The stark horror of the moment replays over and over.

I can't forget that Caldwell is a monster. And monsters lie. God, I wish he was lying about the end of the world crap. But Gabriel hasn't said a word to contradict him.

I squeeze my phone until my fingers turn white. I push the scroll down button until Brinkley's name disappears. I come to a stop on a second name.

Lane.

I haven't even thought about him. Okay, so this is what he wanted anyway—a break. And who said I had to think about him while I'm on this break? At first I thought about him a lot. I imagined what it would be like when we made up. I pictured fantastic makeup sex of course. I also imagined eloquent speeches where he explains what a fool he is for dumping me and how he knows now he can never live without me. But I haven't had one of the makeup-sex-I'm-an-idiot-forgive-me fantasies in a while.

Then I find out I'm going to explode the world and who's the first person I think about?

The woman you love.

"Ah, shit." I sink into the sofa. "I've just learned I'm going to die like forever, and I haven't even thought about Lane."

"You do not love him," Gabriel says. "You love Alice."

I grit my teeth. "Yes, thank you."

He frowns. "You seem as though you would like answers. I am providing the clarity you desire."

"Okay, really, I do want you to leave now. Do you sense that? Go on. I'll call you if Caldwell shows up with a machete or something."

Gabriel flickers and disappears, leaving me alone to stare out at the beautiful expanse of blue grey water.

You love Alice.

I press my forehead to the cold glass. I know what he means. I love her like *that*. I want her like *that*—no one else. Fuck. I can't argue. I kept my distance because she didn't want it to be just about the sex for me. But it isn't about the sex. I'm trying to picture this happily ever after. I don't know what that even looks like, except that it's just me and her. It's not even sexy, it's—happy. Peaceful. Sweet.

"You were afraid it would hurt to lose her. Now

you understand you will lose her no matter what."

I whirl to find Gabriel standing behind me.

"Oh my god, do you mind?"

"You are trying to understand—"

"I know!" I yell. "But can I have a little privacy?"

"I am here to help you."

"If you don't go away, I'm going to rip your feathers out."

Scowling, Gabriel flickers and then disappears.

Maisie is standing at the edge of the hallway, looking at me with curious stare.

I put both of my hands on my hips. "What do you want?"

She grins. "You're a little crazy, aren't you?"

"Don't I know it."

Chapter 19

Ally

"**W**ho did you ask for help?" I accept the bowl of chili mac that Nikki hands me before she sits down on the chair across the room. "Do you want to sit here?"

"No, I'm fine." She winks at me. It makes my stomach knot and my cheeks warm. "I have a better view of you from here."

I'm grinning like a fool when I turn back and see Gloria staring at me, chewing her own chili mac. Her expression is carefully neutral.

"Actually Brinkley asked for their help," Gloria says, putting her bowl down and wiping her mouth with a paper napkin.

"Oh that's right." I remember Brinkley's letter, which came with the first journal.

I trust Gloria to make sure the information makes it into their hands. But I only know one who will come for sure. If I'm wrong and no one steps up, I want you to know that I trust you too. You've always had Jesse's interests at heart, and I think that's the real thing that scares Caldwell.

I can't count how many times I've read that letter, over and over. "It's been two months. Shouldn't someone have stepped up by now?"

"They have." Gloria cuts her eyes to Nikki who is lost in her own bowl of food. Gloria's eyes say the rest.

They just won't come near Tate Tower. "So are they coming here?"

"They're already in Chicago, surveying the situation," Gloria says. "They're investigating The Needle."

"So, what, they'll call us?"

Gloria scrapes her bowl clean before I've finished my fourth bite. "You need some sleep and I need to draw."

"I'll take first watch." Nikki takes her bowl to the sink.

Gloria accepts her guard duty offer with a nod and begins setting up her papers and pencils on the table in front of her.

Nikki takes a seat beside me, pushing the hair back behind my ears. "How are you holding up?"

"Okay." I shrug. I put my bowl on the side table.

I was so hungry before, but now I can't seem to shovel the food into my mouth. "What about you?"

"Fine. Believe it or not, this is a rather calm day for me."

I smile. "Jeremiah works you too hard."

She shrugs. "The price of trust, I suppose."

"The price of skill. You're amazing."

She turns toward me. "*You* were amazing in the tunnel. Any other girl as pretty as you would've squealed at least once, and I even stepped on your fingers."

I'd forgotten about that. I look down and see the red line across the knuckles of my left hand.

Nikki leans forward for a kiss. I let her have my lips once, a soft brush of skin on skin. She pulls me into her lap and runs a hand through my hair.

"It's going to be okay." She reads the lines on my face. "We'll get her back."

"I'm so worried—"

She rubs my back. "I know."

Nikki wants to kiss and cuddle and while that is comforting to an extent, I also feel like I can't sit still. Maybe a shower would help.

I kiss Nikki's cheek and climb out of her lap. "I

don't know if I'll have another chance to wash my hair. Better do it before anyone else comes pounding on the door."

I gather up my toiletries and the few things I took from the room before we left Tate Tower. I close myself in the bathroom. I turn on the shower and exhaust fan but I don't get in.

I wish I could hide in here with the laptop. I want to continue my research, learn more about the handful of people that Caldwell hasn't yet managed to kill. But I don't want Nikki to ask questions. If it were just Gloria and I, I would share my secret.

So I let the water run, using the toilet as a seat as I pull the last composition notebook out of my bag— the last, because it contains Brinkley's final entry. It's not the research I want to do, but it is important information that could help us.

I glance over the last page for the thousandth time, for anything I could have missed. When I find nothing, I flip back three entries.

I was on the bench when I saw Sullivan.

He just appeared, his back to me as he watched the water. The wind was rippling the surface and the high noon sun made everything shine, even the dingy iron of the bridge.

"I was wondering if I'd ever see you again," I said. I set my back against the bench and felt the heat from the wooden planks through my leather jacket.

"I wanted to say thank you," he said, turning around. He faced me and I got a good look at him. He squinted against the sun in his eyes, his freckles scrunching up. I knew immediately that he'd changed. Somehow. "The camps are actually closed and that's thanks to you."

"I should thank you," I said. "Jackson still has her brains in her head."

I try to picture it: Brinkley, Gloria and Caldwell—working together toward a common goal. Even then Caldwell was a liar, manipulating Brinkley in order to gain his help.

I flip the page.

"I know you have questions about Maisie. She's safe. Happy."

"You're her father," I said. I sat forward and rested my elbows on my knees. "Her biological dad."

"I wasn't lying when I said I met her mother in the camp," he began. "It's amazing how much a man's feelings can intensify

in a place like that. We avoided sex for months. We were scared of exactly that kind of thing happening. Georgia—Maisie's mother— knew having something happen to her baby would kill her. And it almost did. I didn't take Maisie for me. I took her hoping it would heal some broken part of her mother......We're together again, and that's what matters. Georgia needs her."

I read this paragraph again. And again.

Maisie.

The fact that Caldwell mentioned Maisie to Jesse means she is no secret. He is going to use Maisie somehow, use her like he uses everyone to get what he wants. I'm not worried Jesse will have a soft spot for the girl. Jesse doesn't do well with kids as a rule, and a sixteen year old is probably even less cuddly than a six year old. But the idea that Maisie somehow fits into this, another innocent girl, makes me nervous.

I close the composition notebook and test the water to see if it's warm enough to do my hair at least.

I strip down and step into the stream. The image of Brinkley and Caldwell talking by the water replays in my mind. I'm more than a little irritated at Nikki. It isn't her fault. She can't be blamed for the inconvenience she's causing.

I know exactly what Brinkley would say to all this—all my pointless obsessing and attempts to prepare for a future I can't predict.

Hindsight is 20/20, kid.

And he's right. Why obsess about hypotheticals? Soon enough, I'll know exactly how this will end.

Chapter 20

Jesse

"**I**f you want to leave, you'll have to let me touch you," Caldwell says for the billionth time.

"Uh, *nope*." I've got Winston in my arms, belly up like a baby. I refuse to let him run around this prison cell, lest Caldwell decide he is going to snatch him up again. Lucky for me, Winston likes to be cradled like a baby, or this would get old quick.

"I've told you what you need to know," he says. "Now you understand the gravity of the situation. Let me return you to your friends."

"Do you think I'm a complete moron?" I ask. "The last time you transported me, you used Liza's snappy power and knocked me out. Who knows what you'll try to use on me the second time."

"I *told* you." Caldwell's voice strains with the tension. "I only wanted you to meet your sister. You've met her and you understand what I have to offer. We don't have a lot of time left. We should make amends and be a family while we still can."

"You know, this whole sales pitch would work better if you weren't grinning like an axe murderer."

Caldwell laughs. Throws his head back and laughs like he's having the best time in the world.

"Yeah, see. Your crazy is showing."

I'm brushing off his remarks, but the truth is, he's hit a chord. A family. Yes, I do want one. I've wanted one since I was eight and Eric Sullivan—Caldwell—dropped out of my life. What I got instead was a rapist stepdad, a shitty childhood, and the tumultuous life as a death replacement agent.

"You can't just take it all back," I tell him.

"I can. That's what I'm trying to make you understand, Jesse. I *can* take it all back."

It's like someone has kicked me in the chest. "I'm not going to let you brainwash me."

"Your death replacing has already erased some of the worst memories. Why not let me take the rest? In exchange, I can give you Maisie and Georgia—and me. We wouldn't have to fight anymore. We could be on the same side."

My jaw drops. "What kind of new mindfuckery is this?"

But even as I say it, my heart aches. I want it. I can't deny that I want it.

He steps toward me, little more than a silhouette in front of the great window. "Let me prove it to you. Let's kill Jason together."

"Uh, no. Jeremiah couldn't make me kill him, and I sure as hell won't let you make me."

A flicker of frustration screws up his face before he regains his calm. "He's hunting your friends now. We have to protect them. I will let you absorb his gift. Just let me prove to you that we are on the same team."

"I am not sure Team Jesse T-shirts and a Team Jesse parade will prove anything at this point." I say, but he'd hit another nerve. *He's hunting your friends.*

Gabriel?

Gabriel tries to appear, but only the scent of rain bleeds through. I wish I could understand why he can't be clear around Caldwell, but I can't expect Gabriel to explain that to me. He can't even explain why grape flavoring doesn't taste like grapes. Useless.

Is Jason hunting them? Are Ally and Gloria in danger now?

Yes.

"Let me prove it to you," Caldwell says.

"Put on gloves."

He arches an eyebrow. "What?"

"Put on thick snow gloves so you can't snap. Hell, mummy wrap your hands actually. Call your offspring in here and have her wrap medical tape around your hands. Then when no one else is in the room—no one for you to command to kill or sedate me—I want to search your pockets for sedatives. Only then will I let you take me *and* Winston somewhere."

His eyes narrow. "Paranoia doesn't suit you."

I shrug for added nonchalance. "Take it or leave it."

"We can't take the pug."

"I said—"

"Do you really think it is wise to bring a pug to a firefight?"

I look down at the little squished face in my arms. He has a point.

"He'll be safe with Maisie."

"No, no, *no*," I say. "That means I have to come back here."

"You're safest here. We all are."

"Winston." Maisie calls from her room down the hall. Winston hears her and squirms in my arms.

"Winnie Pug, come here boy."

It's either set him down or let him fall and break a hip. I put him on the floor and the little traitor runs down the hall toward the thin sliver of light coming from Maisie's door. He nudges it open wider with his nose. Her voice breaks into a sing-song chorus.

I turn back to find Caldwell smiling.

"You did that didn't you? You like mind-melded and told her to call him."

"Jason is going to kill your friends, and I'm offering to help you. Do you want my help or not? Last chance."

Gabriel's shadow flickers in the corner.

Is he going to kill me and leave my body to freeze in Lake Michigan?

No.

Why should I believe anything you say? You set me up to die in the first place. All of this is your fault.

He says nothing to this, or his words are drowned out by Caldwell's approach. I keep my shield up, shimmering in place.

Caldwell stops short of me, looking down on me with a really good imitation of fatherly concern.

"Let me help you." Caldwell grins like I'm about

to sign over a blank check. "I have so much to make up for."

I snort.

I think of Ally running for her life, and Jason as indestructible as they come, trying to beat her half to death—just like Caldwell did.

I meet his eyes. "Wrap your hands and we have a deal."

Chapter 21

Ally

"**F**uck!"

Gloria's yell jolts me awake. I come to a sitting position with a sharp intake of breath.

Nikki is already on her feet with her gun. "Grab your bag." She slides my bag across the floor toward me. She's already packed it up.

I stand and pull on each of my boots with a tug. "What's going on?"

"Jason is here. He's beating the hell out of the keypad outside, trying to get into the building."

Gloria opens the window and turns back to face me. "Remember what I said about parachute jumping?"

"*What?*" I'm trying to bring the world into focus despite the frightful thrashing of my heart, but I'm still half wrapped in dreams. On instinct my hand goes to my bag, but my laptop is closed and screen locked, and

Brinkley's papers are undisturbed.

Gloria lifts her cast covered leg and sticks it out of the window.

"Are you sure this is a good idea?" I ask.

Her legs are out of the window and after a precarious moment of balancing on the window sill, she jumps through. A heartbeat later, I hear a soft thud of feet connecting with earth.

I stick my head out of the window, sucking in the cold air. Gloria pulls herself to standing. She looks like she's putting even more weight on her uninjured leg, but otherwise, is moving okay.

The apartment's door handle rattles. Then fists pound at the front door.

"Go on." Nikki puts a hand on her back. "I'll help lower you down."

On the ground, Gloria motions for me to hurry. I take a deep breath and sling my legs over the lip of the window. Nikki grabs onto my arms, forearms clasped with mine, and begins to lower me down. My toes stretch, desperate to find earth beneath them, but I'm too high up. The side of the brick building scratches at my jacket, smearing dead leaves and dirt along my side.

I look up to see Nikki patiently holding my arms.

"Put your legs together and let go. As soon as you feel the ground touch your toes, bend your knees. Okay?"

I let go and fall.

I slam the ground, rolling to the side as a sharp pain shoots up my hip.

Gloria helps me to my feet. I lean on her, testing my weight on my feet. My ankle hurts, but it isn't so bad. I've had worse.

I turn at the sound of Nikki's feet connecting with the ground. Just as she does, Jason sticks his head out the window above. Then he's trying to climb out the window after us.

He jumps, lands and starts coming before we even have a chance to react. His face is a mask of fury and he swings at Nikki, but she ducks, driving an uppercut into his sternum.

"Move!" Gloria limps across the small patch of earth and shoves a gun under Jason's jaw.

He tries to yank himself free, but Gloria grabs onto his throat and squeezes. Forcing his chin up with her muzzle, she pulls the trigger. Brains shoot out of the top of his skull and into the oak tree overhead. The branches and leaves are splattered red. Jason hits the ground like a sack of potatoes.

"Jesus." I swallow a wave of nausea and stumble back on my weak ankle, my hip throbbing.

The three of us crowd around his body. Thankfully, his face isn't disfigured, but I keep my eyes carefully pointed away from the wet mess that clumps around the top of his head.

"Did that work?" Relief washes over me.

"Shit." Nikki's grip tightens on my arm.

"What?" But I don't need her to answer my question. The hole at the bottom of his chin is closing.

Gloria motions toward the bridge. "We have to go."

We reach the boat, a little dinghy hidden in the shadows beneath the bridge. We climb in. The three of us will be a tight fit, but we pile in anyway, with me nestled between Nikki's legs and our bags. Gloria yanks on the pull cord.

The boat roars to life.

"How did he find us?" I ask Gloria. "Is he using an A.M.P.?"

Like Caldwell used Micah. I don't dare mention her baby brother aloud.

"I don't know." Gloria glances behind her once more before focusing on the river ahead. "But I'll find out."

She steers the boat into the middle of the small canal and turns the motor on full blast. The little boat lurches forward, kicking up mist and wind in our hair.

I don't look away from the illuminated bank, waiting for the next monster to show his face.

Chapter 22

Jesse

Caldwell steps from the bulbous head of The Needle and in a heartbeat, we're outside a brick building in some godforsaken part of Chicago. Godforsaken because I've never seen a shadier, more depressing street. Most of the lights have been busted out, with the exception of one tangerine colored bulb that flickers about half a block up. In the spotlight below, a mangy cat licks its paw.

"Where the hell are we?"

"You don't recognize it?" He spares me a glance. "I suppose your friends don't tell you all their secrets."

"Don't imply that you're the god of truth."

He gestures with his wrapped hands toward the building directly in front of us, its front door busted in on its hinges. I peek inside and hear people talking. A closer look reveals a small huddle of bewildered tenants clustered together.

"What's going on?" I ask him. I don't like the wide eyes of the woman holding a baby in her arms.

"We're too late," he says and grabs on to me. The world disappears for a heartbeat, and we step into a room. The kitchen table is overturned and the bed has some crumpled sheets on it, as if someone had just woken up. With my head out the window, I see nothing on the ground below. Caldwell moves me again.

"Hey—" *Stop yanking me around.* I'm about to say. I don't get it all out.

Now we are in the backyard, or whatever you want to call this. A stretch of grass runs from the back of the building to a canal, one of the many that no doubt connects to Lake Michigan.

Caldwell is frowning at the ground. I turn away from the canal and come to stand beside him. He's staring at a thick slick of something gooey.

"Is that—?"

"So he can even heal brain damage. Interesting."

"Oh god." I search for the bodies of my friends, but I don't see anything.

"They're not here," he tells me. "But he'll catch up to them sooner or later. We would've been here sooner if you hadn't argued with me."

I snort. "Don't you get enough blind followers from your congregation?" I frown. "Gloria must've brought them here thinking it was safe. Guess that means you know all of our supposedly secret places?"

"Unless you have a sealed underground room without windows, doors, or cameras—you can be found."

"Assuming you killed everyone who knew about the room." My breath billows white around my face in the icy air.

He gives me a wicked smile.

"Of course you had your builders killed." I'm not even surprised. "So now what?"

"We have to catch up to them before Jason does. Are you ready?"

"Oh, you're asking my permission to manhandle me now?"

Caldwell looks away from me for a minute, his head cocked as if he's listening to something. "The police are coming."

"How do you know?"

He gives me a malicious grin and taps the side of his head. "I'm listening. Frances of 1212 Ducet street just saw a car creep past her house. They're coming with no lights or sirens on. They must be canvassing for the gunman."

"How are we going to find them?" I ask, unwilling to take a step toward him yet.

His fox grin grows wider. "Let me show you how useful I can be."

He steps toward me, his wrapped hands raised up like little crab claws. I have to admit that I'm surprised he wrapped his hands just to placate me. When he can use his mind-whatever to control people and has unlimited freedom with his teleporting thingy—I guess having your hands tied isn't much of a sacrifice.

I hold my hands up to stop him. "Stop looking so creepy or I'm not going anywhere with you."

The moment the words get out of my mouth, several colorless forms whip around the building.

"Police. Hands up."

Caldwell grabs onto me and we disappear. There is a moment of darkness—no, darkness isn't right. When I'm in a dark room and there's simply no light, the room hasn't disappeared. I can still see the furniture and belongings, and after a moment, their shapes begin to come into focus. Stepping between places with Caldwell was more like stepping into nothing than into a dark room. A heartbeat of void, and then we are on the Magnificent Mile, watching a single pair of skaters take a turn about the ice.

"What time is it?" I ask, as a man lifts his female partner up into the air before placing her on her skates again.

"Almost eleven."

I point at the skaters. "Can they be out here?"

"They can do whatever they want," Caldwell says and points at the empty box-office. No one is here to chase them away.

"So where are they?" I don't see Ally or Gloria or even Sasquatch anywhere on the illuminated streets stretching out around me.

Caldwell turns left and heads north. I follow him, my breath huffing white around my head as I struggle to keep up. We scurry past a bank, a burrito place, and a coffee shop. A few blocks up, the canal comes into view. Caldwell stops on the bridge and leans over so he can peer beneath. I try to do the same but I'm too short.

"There's her boat." Caldwell straightens and turns in all directions. He squints as if trying to see something far away, with his head slightly cocked as if also listening. Then a grin spreads across his face.

"There."

I follow his finger. I don't see anything through the herds of people walking from one destination to another. Some women are dressed in ridiculous heels and short skirts that are definitely giving them vaginal hypothermia. Whatever bar they're heading to can't possibly be worth it, right? I mean, I never wear that stuff, and I've never had a problem getting laid.

"There," Caldwell urges again, turning my chin slightly to the left.

Now I see her. The red coat is a dead giveaway. Not to mention Sasquatch standing beside her.

"Ally." I call her name. She's still talking to Sasquatch as they wait for the light to change and the crosswalk to illuminate. I cup my hands over my mouth. "Ally."

Someone screams and several people stagger back.

I see Gloria's gun go up, and I'm running.

Caldwell slips his arm under mine mid-step. There's a step of nothing, and then I'm almost right on top of them.

"Ally," I scream again. The shield goes up around her, knocking Sasquatch back a pace. Gloria's face washes with relief when she sees me, her gun faltering for a second. Jason tackles her, slamming her into the ground. She cries out as the two of them connect with the pavement, knocking back a second time as they roll into Ally's shield.

"Get off of her." I bend down and grab Jason's head. I twist his hair in my hands and yank him backward off of Gloria. As soon as he realizes it's me, he drops her and grabs onto my throat.

He starts to squeeze and I see stars. I wrench myself out of his grip and expect for him to try again, but his body convulses and doubles over. My eyes follow the wires sticking out of his back to the black electroshock weapon held in Sasquatch's hand.

Caldwell is just standing to the side watching us, a huge grin on his face as if this is the best show ever.

I throw my hands up. "I thought you said you were going to make yourself useful!"

All eyes go from me to Caldwell. Ally, Nikki, and Gloria all take a step back from him, bumping into a few of the closest lookie-lous. I think he likes their fear. His grin certainly deepens.

Jason slams into my midsection and knocks me off my feet. My head connects with the pavement and the world spins. For a moment, I see nothing but color, smeared and unrecognizable.

Ally screams and I force the world into focus. Someone is pulling me to my feet, and I see Jason dragging Ally away from Caldwell, using her as a shield, as if Caldwell gives a damn about saving her life. The sight of Ally being used against me, *again*, sends me into a rage.

I power up without thinking. Blue flames erupt around me and the crowd screams. A few "holy shit"s and "what the fuck" exclamations ripple through the crowd. Jason shoves Ally down onto the street.

"About time." Jason launches himself at me.

"Run." I motion for Ally and everyone around me to take cover.

Jason doesn't stop coming. He sticks his arms right into the blue flame and his flesh ignites. I take a step back and punch him in the chest once, a poorly aimed strike. The second blow connects with his solar plexus and he stumbles back. The burns all along his body start to heal themselves.

Jason grins. "I can do this all night."

"Well, I haven't the time for that." Caldwell shoves his taped hands into the blue flames and lets the fire burn off the bindings. He steps back, hands in flames and shakes off the remnants of tape.

Ally and Gloria are hiding in the alcove of a Starbucks, using a concrete pillar as their shield. I put the shield around Ally again, realizing it must have faltered as my head bounced off the concrete.

I prepare myself for Jason's second attack.

Caldwell doesn't let him get that far. With his hands free of the tape, he grabs Jason and disappears.

"Hey," I yell. "*Hey.*"

My fire pulses and the few remaining people around me run screaming.

That jerk. I should've known his goal was to get ahold of Jason and kill him for his power. I should've known he wanted it all for himself. What an idiot I am—

Something slams into the pavement ten feet in front of me. Caldwell appears beside the sack of meat, looking down at the busted mess that was Jason.

I look up and then down at the body again. I turn to Caldwell. "You threw him off a building?"

"Heal *that.*" Caldwell tugs at the bottom of his suit jacket. When Caldwell sees me staring, he starts to laugh like he's just made a joke. It's infectious. Before

I know it, I'm giggling too. That is, until I see Ally giving me the most horrified look, like she just caught me bludgeoning baby seals or something.

"Go on," Caldwell encourages me, his smile still bright. "If you scatter his brains, he can't regenerate. Just smear them all over the concrete."

I blink several times, search for the right thing to say. "Uh, that's a sweet offer, but I don't really have any interest in plunging my fingers into someone's mushy brains. Thanks."

"It's how you'll absorb his power." Caldwell kneels down and points at the split skullcap. "You have to be the one to finish him. Go on."

I take a step toward Jason's body. It's completely busted. It's not murder if he can't heal, right? And I'm not the one who threw him off the building. Mega healing powers *would* be pretty great.

"Hurry," Caldwell urges me as I step closer.

"Jesse, what are you doing?"

"Isn't this what you wanted? You said you want me to be invincible."

"Not here." She looks around the crowded street. "Not like this. Everyone can see you. This is going to be all over the news."

"Oh, right." Caldwell snaps his fingers.

I suck in a breath, waiting for his power to disable us. Ally should be okay. She's in the shield, but Gloria and I are completely exposed.

He cocks his head and snaps his fingers again. "As in, I have an idea? Eureka?"

I'm not comforted.

"To be clear, I will take care of the crowd." Caldwell turns toward the mass of people. Several step back, except for one woman who actually looks a little closer at Caldwell's face.

Her face alights with recognition. "Are you Timothy Caldwell? You are, aren't you? I've been to one of your shows."

"No." Caldwell meets her eyes. "In fact, you've never seen me before. Go home and feed your cat, Dorothy."

The woman blinks, shakes her head. Without another glance, Dorothy shuffles past us toward the subway, on her way home to feed her cat, presumably.

I meet Caldwell's gaze. "You can't mind wipe everyone."

He bristles at this, tugging the end of his suit jacket. "Ye of little faith."

Concentration overtakes his face. He turns toward the crowd and the emergency crews on the outer edge of the cluster.

A strange feeling washes over me. A sort of buzz that presses on the inside of my skull, like my head might pop off. I stick a finger in my ear and it doesn't help. I feel like my ears need to pop, but holding my nose doesn't help.

Something happens to the crowd. Everyone has stopped moving. A general shuffling or bewilderment has prevailed amidst the chaos. Now, people are standing around zombiefied. The atmosphere changes again. People begin to blink and shuffle away. Several people step around Jason's body as if it isn't there— and not in an oh-my-god-a-busted-body kind of way. It's more like a hobo-sleeping-in-the-street kind of way.

"Wait, what?" I watch the crowd disperse. "What's happening?"

"Nikki," Ally yells. "Nikki, stop."

I turn to see Nikki walking away from us. She has her shoulder bag lifted high, and she's walking away from us like she can't hear Ally.

Ally turns wide fearful eyes on me. "Stop her."

I try not to smile, but I can't help it. Sending Nikki away is a fantastic trick. Why shouldn't she walk to the end of the Earth and never come back?

I giggle and catch Caldwell smiling at me. That sobers me up.

"Jesse. Help me." Ally screams again. She's pushing both her hands against Nikki's chest, but she won't stop trying to walk to the subway entrance.

"Can you stop her?" I ask Caldwell.

He arches an eyebrow. "Are you sure you want me to?"

I consider this, but another yelp from Ally and I concede. "God, yes. Okay."

Nikki stops trying to push through Ally and descend the subway stairs. She blinks at all of us for several heartbeats and her eyes focus on Ally. "What happened?"

"He's healing." Caldwell nudges me, bringing my attention back to the mess at my feet. "You don't have much time."

Gloria steps out of her dim corner in the Starbucks alcove. ""Don't do it, Jesse. It will change you."

I arch an eyebrow. "In a good way? Like teeth

whitening or a dye job?"

"No," Gloria says.

"Don't frighten her, Jackson." The malice returns to Caldwell's voice. The fun is over. "You don't know what you're talking about."

"Don't I? I was with you when you took Henry Chaplain's gift."

Caldwell's eyes narrow on mine. "This is your last chance. You can't expect me to throw a man off a building for you *every* day."

"Really? You seem to like this sort of thing."

Caldwell grabs my arm and wrenches me forward. "Just scoop out his brains with your hands, and it'll all be over. No more worrying about him hunting your friends. You'll be indestructible, and you can use your shield to protect Alice. It's perfect."

It sounds perfect.

Ally's face is a mixture of fear and worry. "It's too good to be true. There must be a catch."

Caldwell shoves me down onto Jason's body.

My hands shoot out to protect myself from the fall and I connect with something warm and mushy. My hands are *in* Jason's skull. *Ugh.* My gag reflex is activated and I'm about to puke. I stand up and come away with a fistful of Jason's brains.

Oh shit—

It's all I manage to comprehend before white fire erupts in my eyes. I'm convinced I'm being boiled alive by my own firebomb somehow, but this seems like a strong reaction to touching some brains. Super gross, but not spontaneous combustion worthy.

I can't stop screaming. I fall, a moment of weightlessness overtakes me before I connect with, presumably, the concrete. At least it feels like rough concrete as I grope for anything to grab on to. But I can't open my eyes. I can't see anything or feel anything but the white hot pain ripping me in two.

Chapter 23

Ally

Jesse pulls herself away from Jason's body and they erupt in blue fire. Jason's corpse disintegrates immediately, but Jesse just burns.

In color and intensity, the flames are similar to Jesse's firebombs, yet this blue is more pure, white almost, and not tinged with the red of her initial start-up. Blisters spring up along the side of her hands and face, running up her body as she screams. She tries to stand and collapses. She howls in pain, clutching her head and wailing.

I search the ground for anything to throw on her, a piece of cloth or heavy blanket that might put out the fire. I tear off my coat and jolt forward to wrap Jesse in it, but Nikki grabs hold of me.

"Hey—" I try to wrench free of her. "Let go."

"You'll burn before you ever get close to her," Nikki says, tightening her grip. I try to wrench myself free. "Look. *Look*."

I crane my head around to see what she's talking about. A thin sheen of gas, a cloud about a foot in diameter is burning the atmosphere around her. Caldwell's pants catch fire and he steps back, patting at the fabric. The sidewalk is charred black in a radius beneath Jesse.

"I can't let her burn," I scream.

"She'll heal." Nikki insists. "You won't."

"What did you do?" I yell at Caldwell, finding a target for my anger. His smug smile and wide expectant eyes incite me more. I move toward him, but Nikki's hold on me tightens.

Finally, the blue fire flickers, dies down, and Jesse's screams cease. She hits the ground hard and doesn't move again.

"No." Gloria jumps forward from her place in the alcove.

Caldwell grabs hold of Jesse's head, exposing her long neck for the blade he's pulled from somewhere.

Gloria shoves her gun into his temple, placing one hand on his shoulder. He can't teleport unless he wants to take Gloria with him, and he can't move unless he wants a bullet to the brain.

Or so I think.

Caldwell pivots on his heels and Gloria's gun goes off, firing two bullets into the pavement and one into Jesse. Then he's upright beside Gloria, and I think I'm going to see it again—Caldwell snapping someone's neck. But Nikki is firing her gun into the space where Caldwell stands and he's forced to teleport again. He reappears over Jesse's dead body and grabs a hold of her. He disappears.

Jesse disappears with him.

We stand beside Jason's ashes, in the radius of the charred pavement.

"Oh my god." I'm shaking. "Oh my god, what just happened?"

Gloria shoves her gun into the holster hidden beneath her coat. "He's going to kill her while she's dead."

"She was dead?" As the flames died, so did the shield around me, just like when we jumped from the building.

"Taking Jason's healing power killed her." Gloria kicks at the pavement. "The same thing happened when Caldwell took Chaplain's power. We just have to hope she wakes up faster than he can kill her. Or wakes up enough to at least erect her shield."

"It's a reboot," Nikki holsters her own gun. "When you install new programming, you have to reboot."

God, no. Jesse wake up. Wake up while you still can.

Chapter 24

Jesse

This is the weirdest dream yet. I must be dead. Gabriel and I stand in another one of those ethereal dreamscapes. It's like I'm floating in a giant red Jell-O mold.

"What the hell happened up there?" I'm not sure why I should think that living is *up there*, but it's what comes out of my mouth nonetheless.

Gabriel looks me over, circling me as if inspecting me more closely. "You assimilated Jason's healing powers."

"Uh, okay. And that killed me?"

"It is a tremendous influx of power." His voice holds a hint of chastisement. The insubstantial dreamscape solidifies to a jungle landscape. Small chattering monkeys jump from limb to limb. Enormous colorful birds take flight, pushing themselves up through the dense canopy.

"This is nice," I say, taking a turn about the place. "A little humid, but it's pretty."

"You favor life?"

"Uh, what kind of question is that?" I ask.

"You want a world full of life."

"Oh god." I throw my hands up. "Are we back at this again? Here's an idea. How about we don't destroy the planet we already have, and then we won't have to build a new one."

"Fire brings growth. Fire brings rebirth and improvement."

"It also brings death, destruction, and an end to M&Ms and French fries. What kind of world is that?"

I instantly regret this question. Gabriel envelops me in his wings, blocking out the light of the jungle.

I see myself standing in a frozen wasteland, as if through someone else's eyes. About ten feet away, my eyes are feral, clothes askew. Then a deep purple light begins to glow inside me. The light shines through my eyes and mouth as I part my lips to scream. I throw my head back as black wings erupt from my spine, falling out onto the white snow. The violet light explodes from my mouth and shoots up toward the sky, growing brighter and brighter until I can't see my other self anymore.

I push away from Gabriel. "That's what's going to happen to me? That's me? Exploding?"

He doesn't answer. He only watches me with cautious eyes.

"And what does that do? What the hell will that change?"

"Calm yourself." Gabriel extends his hands as if to take hold of me again. I jerk away.

"No. You're telling me I'm going to grow angel wings and explode. There's nothing to be calm about! And my only alternatives are worse. Either let myself be murdered by a sociopath or be responsible for the whole world going down in flames."

Gabriel grimaces. "Your heart is beating too fast. You must protect your body."

"Oh because if I just die, then what? What happens to a partis whatever if they're *dead* dead, but no one absorbs the power?"

"Then another is called."

For half a second that sounds great. If I just die, then some other person can be partis and deal with this crap. But then who would resist Caldwell?

"You're sad," Gabriel says.

"No shit, Sherlock. Did you think this was happy news?"

He reaches for me.

I step back. "No."

"You want to understand. It will be easier, if you comprehend what you must do."

I stay out of his reach. Do I want to comprehend what I must do? No. Not really. I want to be eating an ice cream sundae and watching reruns of *Dead Like Me*. How did I get here? What the hell am I doing with my life?

"Ugh. Fine. Show me whatever."

Gabriel stretches his wings out to envelop me once more. In the darkness, he places a finger on each of my temples.

The visions come again.

The Earth began beautiful and pristine, with its blue skies and cool waters. I watch it turn black. Green land becomes a landfill. Blue skies fill up with gray smog. Thousands of animals running through open plains fall dead, laying scorched in charred forests.

Make a new world, or there won't be one.

That is the choice.

"And what will happen if I don't?" I look up and

see his green eyes glowing in the dark. "What happens if I refuse to explode?"

Gabriel opens his wings to reveal another world. This place is the apocalypse—there's no other word for it. The world burns. Buildings are in ruin, remnants of concrete crumbling in a gaseous backdrop the color of cinnamon and amber, reduced to monotones in their degradation. To my right, the body of a woman sits bent over, her hands over her head, frozen forever as a statue of ash.

I recognize the ears, the fingers, and the curve of the jaw.

Ally.

I reach out to touch her ashes and they disintegrate under the lightest pressure.

"No." I step back. "What you're asking is impossible. I can't do this."

His wings stretch wide. His eyes grow brighter. "Wake up now, Jesse. *Wake up.*"

Chapter 25

Ally

I turn around twice, but see no one. People shuffle along the street as if completely unaware of anything that just took place.

"She's gone," I say. It's a horrific declaration that shreds my insides. "He's probably cutting her head off right now."

I sink to my knees and cover my head with my hands. I pull at my hair until I feel some of the tension release, and I draw deep unsteady breaths.

"We don't know that." Nikki places a hand on my back. I shrug her off.

Dead, dead. I'm never going to see her again. Or if I do, it will only be because Caldwell will want me to see what he's done to her. He'll relish in my pain.

"Hey." Nikki kneels down beside me. "Just breathe, baby. Be positive."

"Be positive?" I throw my head back and laugh. "You saw the knife. You saw what he was trying to do.

We distracted him for seconds at best."

I press my palms to my eyes and they come away wet. I try to blink back the tears and pull myself together, but I can't even see the sidewalk beneath me; the pavement is blurry.

"She's not dead," Gloria says.

I lift my head to look at her. "How can you be sure?"

She motions for us to follow her down the sidewalk. "There's one more thing that has to happen."

"But you were the one who screamed *no*. You looked convinced he was going to kill her." I wanted to point out that it was her reaction more than anything that had sent me into a panic.

"I wanted to slow him down." She searches the surrounding street and frowns. "We need to get moving."

We march away from the scene of the crime. I cast one look over my shoulder at the black circle of evidence we're leaving behind and hope that we can benefit from Caldwell's deceptions this once.

"What's going to happen to her now that she absorbed his power?"

"The more power she has, the less stable she'll

be." Gloria looks both ways and then jaywalks across the street. A taxi honks and she flips him the bird. "This is the first time she's absorbed someone else's power. I suspect she'll need time to adjust."

"We should go back to Tate Tower," Nikki says behind me. "We still have time before the so-called explosion."

Gloria stops walking and turns toward her. "If you want to go back, that's fine. We aren't going back."

"With all due respect—" Nikki's voice is steady and placating. "Jeremiah needs to know that Jason has been eliminated. He should reallocate those resources to better use."

Gloria squares her shoulders. "Call him now and tell him."

Nikki pushes the earbud in her ear, holding it down until it glows blue.

"Tamsin here. Jason has been eliminated. Reallocate resources." She listens for a moment. "Understood."

Gloria shifts her weight. "What did he say?"

"He's working on the evacuation. He's also doing damage control. Caldwell missed a few minds I guess, but Jeremiah said he'd make sure we aren't implicated in anything."

Gloria's shoulders inch down away from her ears. "Good, because we have work to do."

Chapter 26

Jesse

I wake to strange purple light shining in my eyes. I blink and rub my lids, but the light is still unbearable.

"Gee-*zus*." I try to sit up, using my hands to shield myself from the godawful light. "Can we get a dimmer switch in here or something?"

"It's your shield," Caldwell says.

I peek through my fingers and find him sitting in a chair on the opposite side of the room. He's the picture of composure. His eyes are downturned. He runs one fingernail under another, scrapping out something beneath. His legs are crossed and he clasps one knee with his hand. It's the lip curl that gives him away.

"You control your shield, don't you? If you don't like how bright it is, tone it down."

Gabriel?

The shield dims but doesn't fade completely. A

lighter purple sheen continues to throb around me.

"Why is it so bright?"

"Your original power gets stronger with every ability you absorb. The power I have now with four gifts is exponentially more than what it was when I first left the camp."

"So my shield is stronger?"

"And your fire, I suspect. Try not to incinerate us."

I look around the room and realize it's not The Needle. This room has a door, first of all, and it's square.

"Where are we?"

"You're in the Unified Church compound. I can't take you back to The Needle in your current state. It isn't safe."

"What about my dog?"

Caldwell gives me a look, not unlike if I'd just spit on his shoes. "He remains unharmed."

For how long?

"How do you feel?" he asks me.

I examine my arms and legs. The blisters I had from Jason have healed. My skin is smooth, flawless. Well, unless you count the gross, crusty stuff on my hand and under my nails, which I'm pretty sure is brain. But no scratches. Hell. No bruises even.

"It's your fault I got his power. I wasn't going to touch him. So why are you being pissy about it?"

Caldwell's eyes cloud over. "What did your angel show you?"

"A bunch of gibberish. Why?"

"*Think.*" Caldwell hisses. "Can you remember any specific images?"

Like all dreams, Gabriel's visions are rushing away from me, dissolving in deep water.

"It was just more crap about how I'm going to go all super nova."

"Did he explain the Big Bang? Did he show you that this won't be the first, or the last such explosion? They occur all over space and time and will continue to occur forever. Once a species develops consciousness, then the rebirth is made possible. Consciousness is one of the primary elements of a universe, yet it's more than that. The apex's responsibility falls to the most destructive of species. Elephants for example, are highly intelligent. But they aren't being asked to die and give new life to our corner of the universe."

"So it's punishment?" I ask. "For being dicks."

"There are twelve partis who house this power, and so it will be until there is one—the apex."

Here we go with The Highlander shit again.

"And the apex will become one with the Thirteenth element—"

"Whoa, what? Did you say *become one*?"

"Yes." Caldwell blinks. "Join together."

"No, no, no. I haven't accepted the idea that I'm going to die no matter what. Now you're telling me that I have to *become one* with an angel?" I pull at my face. "You're talking about sex, right? I only know one way to *become one*."

"The interpretation is unclear."

I rub my eyes. "God, I hope so."

"But you would join. Intimately."

"Ew. Just stop. You're making me sick," I say, pinching the bridge of my nose. This does nothing to alleviate the pressure building there.

Caldwell stands, running a palm down the front of each pants leg. "I have to go."

"Fine, let's go." I stand and feel a tug on my arm. My right forearm is shackled to the bed. "Oh god, no. Not this again. We've done the shackled to the bed bit.

It never ends well."

"It's for your own good."

"Said every abuser ever."

"I've been gone for too long. I need to attend to my affairs, but I can't have you running around until we are sure you can handle the extra power."

"Don't pretend like you're doing this for me. You're still trying to figure out how to use and manipulate me."

He doesn't gratify me with an answer. Instead, he goes to the door and throws it open. He casts one last look at me from the frame. "Stay out of trouble."

Don't count on it.

Gabriel appears in the small room, looking around him as if expecting to find someone else.

"Thank god," I whine.

"It is difficult to penetrate the magnetic field when you are close to one another," he says again.

"Yeah, I still don't know what that means. Can you get me out of here?"

"I cannot open locks."

"You better. Not only are you going to kill me, but you're going to try to get sexy with me first? You're in so much trouble. That's *entrapment*. They have lawsuits against this sort of thing."

"I have never lied to you."

"That's what a liar would say."

I search every remembered conversation that Gabriel and I ever had. Some of it suggests maybe this is where it is going. *Be human while you still can. I'll be everything you need.*

Then there was that time that he actually touched me, took my hand, and tucked it into the suit jacket so I could feel his lack of heartbeat.

"Man." I fall back onto the bed. "I should've seen this coming."

Gabriel kneels in front of me, placing one hand on the thin mattress cot beside me. He looks at me with upturned eyes.

"Oh *no*." My voice climbs toward hysteria. "Don't start giving me bedroom eyes."

"I want you to be happy. It is easier for both of us, if you are happy."

"You want me to be happy?" My voice spikes. "For starters, never give me sexy looks again. I can't have an invisible boyfriend! Then once your chastity belt is on good and tight, get me out of here. Give me Winston. Make Caldwell stop being a homicidal maniac and killing people so I can go live somewhere boring and normal with Ally. "

"You want to be with Ally."

Yes, I almost blurt it. For some reason, I bite my tongue.

"She is the companion you wish for most?"

"I feel like this is a trick. If I say yes, are you going to kill her and stuff her in the apex or something?"

His brow pinches in confusion. "No."

"Because I don't want her involved in the sexy-world-blowing-up whatever."

"She is already involved."

"Wait, whoa. What? What are you saying? Are you saying you're going to kill her? That is *not* okay. If I get to pick the new world, I'll pick one where she is alive and happy. Got it?"

He blinks those green eyes at me.

"No," I shout. The air glimmers around me. "*No. I will totally lose my shit right now if you don't tell me you understand. Ally lives. Do you understand? No matter what, Ally *lives*. She's going to be a grandmother that dies in her sleep with a fat pug sleeping on her feet, you got that?"

His wings twitch against his back. "I understand

what you want."

"But?"

"But we do not always get what we want."

"No." It's all I can think of. No, no, *no*. "If she is going to die, you might as well kill me now. I'll never be your apex."

"You will be the apex."

"No. Because I can't imagine a world without her and I wouldn't save a world without her in it."

As soon as the words leave my mouth, I realize I've cursed myself. Never say never.

Chapter 27

Ally

While regrouping in Gloria's apartment, I've had nearly two hours of uninterrupted research. And thank God, because if I had nothing to do but sit here and obsess about whether or not Jesse has been beheaded, I would lose my mind.

Fortunately, Nikki was distracted with her own work. Jeremiah sent her tasks, which she addressed remotely. And once that was done, she took inventory of her guns, stripping and cleaning each one thoroughly.

I've also spent my time wisely. Since, thanks to Gloria, I knew only seven of the twelve on my list were partis, I worked to eliminate the others. It helped once I took Cindy, Jesse, and Rachel off the list—all known partis.

What I was left with were nine names for the four remaining partis that we needed to unearth and investigate. I eliminated three more names right away:

Sharon Ortega, Chris Trinidad, and Paul Lang. All are dead and can't be one of the eight partis, including Jesse, that Gloria thinks still walk the Earth.

In my search, I stumbled across an interesting BBC article about a woman named Jin Go who lived in an apartment complex in South Korea. The 67-year-old grocer claims that one day a woman she knew, Minli Yang, had stopped to buy vegetables. Only when Minli went to pay for the vegetables she'd selected, Jin Go couldn't accept the money. Go claimed that as she reached for the money, a horrible light shot out of Yang's hands and into Go's eyes. Go was permanently blinded and the authorities are searching for Yang, whom they've been unable to find.

Go claims she was not surprised that the girl would shine a terrible light into her eyes and steal her vegetables, given her recent poverty since the death of her father. Neighbors of Yang's living complex confirmed they too had seen strange lights coming from Yang's windows at all hours of the night, leaving authorities to believe that perhaps she'd been practicing with the light-emitting device before actually using it on the grocer.

The article encourages anyone who sees Yang to

report her whereabouts to the authorities. A picture of a petite woman with long sleek hair and big black eyes accompanied the article.

Monroe Dupree was also on the run.

A neighbor told authorities that he heard gunfire next door and ran to check on Dupree, believing the man had attempted suicide for a third time. However, when he arrived, he couldn't find Dupree or anyone else in the house. When he searched the yard, he believed he saw Dupree running off in the direction of the swamp, but told authorities that couldn't be right. *I must've seen a shadow 'cause no one would wander out there with them gators at this time of night, with the wind a-howling like it was.*

The neighbor also claims he saw a black sedan speeding out of the shared gravel driveway, heading in the direction of town.

Now I have two names at least. Two potential threats or allies.

"Got her." A grin spreads across Gloria's face. She leans forward on her elbows, coming out of her seat at the table and grabbing a pad of paper and a pencil resting a foot away. "He's holding her in the First Church of the New World."

"Goose Island?" Nikki reassembles her clean gun and smiles.

I give her a definite, do-you-have-to do-that-at-the-table stare. Really though, I'm thrilled she's found something to occupy herself.

"Yes." Gloria turns the laptop toward me so I can see the blinking red dot representing Jesse. "I'll notify our backup."

Nikki and I exchange a glance. I wet my lips and turn to Gloria. "Gloria, when are we going to meet this backup?

Gloria doesn't even look up from the computer. "When they decide it's time."

Nikki puts the clean gun to the side and selects another. "So what's the plan? Just go in guns blazing?"

"I don't have a gun," I remind them.

Nikki arches her eyebrows. "You need one."

"Do I?" My sarcasm is loud and clear. I don't believe violence can be ended with more violence. It seems like an idiotic idea to me. Why would doing the thing you want to stop, make the thing stop?

"You don't have to carry," Gloria says. "Not everyone in a war carries a gun."

"What she said."

"Of course, those soldiers usually die first. Or become POWs," Gloria adds with a shrug.

I like this answer a little less.

Gloria closes the laptop and reaches across the table to grab her sketchbook. "I'll view the church, the situation, and based on what I see, we can finalize the plan."

"And while you're doing that, I'll keep researching Monroe Dupree." I search for my bag, computer and notes. I was so footsore when I came through the door, I don't even remember where I dropped them.

The television kicks on behind us. Nikki and I both jump to our feet.

"What the hell?" Nikki asks. "Do you have a ghost?"

"I don't believe in ghosts," Gloria says.

The fact remains that the TV in the room came to life all on its own. I take a step toward it.

"Maybe you shouldn't do that," Nikki says, her voice higher.

"Are you scared of ghosts?" I'm trying to sound casual, teasing. But it is a little strange.

"What is it saying?" Gloria asks.

As if on command, the volume on the television

goes up. I can actually see the button moving.

"—continue to argue about the condition of Earth's magnetic field. Scientist Ralph J. Grangerson says this: 'While it is true that the magnetic field is weaker today than it was fifty years ago, we do not have enough data to understand the ramifications of this observation. It could well be true that the field weakens and strengthens regularly and has for billions of years. Much like climate change, it could be part of a larger cycle.'"

"Other scientists argue that the weakening magnetic field is a serious problem. "Dr. Taylor Rickets of Henrichs University has this to say: 'Without a magnetic field, life on Earth won't last long. One solar storm could exterminate life on the planet, or render it uninhabitable. And if that doesn't kill us, the radiation will, slowly.'"

Caldwell appears on the television, his legs crossed and fingers laced in the perfect portrait of composure. Even his hair is slicked back into place. The word LIVE flashes on the bottom right side of the screen.

"He changed his suit," Nikki says, as if this is the most important thing to notice.

"The Bible tells us that the end times are near,"

Caldwell pantomimes sympathy and seriousness. "This may put fear into your hearts, I know. But have faith, for we are the children of God. And he will keep us safe under his wing."

The television clicks off.

"What the hell?" Nikki stands, knocking back her chair.

"I'm sure there is a rational explanation." I struggle to keep my breath steady and my mind clear.

"Do ghosts frighten you?" Gloria asks her, a small smile tugging at the corner of her lips.

Nikki's cheeks flame bright red and her nostrils flare.

"Really? In a world like ours?" Gloria says as if Nikki had spoken.

"The dead stay dead." Nikki puts her hands on her hips. "They're at peace."

It sounds like a bizarre mantra that one might tell oneself in order to not be afraid. Though why Nikki has a readily available mantra about the dead, I'm not sure.

"It's strange," I agree, not wanting Nikki to feel like we are excluding her, making her out to be paranoid. "It turns on for some program about magnetic fields and shows Caldwell's face and then turns off again? Why? And did you see the way he snake-eyed the camera. How many people do you think he's manipulating?"

"Millions," Nikki says, some of her calm returning.

Gloria says nothing. Her eyes fall to her sketchbook again.

"Gloria," I ask. "Do you have an explanation?"

"It's your TV," Nikki says. "Does it do this?"

"Sometimes," Gloria admits.

Nikki continues to stand in the middle of the room looking from the television to me to Gloria as if waiting for instructions. When neither of us give her any solid ground, she's forced to recover herself. "It is an old television. Maybe there's a bizarre electrical problem or something. My grandfather had an ancient alarm clock that would click on and play Etta James all by itself once in a while."

Gloria doesn't look worried, so I find it easier to keep my own panic under control.

I try to remember what we were doing before this happened, but my mind is distracted doing the math. If Caldwell is dressed and giving live press conferences, he isn't cutting off Jesse's head. And it seems unlikely that he could give a press conference if he was recovering from having killed her. After all, he'd have to reboot just as Jesse did, right?

I look up from my thoughts to find Gloria watching me.

"No she's not dead," Gloria confirms. "Not yet."

Chapter 28

Jesse

No. I roll over on the bed, turning away from Gabriel. *I'm still not talking to you.*

"You are talking to me."

I cut off the mind speech, refusing to say anything else. This is punishment for him being so secretive and getting me into this mess. I stare at the cinder-block wall of my little cell, noting the thick lines between each stone and flecks in the white paint that reveal the gray rock beneath.

Die to save the world. Don't die and the world dies.

I can't wrap my head around the idea, though I know I should be able to. This is just a larger representation of what I already do, right? I die so others don't have to.

So why is it so crazy to think I am going to do it for the whole world?

My throat contracts and a little sound escapes.

"Would I wake up?" I roll over and stare up at the ceiling. "Like all the other times I die for others. Would I wake up again?"

"No." Gabriel leans over, blocking my view of the ceiling. "This death will be different."

Why?

"The process will destroy your body."

So I'll never be alive again. I'll never see Ally or Winston. I'll never eat chocolate or potato chips or watch reruns of *Dead Like Me.*

I adjust the pillow under my head and my mind starts to chew on the idea, broken up with grievances like *god I wish I could wash the brains off of my hands.* I see Kyra, Umbri, Gloria, Cindy, Ally and Lane—all of us at the table eating, laughing. I see Ally sliding a coffee into my hand and pushing a stray hair off of my face. She's smiling at me. She's laughing at my sarcasm.

I see Lane offering me a helmet to his bike, helping me fasten it under my chin before he climbs on and waits for me to do the same.

The life I built—this good life full of good people—gone.

"I worked so hard for this life." I worked so hard

to get away from Eddie and my shitty childhood. "Now you want me to give it up?"

"A human cannot live forever and you *are* human, Jesse."

I roll onto my side and curl into a tighter ball. The chain on my wrist bites deeper into my skin. I lift and lower my arm until I can figure out how to lay it just so without it squeezing my wrist bones.

Springs in the mattress poke through the thin cot, causing pain in my side. *Pain* I understand. That people are mostly assholes, I understand. But the rest—?

"Why twelve?" I'm not sure why I latch onto that question of all questions. "There could be twenty or a hundred partis. Everyone with NRD could have their own funky power, but there's twelve. Why?"

Gabriel sits on the bed. His suit brushes against my leg and surprises me. I reach out and touch his arm, finding it solid. The cot even groans under his weight. I slide my hand from his arm to his wings, and gasp. They're real. It feels like I'm petting a bird, the feathers soft except for the small ridges bisecting the center. A scent of rain overtakes the room. I search his face, waiting for him to tell me to stop. After all, touching someone's wings seems incredibly intimate. He says nothing, his green eyes wide and watching. His jaw is covered in flesh, pink enough that it could actually have blood and bone under there.

I pull my hand away. "So why twelve?"

"It is difficult to explain, given your limited comprehension of the universe."

I frown. "*Try*."

"Creation," he begins. His gaze rolls up to the ceiling, and then falls to his hands clutching his knees. "Creation is also destruction, it is a force. It is an energy."

"Still with you." I sit up on my elbows.

"It is difficult to channel such force into an organism as limited as a human being. Each of you are born with a spark of it, the power that roots you eternally to the universe, but to make the universe anew, you must house more."

"The Big Bang?" I remember Caldwell's words. "The creation slash destruction force goes through a person and boom?" I make an exploding motion with my hands. "Well what if I don't want the universe to go boom?"

"That is your choice."

"But that doesn't explain the twelve partis or

NRD."

Gabriel's eyes fall to his hands again. "When something so large tries to move into such a small space, it must often be broken into pieces, to be reassembled on the other side."

Gabriel shows me a simplistic image. An orange, sliced several ways, is fed through a tiny hole that the whole orange couldn't have fit through. "So I have a slice of the orange, two actually," I tell him. "And there's twelve slices of this orange."

"Yes." He smiles, seemingly pleased that I'm not a total moron. "And the orange must be made whole again."

"So it can explode and juice the world."

He frowns.

"You chose the orange metaphor, not me. But what about NRD? Why does it exist? Did you really choose me because I wanted to die?"

He considers my face for another long moment. I feel an urge to squirm. His tie fades from black to green, tinged with red. He never has explained the reason for the mood tie. I could ask about it now, but I feel like it would distract him from the more important questions.

At last, he speaks again. "Energy exchange is complex. In this case, like attracts like. You received a piece of the orange, because in a way, you are very much like the orange. Some humans desire only to live, to be part of creation. In others, the desire to live is as strong as the desire to destroy. The desire to create is equal to the desire to destroy. Both must be present."

His tie deepens to midnight blue.

"Humans believe they have NRD because the brain, upon birth, gave them this condition. However, this is not true."

I sit up straighter. "Whoa, *what*? Say that again."

"Humans use science to justify the existence of NRD. They manipulate the facts to fit the theory. NRD occurs at death, not birth."

That would explain why researchers have yet to create a reliable test for NRD that would be administered at birth.

"But we have blood types and magnetite and all the reasons for NRD. It's science."

"It is your limited comprehension of a much larger force. You overlook several factors."

I collapse onto the cot, letting the circulation return to my hand. "Here you go, calling us stupid again. I'm not dumb. I understand what you're saying."

He blinks at me.

I throw up my hands. "There's a giant orange and you like, cut it up and shoved the pieces through the tiny door known as Earth, and now you're like trying to get the monkeys who got a slice to kill each other and put the orange back together again, but once we do, the orange is probably going to blow up in our faces. Right?"

"Things must be allowed to die, so they may be born again. This planet is dying. Mankind is at the end of its era. All species have their time."

"And what does that make you guys—the angels? The compassionate hospice nurse?"

His eyes darken. "We are the midwives of the new world."

Chapter 29

Jesse

I must've fallen asleep. I wake, disoriented by the sound of footfalls. For a moment, I think I'm back in Jeremiah's compound, Tate Tower. Some drill is being run or some unit is being dispatched, and that's the reason for all the chaos, all the running and screaming.

But as I go to stand up, a sharp tug yanks at my wrist. The shackle. The unfamiliar room. The white tiles beneath my shoes, which is different from the soft gray carpet of my room back in Tate Tower.

Caldwell still has me. And he must be close, because Gabriel is nowhere to be seen.

The door swings inward and Caldwell steps into the room and closes the door after him.

"Did you just *walk* in here?" I ask, baffled.

"Sometimes I like to see what happens in-between." He yanks at the bottom of his suit as if it has ridden up too high.

An explosion rocks the church and plaster rains

down from the ceiling.

"They never give up, do they?" he asks, with an air of agitation.

"Who?"

"Your friends," he says.

My heart leaps. But before I can fully appreciate the sentiment of their rescue mission, I realize that Ally is trying to save me. Again.

If I survive this, I think, *I'll have to follow Ally everywhere. She can't risk her life trying to save me if I never leave her side. Nikki will* love *that.*

"Why are you smiling?" Caldwell says. "I'm going to kill them."

My shield brightens, shimmering to life around me. It extends out far enough that it knocks Caldwell back, his tie askew.

"Thanks for reminding me that you're a fucking monster." The shield glows brighter, and he steps back, connecting with the wall behind him.

"I need to unlock your cuff. We're leaving."

"My friends are coming," I say. "They'll unlock it. Or at the very least, they'll saw this off, and I'll have this cool retro bracelet. Very *Château d'If.*"

"Do you understand what he wants you for?"

An explosion rocks the building, and he cuts his eyes to the right. He turns his head as if he is actually following something, and then I remember he has Liza's vision. He can see through anything. These walls and so called barriers are nothing for him.

"I should've left you in The Needle." His eyes widen at the invisible threat that is presumably closer than before. He takes a half step away from the door.

"If I leave you here, he will use you, manipulate you far worse than I ever will."

"Who are you talking about?"

"Tate."

"Jeremiah?" A wave of confusion washes over me. Did Ally go back to him? No. That seems less likely than the fact that he simply tracked me himself and is trying to *reacquire* me. Reacquire. Ugh. I've heard him use that word in the past for people and objects that we were sent in to retrieve.

"Who did you think I meant by friends?"

Relief washes over me. *Not Ally. Ally.*

"So you're going to kill Jeremiah?" I shrug, the chain rattling at my side. "Okay."

Caldwell gives me a curious look.

"He's almost as bad as you," I tell him. "He's got

all these resources, but he didn't even *try* to save Brinkley."

"Don't leave with him or you'll regret it," Caldwell threatens.

"Or what? He'll torture me? Kill my friends? Kidnap my dog? Abandon me and have a whole second family with some *other* daughter? Oh wait, no. That was all *you*."

Caldwell growls his frustration and disappears.

I exhale a long breath. The church rocks again with another explosion somewhere, followed by the *pat-tat-pat-tat* of guns going off. It never ceases to amaze me how willing Jeremiah's people are to fight out in the open like this. After seeing how Caldwell does crowd control, I know why he isn't afraid. He'll mind-wipe everyone back to obliviousness. Jeremiah doesn't have any such talents that I know of, yet clearly he's got money. Money must be its own superpower.

The door to my room is thrown open and there stands Jeremiah, sweater vest and all.

"Jesse," he says, sighing my name. He adjusts his glasses. "Thank god, you're all right."

"My hero," I say with thick sarcasm. "Get me the hell out of here."

"You'll have to lower your shield."

"Ha, *no*. Not happening."

"But I came here to save you. I'm not going to hurt you."

"Save it. If I had a dollar for every time some dude said that to me, I'd be *so* rich right now."

"How am I supposed to get you out of the building without you lowering your shield?"

Good question.

I look down at my wrist and wonder if I can expose just the chain. It requires a little more control than I think I have over my shield. Threatened equals shield up. Fear equals bigger, brighter shield.

"I'll try to expose just the chain," I tell him.

Jeremiah looks like he might refuse me. His gaze is steady and unforgiving, but I don't waver. I am tired of being lied to and misled. I'm tired of the men around me telling me what I should do with my own power.

Jeremiah issues an order for a bolt cutter and someone barks compliance through the speaker. A wave of heat rolls from the hall behind Jeremiah, along with the distinct scent of something burning.

"Where's Alice and Nicole?" he asks.

"How am I supposed to know? I've been catching

up with dear ol' dad."

"You were foolish to go with him. You have nothing to show for it."

The sharp truth of the assessment pisses me off. I don't have Winston, and Jason almost hurt Ally and Gloria.

"Fuck you. I have a fancy new healing power."

"When will you figure out that you have to work with people in order to achieve your goal?"

A man appears with the bolt cutter. "Brinkley tried to work alone, and look where it got him."

"You don't know anything about him." My temper flares and my shield gets bigger, knocking Jeremiah back out of the room. The door slams shut after him, and the terrified minion with the bolt cutter is pressed against the wall as if I intend to crush him.

My shield shrinks as the man starts yelling.

"Sorry, sorry." I throw my palms out in apology. "I wasn't mad at you."

He runs his hands over his body to make sure it's all there. Then he picks up the cutters he dropped. "May I?"

"Yes, please." I drop the entire shield long enough for him to cut the chain quite close to my wrist.

Jeremiah throws the door open again and the shield goes back on, bumping the man with the cutter.

"Thank you," I tell him. "Sorry about squishing you."

"Follow me. I have a helicopter waiting." Jeremiah exits the room, the minion with the cutter lingers behind to take up the rear.

I consider my options. I can refuse to go with Jeremiah. He did sedate me and he wanted me to kill Jason as badly as Caldwell did. There's got to be some horrible reason for that. I should slip away and find Ally and Gloria on my own.

The problem is, I don't know the first place to look for them. I don't have Gloria's people-finding skills. I can't pop anywhere in the world like Caldwell. If I go with Jeremiah now, at least I could find Ally and then leave whenever I want. He can't stop me. And if anyone is keeping tabs on Ally and Nikki—Caldwell aside—it's Jeremiah.

"Coming." I catch up to Jeremiah, Gabriel at my heels. We take a series of twists and turns through the church, and once or twice, I think I see Caldwell's face for an instant in an unlit doorway. But whenever I look for a second or third time, he's never there.

I must be imagining it.

"No," Gabriel says. His voice is velvet in my ears. "He is waiting for the chance to grab hold of you."

Better make sure my shield stays up then. God, this is getting old.

"What is getting old?" Gabriel asks, those emerald eyes falling on mine.

All these dudes fighting over me. Girls like this shit? It's not flattering at all. It's suffocating.

Life is hard enough without Jeremiah and Caldwell circling me like sharks, each one waiting for the chance to chomp off one of my legs.

We turn yet another corner in the labyrinth of the church.

"Down," Jeremiah screams. His hand connects with my shield, but instead of moving me, my shield rebuffs him, his own body hitting the floor.

Caldwell's men fire. Bullets slam into my shield and ricochet, zipping off in other directions. My shield shimmers and blurs on impact, but remains solid and impenetrable.

"That's cool." I can't help but be impressed with my awesomeness. I'm bulletproof.

The bolt-cutting guard yelps as a stray bullet slices

through his upper arm. Blood wells up through the hole in his black clothing.

"Less cool," I say, worried it was a bullet bouncing of my shield that got him. Another one of Jeremiah's men reach forward and grab the bolt-cutting guard, dragging him around a corner, out of sight.

Jeremiah shouts more orders into his earpiece and men flood the small corridor.

Caldwell appears in the middle of the hall and all gunfire ceases. Jeremiah's soldiers go stiff and jerky like puppets on strings. A swirl of black shadows emerge from Caldwell, ribboning around him.

"What the—?" I take a step back.

Men start falling at his feet. Anyone who brushes against the black ribbons falls down.

Dead.

Totally *dead*.

Because unconscious people don't pass out, eyes open and vacant.

Jeremiah's wide eyes meet my own. He considers the scene, mouth ajar.

Georgia, Caldwell's wife-woman-whatever the hell she is steps out from behind Caldwell and as soon as I see her I realize the black ribbons of death are coming from her, not Caldwell.

Her palms are turned up toward the ceiling, but her arms hang low by her side. The ribbons follow her gaze, reaching out and attacking whatever object her eyes fall on.

She's controlling them with her eyes. Shit.

"She's partis," I tell Jeremiah, just in case he can't see the ribbon dancing. "She's sucking the life out of people. Uh, you should go."

Jeremiah stops calling his men into the room. Smart.

Caldwell seizes this opportunity to take his men out of the church. First they are here, fighting Jeremiah's men. Then they're gone, his men gone with him.

I don't think Georgia can penetrate my shield, so I step forward, putting myself between her and Jeremiah's men. It isn't that I like any of them enough to save their lives, but it seems like a jerk thing to do, just standing over to the side with a shield, watching people die.

I try to gain Georgia's attention. "You should join a circus. You can be in the freak show."

She turns her cold eyes on me.

"Your stage name can be Rigor Mortis Ribbons. No. Dancer of Death. Or maybe Death and Ribbon Dancing."

Her jaw tightens, but I think it's working. She's stopped looking at Jeremiah and his men and in my periphery, I see them sneaking away, sliding into the hallways behind us.

"It'd be a *killer* show." I grin. "Get it?"

One of her black ribbons snaps forward and slams against my shield. My shield hisses like water thrown on a hot skillet. Sparks even fly.

"Why the hell hasn't he tried to kill *you*, Georgia?" Anger makes my face and neck hot.

My shield throbs wildly, half-blue fire, half-purple.

She takes a step away from me.

Caldwell reappears behind Georgia and they exchange a glance. Then she takes a step back into his arms. He wraps himself around her. It's tender, like she's the most precious thing in the world.

They disappear, leaving me alone, standing in the center of the hallway.

He *loves* her.

It's like a fist has been shoved into my chest and is squeezing my heart.

My shield fails altogether.

For a long time, I thought maybe my father was broken. He'd died and then suffered in a camp for years. Maybe he just lost his ability to relate to others. Then there's this Maisie shit. But again, I thought maybe he was only going through the motions. After all, it wasn't like Maisie and Caldwell appeared to have this amazing connection or anything. Teenage angst or not, there was a distance there. Nothing to be jealous of.

But this.

The way he took Georgia in his arms. The gentle, sweet way—it wasn't fake at all. The way she folded into his chest, with trust and love—he's given her a reason to believe in him like that.

He loves her. But not me.

So it *is* personal. All the attempts I've made trying to say *it's not me, it's him*, crumble away.

"It's me." I can feel tears welling, my throat constricting under their weight. It's why Lane didn't want me. It's why Ally found someone else. It's why—

"Jesse," Gabriel takes a hold of me. "Breathe."

"It's *me*," I scream and the church explodes with blue fire.

Chapter 30

Jesse

Jeremiah is dead.

Blackened flesh. The scorched glass of his spectacles. Almost nothing is left of the sweater vest. The three other men lay dead in the hallway with him. Jeremiah's men no doubt.

I've been responsible for someone's death before. I was present when Caldwell killed Brinkley and I couldn't save him. That was my fault.

This is different. I killed someone.

Four someone*s.*

I slump against the wall, sliding down its unforgiving stone until I'm on my knees beside the body. Jeremiah's body.

I breathe. In. Out. I try to think, but my mind is a clear shocked buzz. White flames burn around me, then fizzle to smoke. I can't process what I've done, a single mantra repeating in my head.

I don't kill people, I save people. I don't kill people, I save people. I don't kill people, I save people. I don't kill people—

"You need to leave this place." Gabriel warns. "You cannot stay here."

"Jesse. Move. He's coming."

Nothing Gabriel says can make me get up from the floor. My eyes fixate on a place where two stones jut together, one pushing the other up and out of place.

Gabriel gives up and disappears. Or he is forced out by the owner of the polished black shoes that step into my field of vision.

Caldwell kneels down in front of me. "Jesse."

He is able to get quite close, because my shield doesn't erect around me.

"You don't understand what is happening to you." He lays one hand over my knee. "But I do. I have gone through this, and I can help you. The longer you fight what you are, the more grief you will experience."

"I don't know what you want from me." I look up and search his face. It's as unreadable as the scorched stones surrounding us.

"I want you to accept your role in this. Stop trying to play the hero. Stop trying to escape, and embrace what you are. It will make this—everything that must happen—easier."

"For you or me?" I ask, but I know the answer. I saw it in the way he wrapped his arms around Georgia. I'm just a chess piece he's trying to maneuver. But can I get something from him too? Should I play so I can help myself?

"Come with me. It's almost time for the main event and I want you there." He stands and offers his hand. "Please."

I look at the four dead bodies.

I did that.

Me.

If Caldwell kills me, maybe it would be better. I'm going to die anyway. The world will die anyway. And if he kills me, at least it will keep me from hurting anyone else.

Chapter 31

Ally

"**G**oddammit!" Gloria slams her laptop shut. I let go of the steering wheel just long enough to reach over and slip the device out of her hands before she throws it into the windshield. I hand the computer to Nikki in the backseat.

"What happened?" Nikki asks, sitting forward to accept the laptop.

Gloria turns toward the passenger window. "He took her back to The Needle. Fuck."

"There goes our window of opportunity." Both Gloria and Nikki give me a cold glare. "I'm sorry. You're right. Now is not the time for pessimism."

My chest constricts as I turn on Gloria's blinker and switch lanes. It's as if I can see an ever-expanding ocean between us, taking Jesse farther and farther away from me.

Nikki's ear glows blue, her wireless device blinking to life. "Tamsin."

Her brow furrows, the creases above her eyebrows deepening. She exhales. "I'll be there soon. Follow protocol three until I arrive."

The blue earbud goes dark and she meets my eyes.

"You'll have to drop me off at Tate Tower."

"We can't stay at Tate Tower," Gloria says, unyielding.

"I understand," Nikki says, her voice calm. "But I have to go back. Jeremiah is dead, and I have to assume control."

I tap the brake without meaning to, my eyes flicking up to meet hers in the rearview. "Jeremiah's dead?"

"Jesse killed him." Nikki measures my face. "If my report is accurate."

"Shit," Gloria says.

"What happened?" I ask Nikki.

"They were trying to rescue her from Caldwell, and she lost control. Four men were killed."

My heart lurches. *Four men were killed. She will become less stable, the more power she absorbs.*

"I have to run things until Jeremiah is able to. We—"

"Wait, what? You said he was dead."

Gloria turns away from the window. "Jeremiah has NRD."

"So he'll only be dead for a little while?" I ask.

"Right," Nikki says. "So until he is able, I have to coordinate the units. It'll be easier for me to monitor everything from control at Tate Tower. So, please, take me back."

"You can't stay there," I remind her.

"We'll only stay until Jeremiah is awake. Our secondary location doesn't have the medical ward up and running yet. Once it does, or once he's stable enough, we'll move. We should still be able to clear the building before Jackson's prediction catches up to us."

I hook a right at the next light and carry us east.

"There's something else." Nikki settles back into her seat as if bracing herself for my reaction.

I don't tell her to spit it out. I just flick my eyes up to the rearview and meet hers in an invitation.

"There are more partis in the city," she says. "Besides Jesse."

"How do you know?"

"When they use their power, it produces gamma rays. In addition to Jesse's output, we've registered three other sources in the city in the last 24 hours. No doubt one is Caldwell, but we don't know about the other two."

Another Jason—*two* Jasons—loose and prowling the city. I think back to Minli and Monroe. Could they be in the city looking for a fight? Or maybe someone even worse.

God, no.

"There was a reading quite close to Jackson's apartment while we were there," Nikki adds. "It's quite possible that we're being watched for weaknesses. We should be on our guard."

"Okay." What else can I say?

We arrive at Tate Tower, and it's like arriving with the President. Before I can even fully park the car on the street, personnel flood Gloria's Cadillac. Nikki is escorted inside by a team of guards, one man two inches taller than Nikki, quickly debriefs her on the state of things.

Nikki goes up in the first elevator with her guard, and our eyes lock for the briefest moment. She gives me a reassuring smile and I return it.

I can't help but find her attractive at moments like this. A girl in power, self-assured and handling her business, it's a special kind of turn on for me.

We're about to go back to the car but the guard speaks to me.

"Tamsin suggests that you return to your apartment here in the tower," the guard says. I can't tell if it's a man or a woman through the armor, and the head plate masks the voice. "But she realizes you may not want to stay."

"We'll stay," Gloria says.

I manage to keep the surprise off of my face. The guards leave us, returning to whatever order Nikki is no doubt sending them through their little blue earbuds.

I don't say anything as Gloria steps into an open elevator and smashes a button. I don't speak until the doors close.

"We'll stay for a little while?" I ask.

"Get the rest of your things. And Jesse's. We don't want to lose anything in the blast."

I'm relieved we're finally alone. Alone enough anyway.

The door to the apartment Nikki and I share opens this time.

The difference between treason and patriotism is only a matter of dates. The Count of Monte Cristo. I read it in

French class my senior year. It's strange how the mind works. How it can pull up a memory from the bottom of a dark pool of forgetfulness.

Gloria follows me inside and into the apartment and slides the deadbolt into place.

"This room is bugged," she says.

"No, Nikki has special privileges."

"Are you sure about that?" Gloria looks wholly unconvinced.

I think about the sex. Granted, we haven't been able to as much as we'd like lately, given the hectic nature of work, but we've had enough that I shiver at the idea that I did it on camera for whoever happened to be on duty.

"The bathroom," I tell her and her face alights with recognition. It is our best option.

Gloria and I step into the bathroom and shut the door behind us.

"What's going on?" I ask her.

She presses a finger over her lips and turns on the faucet. Then she reaches into the shower and turns that on too. We slide down onto the floor together, and even with all the white noise created by the running water, she whispers.

"We have to wait for our backup before we break into The Needle."

"You said it was impossible. It was designed to be *not* broken into."

"There's a way. I've started to see it while I draw, but I keep getting interrupted."

"So draw," I say, squeezing her knee. "I know you can do it."

She spares me a smile. "Jesse will be okay."

My heart hammers. "Are you sure? She just killed four people."

Gloria looks at the shower, considering the diamond-shaped pattern of the curtain. "Casualties are unavoidable."

I grab her hand and say something I've wanted to say for months. "I'm sorry about your brother, Gloria. I'm so very sorry."

Gloria's gaze falls to her lap. She runs one hand over her short hair before her fingers curl and she scratches her scalp. "Micah made his choices. I made mine."

I hug her. I think she'll stiffen in my arms or clam up, but she accepts my hug, clasping her hands behind my back and returning the squeeze.

"While you draw, I'll pack up, okay? Then we'll get out of here."

"We should try to be gone before Tate wakes up."

"Is Jeremiah really that bad?" I ask.

"You didn't know he has NRD."

"No," I admit, though I'm not surprised to find that Jeremiah kept secrets. On most days, I feel like everyone is keeping secrets. Even me. "Is this the part where you tell me he is secretly partis too?"

"No," she says. "He is something else."

"That sounds so ominous. What is he?"

"I'm not sure." Gloria pulls herself to a standing position, straightening slowly as if her knees are unsure of themselves. "I draw him in the corners of my pictures sometimes."

I frown. "That's strange."

"It is," she agrees, turning off the shower and tugging the curtain back into place. "But that's where I see him. I don't know what it means yet."

"Do you think Caldwell is working with another A.M.P? Is that why he's still able to dance around us so easily?"

"He might have one," she agrees. "They won't be as good as Micah. Or me."

At the mention of her brother's name, the blood slows in my veins. "Did you read Brinkley's journals?"

"No." Gloria pulls open the bathroom door and leads us out.

"You can tell by the way Brinkley writes about you in the journals, you were close. Losing someone close to you—"

Gloria stops in the middle of the hallway. Then she turns and meets my eyes. "Brinkley made his choice. He did what he thought was right. You can't ask any more from a person."

There is a finality to her statement and I can't ask more.

"So tell me about our backup."

"I am not allowed to mention them by name. It was agreed upon."

I choke on curiosity. "But I'll meet them, right?"

She smiles. "You sure will."

Chapter 32

Jesse

Here I am, back in the freaking needle. Talk about two steps forward, four steps back. I walk up to the large windows and look out over Lake Michigan.

We can ride all the way to the ocean.

Lane's blue eyes were bright when he said this, what seems like a century ago.

Yes, I think. *Take me far away from all this bullshit.*

But we didn't go to the ocean that night. Or the night after or the night after that. We just went home.

The fear that Lane has finally called me, but that I can't get the call because I have no cell service up here, creeps in again. Another, more cynical voice says, *No way. He wouldn't pick this one moment to call. He avoided you for two whole months and your cell service was just fine. Get over it. He's done with you.*

He had a hundred moments. A thousand. He didn't choose to call then, and he sure as hell isn't calling now.

I sink down onto a sofa and note how quiet this place is. From here, I can't hear Winston snoring. When we got back, I found him curled up in Maisie's bed, in the crook of the girl's arm. Traitor. One belly rub and he'll give it up to anyone.

Caldwell said he'd be back, that he had to "check on something." I don't care. I'm a little curious why he hasn't killed me yet, or at least tried, but that curiosity is little more than a bee buzzing in the back of my head.

I've killed four people.

Have you ever killed anyone? I asked Brinkley once.

Have you ever eaten a donut? he asked in return. *Sometimes you can't get around it. Even if you'll regret it all your life.*

"Is that what you would say now?" I ask the purpling dawn on the horizon. No one answers.

Gabriel appears, his wings open as if he's just landed. He tucks them into his back and they disappear, making him look like a beautiful man in an expensive suit.

"I killed four people," I say, pressing my hands to the cold glass. I watch the white crests rise and fall between my fingers.

"Nearly 200,000 died today," Gabriel says, mimicking me. He presses both hands to the glass too. "You were not responsible for that."

But I am responsible for these four. What if they have families? What if someone is finding out right now that I killed the person they love most in the world?

"You did nothing wrong."

"How can you say that? Of course it's wrong."

Gabriel shows me the blackened city. The world is in ruin. Building façades crumble. Smoke billows up into the gray sky. A sulfuric wind tears at what remains of the rubble.

"You have the power to make it right."

Chapter 33

Ally

I listen to Dr. York's voicemail for the third time and frown.

"—haven't heard from her in a couple of days and so I was just wondering if Cindy was with you. It isn't like her to miss a seminar without talking to me first. If you could give me a call back and let me know if she's just freelancing with Jesse, this old man would sleep better tonight."

I stretch out on the living room sofa as my mind runs several scenarios: Cindy dead by Minli or Monroe's hands. By Caldwell's. Cindy overtaken with power, half-crazed and wandering the streets of Nashville.

I call the hospital and leave a message for Dr. York who isn't available. I apologize for not knowing where Cindy is and ask him to call me back if he gets ahold of her.

That's four partis that are missing—five if I count

Jess. Is this Caldwell's doing? It has to be, but why? Has he killed them? Or is he detaining them like Jesse?

The intercom by the front door buzzes, and I see Nikki's face in the tiny screen. "Al?"

I get up from the sofa and cross to the door.

"Al," Nikki says, because she can't yet see my face in the intercom.

I press the button that will carry my voice up to the control room. "Hey."

"What is Jackson doing?" she asks with a curious smile. I can see the control room behind her, large monitors blinking blue.

Gloria is sitting at the two-person dinette set to the right of the front door, drawing with a towel thrown over her head.

"So there *are* cameras in here."

"Nowhere important," Nikki says.

"For your sake, I hope not."

"I promise. But seriously, what is she doing?"

"She's viewing. She doesn't want anyone to know what she's drawing, so she's covered herself."

I glance at Gloria. The baby blue towel shivers with the motion of her hand moving beneath. The towel's tag scratches at the tabletop.

"How can she see?" Nikki asks.

"She doesn't need to look at the page. She can just draw whatever she sees in her head. Kind of how we can type without looking at the keyboard."

"If you say so."

"Did you call just to ask me what she was doing?"

"No." Color fills Nikki's cheeks. "I need you to come up here."

"Is that an order?" I ask, grinning.

She returns my smile. "It's a polite request. The crew up here is minimal right now, and I need to tell you some things."

My heart quickens. I glance at Gloria again and the quivering towel. I can leave her, can't I? She usually draws for hours at a time. I'll be back before she's finished. I make a point not to look back at my laptop, where I have several windows open in a search for more information on Paul Kellerman, a name I'm trying to rule out from Brinkley's list.

I force a smile. "I'll be right up."

The screen goes dark. I find a notepad and scribble a message for Gloria. I put it on the kitchen table so that it's the first thing she'll see when she pulls the towel off her head.

I close my laptop and slip out of the apartment.
The elevator is empty and the halls quiet. Either
everyone is out of missions, or catching some sleep.
On the 64th floor, I step off the elevator and walk to
the end of the hall. I stop just before a large metal door
but don't knock. The camera twists down to look at
me. Its large robotic eye dilates, taking me in.

I wave and some mechanism in the door clicks.

I push it open and step into the control room. It's
big and airy in here, a lot of space to move around. The
monitoring stations are pushed to the far walls, leaving
a large space between the computers. This setup is
essential, given the traffic that comes through this
room on any given day.

Despite the volume of bodies the room is used to,
Nikki wasn't lying when she said the crew was minimal.
Apart from Nikki, I count only five other heads, each
watching their own cluster of screens. I walk up behind
her and place one hand on the small of her back. I
count her vertebrae, making it to six before she turns
and wraps her arms around my waist.

She places a kiss on my neck, and I feel myself go
soft inside.

"How's everything?" My voice is a little deeper

than usual.

"It's dying down. It was chaos an hour ago, but that's passed. Everyone is fine as long as they know what they're supposed to be doing."

I picture them, Jeremiah's tactical units, small teams like the one I joined in Nashville, where I met Nikki. They're out there now, looking for the missing or injured people created by Caldwell's relentless search for power.

"Have you learned anything else?" I ask, hopeful as I clasp my hands behind her back.

"She's in The Needle with Maisie, Caldwell's wife Georgia, and probably Caldwell himself—seeing as we can't clock him on any of the other cams right now."

One big happy family. Jesse must be losing her mind.

"He's manipulating her."

"It's pretty easy to see that's her soft spot. Family and *you*." Nikki takes another step toward me. "I don't blame her."

"You wouldn't risk everything to save me."

She wraps her arms around me again. "That's where you're wrong."

As soon as she says it, I know what's coming. My heart speeds up, afraid.

"I love you, Al."

"No."

Nikki laughs, a terse little snort. "No?"

"We've only been dating for a couple of months."

"I've been in love with you since I first saw you, a year ago. You're all I think about. When I picture the future, the *after* of all this, I picture you. A cabin in the woods somewhere. Two huge dogs and maybe a kid, because I know you want one. But only if it's cute and has this little button nose."

She reaches up and brushes the end of my nose with the tip of her finger.

"You don't know enough about me to know if you love me."

She tilts her head, a hint of a smile tugging at the corners of her mouth. "I know you're unfailingly kind. Considerate. You look out for people and put them first. You're fair, with a good sense of justice. You take things seriously and care about the work you do."

Too seriously, Jesse would say. I take myself too seriously.

"You're smart and resourceful, not to mention hot as hell. That alone is enough to spend the rest of my life with you."

The rest of my life with you.

I stumble back and hit the control panel. The screens go fuzzy for a moment until Nikki pulls me up and touches a few buttons.

"I'm not proposing." Nikki laughs. "Breathe."

"I—"

I what? I don't know what I want to say. Not, *I love you too.* Certainly not that.

What can I say instead? Something about *after?*

When I think of *after* I think of Jesse. Always Jesse. I've been by her side since we were eleven. At ninety, I want to look over and still see her there. Frankly, I think Jesse will be a *hilarious* old woman.

Nikki reaches up and tucks my hair behind my ears. "Are you okay?"

"Yes," I manage to say. I release a short laugh. "You just surprised me. I didn't realize this is what you called me up here for."

"I called you up for a kiss actually." She flashes another sweet smile. "I was hoping to squeeze one in."

She leans in for the kiss but I step back. I can't kiss her right now. I need to think about this. Then I remember something. "You never told me there were cameras in our rooms. I walk around naked."

She smiles again, though this time it's strained. I think she's expecting the lecture that is sure to follow. "I love that about you."

"Maybe I don't want whoever the hell is working the controls to see me naked."

"We don't record the apartments. And the chance that someone was staring into the room the moment you went to the kitchen to get some juice is really low."

A thought occurs to me. "Are you the one who installed the cameras?"

It was her apartment long before I moved in. When we came to Chicago, to Jeremiah's headquarters, I assumed that I would get my own room. I assumed that if they couldn't accommodate that request, I'd be fine sharing with Jesse. We share beds so often that it would hardly put me out unless the bed itself was twin. Jesse thrashes in her sleep sometimes.

But then Nikki surprised me.

Stay here with me, she said. *It's one of the bigger apartments. There's plenty of room. And I like to think of you here, in my bed, even when I'm away.*

It had been very sweet at the time.

Another thought surfaces.

"The man who came to check the ventilation was

not a repairman," I say. "He was installing the camera. You installed it after I moved in with you."

"Al—"

"You lied to me. I can forgive that, if you don't *keep* lying. Why did you have the camera installed?"

"It isn't what you think." Her face grows red. Her eyes slide away from mine and back to the monitors. She pretends to survey the footage, but I know better.

"Then explain it to me," I say. "You said I have a good sense of fairness. I'll understand if it's a good reason. Just be honest."

She doesn't look away from the screen, her chest rising in a controlled inhale.

"I wanted to know if Jesse ever came to the room," she says at last.

"You're jealous of Jesse?"

"Shouldn't I be?" she asks. Her voice hardens.

"We aren't," I lower my voice, "*secret lovers*, if that's what you're implying."

She exhales. "I know."

"Because you've been watching me."

"I'm the only one who has seen you naked. I promise."

"It's not that, Nick." I bite off my words as my

voice rises. A few of the other people watching the monitors glance my way, but no one moves to do anything. I drop my voice. "It's the idea that you didn't trust me."

"I do trust *you*."

I fill in her thought. "But not Jesse."

She searches my face but doesn't say anything.

"You said you understood that Jesse and I are a package deal. I won't sleep with her. I promised you I wouldn't do that, but you can't make me change my feelings. That's not how it works."

Her eyebrows round and her gaze falls to her hands. "I know. I'm trying. I'm *really* trying. But it's hard loving you this much and only getting a little back."

Then it isn't love, I think. Because I love Jesse no matter what. I'd go to the bottom of the ocean to get her, if that's where Caldwell put her. And it doesn't matter if she never kisses me again, never touches me, never completely quits that self-centered jerk, Lane. It doesn't matter, because my feelings aren't based on what she does or doesn't do for me.

"What are you thinking?" Nikki asks, a panicked expression on her face.

"Nothing," I say. "Is that all you called me up here for? Because I need you to give me access to Jesse's apartment. We want to move her stuff before the building goes down."

Nikki punches a few keys. "The door is unlocked, but before you go, there's one more thing I need to tell you."

A few more punches of the keys change three monitors. One monitor shows an aerial view of Chicago. Another couple of punches and the streets and buildings go black before erupting in an array of colors.

"Do you see the thermal reading?" she asks, pointing at one of the screens.

"Yes."

"In the car I told you that when a partis uses their powers, it emits gamma rays. The white spots you see are places where gamma rays have been emitted."

I see one in the church where Jesse was being held. The explosion that killed Jeremiah is probably the source of that gamma burst. I see another in the area where Gloria's second hideout apartment was. Not in the apartment itself, but just outside, like maybe someone was watching us from the riverbank.

"Jason?" I ask. "But I thought the gamma output was only for active powers. After all, it's not picking up every time Jesse uses a shield or Caldwell teleports. Did Jason have an active power?"

"Not that we knew of," she says. "Though I guess Jesse can tell us that now, can't she? Maybe she acquired more than healing."

The more power she acquires, the less stable she'll be.

Jesse. Hang in there, baby.

"We need to get her back," I say. "She's going through—something—and the only person talking her through it is Caldwell."

"I know," Nikki says. "We'll seize the first opportunity we get."

I search her face for the jealousy, for the fear. I don't see it.

"So there are other partis in the city."

"When we find out more I'll tell you. I promise."

Her face is so sweet and earnest that I almost forgive her for breaching my privacy. Almost.

"How's Jeremiah?"

"Alive," she says. "But I'm not sure how long it'll be until he's fully conscious."

"I'm going to want to talk to him. I need to find

out what he hasn't told us."

Nikki sighs. "I was afraid you'd say that."

Chapter 34

Jesse

I fall asleep and Gabriel overtakes my dreams. He is holding me somewhere high in the sky, above an unknown city I can't see because my face is pressed against his suit jacket. But I can hear his wings beating around me, protecting me from the icy air and clouds.

My stomach drops as we start to descend. I swallow a terrified wail.

"I will never let you fall."

"That's what they all say, bud. Then you find someone else's lacy panties in the bed and a positive pregnancy test on the sink."

Gabriel never laughs at my jokes.

We land. The air rushes up around my face as his wings stretch out one last time before tucking away out of sight. Gabriel puts me gently on my feet, and I feel the ground shift beneath me.

Sand.

I turn and see a house. It is sky blue with white trim; an A-frame with great big windows and a wooden sidewalk that leads up to the door. Patches of grass peek through the sand surrounding it. At the back of the house, there's the beach, the roar of gray waves lapping hungrily at the sand. The other direction—in every other direction I look actually—there's only open land. No houses, no civilization, nothing stretching out to the dense tree line in the distance.

A gull cries overhead.

"What the hell is this?" I ask, the wind from the water tearing at my hair.

"Go inside." Gabriel motions toward the house.

The planks echo hollow with each step as I cross to the door. I press against the worn wood and the door creaks open on command. A soft light pours over the welcome mat and weathered porch.

A terror seizes me, as if something horrible will happen to me if I enter that house.

"Jesse?" A sweet voice calls. A voice I would know anywhere.

"Ally?"

"Go inside," Gabriel urges again.

This time I do. I cross the wooden walkway and

place my hand on the sand-smoothed door. It groans as I push it open. At the sound of the door opening, a pug, in all his fat glory, comes running across the living room floor. His little nails can't gain traction on the wood and he slips into my legs, colliding with my shins.

"Come in here and taste this," Ally calls.

I scoop up Winston and scratch his belly, crossing through the nautical-themed living room, into a kitchen that features starfish décor on its sand-colored walls.

Ally stands over the stove, stirring something in a pot that smells delicious. Her hair is shorter, pulled up in a messy ponytail on the top of her head. She wears a shirt that hangs off of one shoulder and white capris.

She's beautiful.

She smiles and offers me the spoon. "Did you hear me? I need you to taste this."

I go to her side at the stove and she lifts a wooden spoon up to my lips. Spaghetti sauce. One of my favorites.

Her eyes are wide and expectant, as if whatever I say next is of the utmost importance. I can't remember the last time the most serious thing in our lives was what the hell the spaghetti sauce tasted like—or even when we had the time to make freaking spaghetti sauce.

"What do you think?" she asks, her brown eyes wide.

"It's perfect," I say and look around the kitchen. My eyes fall on a lighthouse figurine perched on the windowsill overlooking the water. "All of this is perfect."

I turn to Gabriel who stands in the doorway, his impeccable gray suit looking even more severe in this bright airy kitchen. "What the hell is going on?" I ask him.

"I was just thinking we'd have a nice dinner on the deck," Ally says, in a perfectly sweet tone. It's Stepford wife-ish actually. Until I realize it's the lack of worry that's weird. The Ally I've known all my adult life is the same Ally who worries and frets over my every move. This isn't the Ally I know. Ally thinking, Ally trying to figure out how the hell to solve this latest, greatest problem that is my bullshit. This Ally is carefree. The only thing that seems to trouble this Ally is how long the noodles had been cooking.

"Then after we watch the sun go down, I thought we could cuddle on the couch and watch some TV."

She reaches up and brushes my bangs out of my

eyes. I see a huge rock on her left hand.

I glance down and see I'm wearing a wedding band too.

"Holy fuck," I say. "We're married."

Ally laughs, the sound high and girlish. Unburdened. When was the last time I heard Ally laugh like that? "It surprises me too sometimes. But I wouldn't have it any other way."

She steps into my arms and clasps her hands on the back of my neck. She kisses me, a soft sweet brush of her lips. I practically fall down, it feels so good.

"So?" Ally asks, her breath hot on my lips. "What do you think?"

"About being freaking married?"

"About my plan? Dinner, a sunset, TV."

"It sounds perfect," I tell her. Too damn perfect.

"I did promise you a happily ever after." She smiles and pulls out of my arms. The beach house wavers, darkening as if the light of this world is controlled by a dimmer switch. It refocuses and Gabriel and I are standing on the beach, looking out over the waves, the smell of salt and fish thick in my nose.

The beach house stands behind us.

"What's going on? What is this?"

"This is your perfect world."

"Is it?" I ask. "I mean, sure a world without people sounds great, but like, where the hell did the spaghetti sauce come from? There's no one on the whole planet? Who grew the tomatoes?"

As if on cue, a small tomato garden crops up beside the house.

"Oh come on." I point at the tomatoes. "I don't know if those can even grow on the beach. And what about the noodles? I'm not harvesting wheat and rolling those little things out, man."

"Why do you resist every paradise I offer you?"

"Uh, *human*," I say. "Don't you know us by now?"

"But this is the world you most want. You respond to this one, unlike the others."

"This is the first one with Ally," I say, and as soon as the words are out, it's true. "I think you were a little heavy handed with the marriage part. I mean, do we have to be married? It's an institution set up by white dudes who want to make sure they aren't playing daddy to someone else's kid."

Gabriel blinks at me.

I shrug. "I'm just saying it's a little patriarchal."

"Wake up," Gabriel says. "He's returned."

I open my eyes and find myself on the couch in The Needle. I sit up as Caldwell steps out of the corner into the light.

"We have a bed for you," he says, placing one polished shoe in front of another. "You didn't need to sleep on the sofa."

I don't even remember falling asleep. But it's good to know that even while I do, my shield works. It shimmers purple around me.

"What's going to happen?" I ask him. "We can't keep going on like this."

"We continue to fish out the partis, eliminate them until it's only us. I think of it as saving the best for last."

"I can't let you hunt and kill people." I haven't forgotten that two of the partis are my friends.

"I'm not hunting anymore," he says, coming to sit beside me on the couch. He crosses one leg over the other in the most casual way. We could be discussing my college education. What did Stalin's daughter talk to her father about?

"Now that all of the partis have been chosen, I don't have to hunt them. I know who they are."

"So do you have them locked away in towers too?

Are you collecting us like beanie babies? Waiting for some moment I don't know about?"

Caldwell stares out over the lake, his eyes twinkling in the low lights. "I will do whatever it takes to be the apex, Jesse. You must understand how important this is. Humanity will no longer exist, if we do not seize this chance. A million lives combined. A *billion* is not more important than seizing the chance to create a new, better world."

A billion lives.

I search the water outside the window, trying to see what he sees. In the distance, there's a lighthouse. A perfect replica of the little red and white tower that I saw on the windowsill in the beach house of my dreams. I think of Ally's smile. Ally's laugh. Her lips on mine.

No, a billion lives aren't more important.

Only one.

Chapter 35

Ally

I'm about to go clean out Jesse's room when someone interrupts us.

"Sorry to bother you, sir, but he's awake and wants to be briefed," the guard says. He is careful not to look at me, keeping his eyes on Nikki's. It always struck me as strange that those under Jeremiah's command were called "sir" regardless of gender.

"Thank you," she says. "I'll be right down."

The guard gives an acknowledging nod and then turns on his heels and exits the control room, hands never leaving the gun lying across his abdomen.

"I should check on Gloria anyway," I say, expecting Nikki to dismiss me now that Jeremiah is awake and she's returning to second-in-command. Whatever momentary privilege I received for being her girlfriend has passed.

"Come up with me." She brushes the back of my knuckles with her fingertips.

I arch an eyebrow. "I'm going to ask questions."

"I know," she says with a sly smile. "He can answer them."

I give her a look as if this might be a trick. She holds her smile just fine.

"Okay," I say. "Just for a minute. I really do need to check on Gloria."

Nikki leans over the control button and pushes a number. A screen on the far right blinks, changing from an image of the parking garage to our apartment's kitchen. Gloria is still sitting under the towel.

"See?" Nikki asks. "You have a little time."

I let her lead me to the elevator, appreciating the fact that she won't let go of my hand. It's not exactly romantic. Too many guns are around, and the hallway's too white, too sterile. But it is sweet, a display of affection I could never get from Jesse. *"What if I need my hands to karate chop someone?"* she'd ask.

We step onto the elevator, and after a brief descent, step off again. Nikki pulls me forward by the hand, content to lead me. She doesn't drop my hand until we step into Jeremiah's room.

He's sitting up in the bed and wearing a dressing gown, which is interesting given that I've never seen him in anything but khakis and a sweater vest.

"Glad you're back." He gives me the briefest of smiles. "I trust Nikki took good care of you in my absence?"

"She did." I'm not sure what else to say.

"Are you here to stay?" he asks, his gaze heavy over the rim of his glasses.

I frown. "Jesse is still with Caldwell."

"He won't give her up if he can help it. He's trying to get her to meld with her power source more quickly."

I frown. "What?"

"Jesse sees angels. Correct?"

I glance at Nikki accusingly, but then realize I've never told Nikki about Gabriel.

"No one told me," Jeremiah says as if reading my face. "I knew about them already."

"Just explain the melding," I say.

"Jesse still sees herself as separate from the angel. She thinks it's her consciousness and his consciousness. She talks to it, rather than *be* it."

"I'm fairly certain Jesse is human. Not an angel."

Jeremiah nods. "She was born human, yes. But she's changing."

I want to argue that we can't simply override millennia of evolution. Jesse is a primate and primates don't simply become advanced creatures in such a short space of time.

"First Caldwell thought he'd get her to accept her power by locking her in the box. It helped her strengthen the connection she'd been denying, but she doesn't truly accept it as her own. I suspect that he has also forced Jason's power on her for similar reasons. More power, less humanity. But he is playing a dangerous game with her."

My heart speeds up, and I can tell Nikki wants to take my hand, but doesn't. Is she that scared about appearing weak in front of Jeremiah?

"He needs her to accept her powers and begin the war between the partis. Jesse was the last called, and has been dragging her feet the whole way. The danger is that once she fully accepts what she can do, he will no longer be able to control her. She is by far the most dangerous of all of them, but she doesn't know."

"How can you possibly know all this?"

Nikki tenses beside me. What does she think he'll say?

Jeremiah looks away, picking at the corner of the

blanket draped over his lap. "You forget I've been watching him for a long time."

Nikki exhales as if she's been holding her breath. "Caldwell is treading a thin line with her. He needs her to fully accept her power in order to complete the energy transfer, and yet take it before she can use it against him."

I search her face. *You knew about this?*

"I think he is playing to her need for family, love, connection. He wants her to see him as her father. He wants to give her a reason to hesitate before killing him."

"Because hesitation will get her killed," I say, searching both their faces. They are sharing more information with me now than ever before, but there is something wrong about this confessional.

"Exactly," Jeremiah says, smoothing the blanket with an open palm.

"Why are you telling me all this?" I ask. *What do you want out of it?*

"I've always been open with you, Alice."

"No, you haven't. You never even told me you had NRD."

"I told you that my sister and father had it. You

knew that meant I probably would too."

A headache begins to form behind my eyes. "What confuses me is your part in all this? Are you partis too?"

"No." He leans back into the pillows. "I am the observer. Think of the Book of Revelations. John of Patmos was the witness to the end times. His role was to observe and chronicle what he saw. That is my role in this story as well."

I grow uncomfortably warm under the bright fluorescents of the hospital room. "Self-appointed or do you see angels too?"

"I was called, yes," he says, evading my question.

I reexamine what I know of Jeremiah to see if this new story holds true. Back in Nashville, when a little boy was shot and killed in the crossfire, Jeremiah practically shook him at me. His little body was still half inside the body bag when Jeremiah unleashed his anger, furious that I had failed to call in Jesse to help with the mission.

"You're not just observing. You're participating," I say. "With all the rescue missions and attempts to go after Caldwell, the word observer is grossly inaccurate."

"I do damage control. I try to keep people out of the way, but yes, I have been pushing Jesse to engage from the beginning. Engage with Caldwell. Engage with the other partis."

My jaw drops. "Why?"

"Because this needs to happen," he says. "She is the final piece that must be in place."

"And here I thought you wanted to keep her safe."

"There is no safe in this world. No one is going to make it out of this alive. You understand that, don't you?"

I take a step back. My heart is pounding wildly. Someone calls my name. It's Nikki, saying my name over and over again as if I've gone deaf.

"You knew," I tell her. "You promised to help me protect Jesse, and you knew he was walking her into the fire."

"Al—"

I turn and storm out of the room.

Chapter 36

Jesse

Caldwell takes a phone call. He slips one hand into his pocket, his head cocked ever so slightly to listen to whoever is on the line. His face screws up in irritation.

"I see. I'll be right there." He slips the phone into his pocket.

I blink and he's gone. On instinct I blink several more times, trying to reconcile the sudden absence of a person that was just there.

"He does that."

I turn and find Maisie leaning against the wall at the edge of the hallway. Light from her bedroom spills past her. Winston is still snoring in her room, his snores audible, even from here.

"Who does what?" I ask, unsure if she is talking about Winston or Caldwell.

"Dad." She comes further into the room and sinks onto the sofa. "He leaves all of the time."

"He's probably out clubbing baby seals."

She shrugs. "Probably."

This makes me look at her. I'm not sure what I expected her response to be, with me implying that her father is a monster. But I certainly didn't expect her to be so...agreeable.

I take a seat beside her. "Why are you locked in this tower?"

Maisie considers me a moment longer and then pulls a pillow into her lap. "He says it's for my protection."

"From *what*?"

She shrugs.

"I guess you're lucky that he cares enough to protect you. He tried to have me beheaded in a basement once. He also gassed me to death and buried me alive."

Her eyes go wide.

"You must be his favorite."

"I'm not his favorite." Maisie looks down at her lap, taking a sudden interest in the design on the throw pillow. "Mom is. He tolerates me because she loves me so much."

This is a sad insight, if it's true. "Sorry."

She shrugs again. "He isn't my favorite either."

A silence grows between us, thickening with each passing second. I'm not sure how to break it. Then my stomach grumbles. "I don't suppose they actually feed us up here, do they?"

Maisie raises her voice. "I can make breakfast. It's about the only thing I can cook actually."

She goes into the kitchen and starts making food. Eggs, bacon, toast. A jug of orange juice is pulled out of the fridge and handed to me, no glass.

I twist off the lid and gulp it down, wiping my mouth with the back of my hand.

Maisie is scowling at me.

I hold out the OJ bottle. "Sorry, did you want some?"

She looks from my sticky mouth to the wet rim of the jug. "No, thanks."

A moment later, two plates are set on the dining table in one corner of the great room. I eat everything but the bacon, which I toss onto Maisie's plate.

Her eyebrows arch. "You don't eat bacon?"

"Nope. I've done so many different death replacements that I can't help but see meat, as well, *meat*. I can't bring myself to eat it."

"You don't eat bacon," she says again, in awe. "No wonder you're not his favorite."

"Have your quad all mashed up like ground chuck on the pavement and I'd like to see you eat meat."

She shoves a whole piece of bacon into her mouth and smiles.

What a little shit. I can't help but smile back at the kid.

I push my empty plate away from me.

"So what's that shiny purple thing around you?"

"A chastity belt. I'll tell you about them when you're older."

She frowns at my evasion.

I change the subject. "How long do you think we're going to be locked in this tower? I don't really understand why we're here."

"Because the only way in and out is through Dad. It's impregnable."

"Uh, I think you mean *impenetrable*. But yes, you want everything impregnable where sixteen-year-old daughters are concerned."

She doesn't smile at my joke.

I decide to test her, see how much she knows about what's going on. "So we're supposed to wait here until…what? What are we waiting for?"

She pushes her own plate away. "Until everyone is dead."

Chapter 37

Ally

Gloria is packing up when I walk into the room with a duffle full of Jesse's stuff. Her sketchbook is protruding from the top of her own bag as she slings it over a shoulder.

"So we're leaving now?" I ask. "Honestly, I can't tell if we are coming or going. I feel like we are running all over the place and not getting anything done. First we try to leave, and Jesse disappears on us. Then Jason chases us all over the city, and here we are again, back where we started. I hope you saw something helpful in your drawing. I want to meet this backup already and go get Jesse."

"That's what we're doing now."

"Thank god." I gather up my bags, in addition to Jesse's. "Let's go then."

Nikki catches up to us in the lobby, and I swear under my breath. Gloria cuts me a side glance.

"I'll get the car," she says. "Meet me out front."

No one tries to stop Gloria from exiting the building. No sedation darts or dramatics. She exits just fine while I'm waiting for Nikki to stop running toward me.

She slows when there's just a couple of feet between us. "I know you're mad, but hear me out."

We walk together across the grand lobby toward the doors. Outside, several people are rushing off to whatever comes next for them—work, home, school. They pay us no attention whatsoever. In a place as big as Chicago, two women standing on a sidewalk talking is hardly noteworthy.

"You lied about the cameras, and you lied about protecting Jesse. You knew from the beginning that I joined all this because I wanted to make Jesse safer. I wanted more protection, not to suit her up and send her to the front lines."

"I didn't lie," she says. "I wasn't allowed to tell you. That's not the same."

I give her a hard stare. "That's lying. You can't expect me to spend all my time and energy guessing what you haven't told me."

Her fingers brush my arm. "I'm sorry. You have

to understand, that given my position, I can't tell you everything."

"So there are still things I don't know?" I ask, my mind reeling. "You could be planning to throw Jesse in a volcano to appease the gods for all I know."

Nikki tugs at her ponytail, tightening it. "No one is throwing Jesse into a volcano. It's not like that."

"How am I supposed to know? You don't tell me everything."

A taxi flies past us and we step a little farther away from the curb. I tug my coat around me tighter. It's really too thin for a Chicago winter.

"I told you I love you, and I mean it. I hope we have a chance for a life together. It's what I hope for most in the world."

"How can you love me and lie to me? That's not how it works, Nick."

She looks out over the crowded street.

"You're as bad as she is." When she meets my gaze her eyes are hard.

"Excuse me?"

"Jesse spends all her energy trying to fight what she is. Sure, she'll run into a burning building if you tell her to. Or play the hero for a paycheck. But she's so noncommittal about it. You can talk to her for five minutes and know she doesn't think her actions mean anything. Worse, it's like she's annoyed that she's got this job to do."

"Tell me how you really feel." My temper flares. I take a breath before speaking again. "You think Jesse isn't enthusiastic enough about dying, or being your lackey?"

"She came here to Chicago because you told her to. Not because she cares about what happens to the world. She isn't altruistic."

A gold Cadillac pulls out of the garage and slides up the street toward us. I watch her come with a mixture of frustration and relief.

"Who took advantage of that? To you and Jeremiah, I'm some tool you can use to make Jesse jump through hoops."

"Aren't you?" Nikki asks. Her eyes go wide. "No. You're not. I don't know why I said that."

"Because you're mad. I'm mad. We'll have to do this later. I have to go save Jesse."

"Of course you do."

I yank open the door of Gloria's car and stand there waiting for her to say whatever she thinks she needs to.

Gloria frowns at my hesitation. "We need to go."

"Bye, Nick."

Nikki throws up her hands and turns back toward the building. I'm about to close the door when she says, "I do love you, Al. For whatever that's worth."

Chapter 38

Jesse

"**W**hen you say 'until everyone dies', do you mean *every*one?" I ask. I mean, I need clarification.

"He's going to destroy the city," Maisie says as casually as 'he's going to pick up milk.' "A lot of people will die."

"Chicago? He's going to destroy *all* of Chicago?"

"My mom told me that it's important I stay in the tower until 'it's all said and done'."

Maisie uses air quotes around the part she stole from Georgia.

My legs feel all wobbly so I sit down at the kitchen table. "So he locked you here to keep you out of the way?"

"My mom asked him to." Maisie shrugs "She doesn't want me to get hurt."

"What does your mom do?" Besides suck the life

out of everyone. "Is she his glorified secretary or what?"

"No." Maisie's brow pinches together. "She's awesome. She has powers like you, and she helps him fight the bad people that come to the city trying to kill us."

"Why would they kill you? You're a kid."

"My mom says that kids die in war every day."

Fair enough. I glance down at my phone again. There's still no service.

"Is there no way to send a message out? I have people I love out there. I need to warn them that he's going to like, blow up the city, or whatever."

"I have email."

"That'll work." I jump up, excited. "Where's your computer?"

Maisie rolls her eyes at me but retrieves her laptop from her bedroom. She places it on the dining table in front of me, but as I reach for it, I immediately see a problem. The laptop and table are shoved backwards as I try to use the computer.

"You can't send an email with your shield thingy up. Hey, be careful," Maisie whines.

"Right." I frown at the screen. "Show me your

hands."

"What?"

"Just do it."

"God, okay, weirdo. Don't spaz."

Her hands are empty.

I consider my situation and decide that warning Ally is worth the risk that this kid is secretly a ninja and about to stab me or something. I drop my shield, count to ten. Nothing happens. So I open a web browser and go to my email.

It's not a beautiful letter or anything. It's short and to the point, in case the computer blows up in my face, or Caldwell pops up behind me with a syringe.

In The Needle with Maisie and Winston. Not harmed. Caldwell planning to blow up the city. Get out NOW.

I hit send.

I don't get any failure to deliver message, so I exhale the breath I'm holding.

"Okay," I say with a little optimism. "That went okay. Can I send another email?"

Maisie shrugs. "Whatever."

I pause in my typing. "Wait. How do we have wifi but no cell service?"

Maisie shrugs. "Dad designed this place. How

should I know?"

I let it go and type up another email. This one is for Lane.

We haven't talked in a long time. Should we?

As soon as the computer makes the little whoosh sound, acknowledging my email has been sent, I sign out and close the computer.

"Who's Lane? Is he your boyfriend?" she asks with a vicious smile.

"Wow, you really must be my little sister. You're sure annoying like one."

She smiles bigger. "If he's your boyfriend, why hasn't he called you or emailed or texted you? Why isn't he trying to rescue you?"

Her words sting. "First of all, I feel like it's important that you know girls don't need to be saved by boys. Secondly, mind your own business."

She harrumphs and falls onto the sofa. "Whatever. He's probably ugly."

"He's not ugly." I get up from the kitchen and join her on the sofa. "He's gorgeous. He's got these sexy curls and blue eyes. Ocean blue, and when he wears this button down blue shirt I got him, it kills me."

"Why'd you get it for him if it kills you?"

"It's an expression. It's horrible. In a good way."

She looks doubtful.

"Anyway, for your information, he's really, *really* pretty."

"Tall? Dark and handsome?"

"That's the one."

Winston jumps onto the sofa and nuzzles between my legs. Maisie looks a little disappointed that it wasn't her lap he chose. I'm thrilled. Damn right he loves me more.

"He's probably got a funny looking nose or something."

"He does not."

"Whatever."

"Oh geez-*zus*, I'll show you." I scroll through my pictures on my phone, noting my low battery. Without a charger it won't last much longer, but I have enough time to choose a suitable picture of Lane. He was stretched out on the sofa, curled around Winston, looking up at me with come hither eyes. Clothes on, totally PG. "Look. See? His nose is great."

Maisie reaches out and takes the phone. Her face drops. "This is Lane?"

"Gorgeous, right?"

Her brow furrows. "This guy? *This* is your boyfriend?"

"Don't sound so surprised." My temper flares. "I'm not hideous."

Maisie gives me back my phone, but the confused look on her face lingers.

"I'm going to bed," she says.

"We just had breakfast."

"I have a headache." She stands and marches toward her bedroom. Winston dutifully trots after her, slipping through the crack in the door before she closes it all the way.

I look down at the picture of Lane in my hand. He looks fine. It's a great picture.

I frown at the closed bedroom door. "What the hell was that about?"

Chapter 39

Ally

"They'll be here." Gloria seems impervious to the cold, while I stand shivering on a street corner.

I've buttoned my coat up to my chin, tucking half of my face into the collar. It's the wind. Chicago wind cuts right through me.

"Can we get a coffee? I feel like I need a warm drink in my hands."

"Go get coffee." Gloria nods at the Starbucks across the street. "I'll wait here."

I leave Gloria on the corner outside the Art Institute, next to a homeless man holding a sign. I glance back and see her giving money to the man with the cardboard sign. He thanks her and hobbles away to find another patron.

The coffee shop is warm. I exhale and unbutton my coat. I want the heat to soak into my bones and warm me through and through. The windows have

Christmas trees and gingerbread men painted on the glass and holiday wishes written in soap markers for all the customers to see.

Christmas music seeps through the radio, some modern version of Jingle Bells, which is far sexier than I think it was ever intended to be, sung by some young diva of the hour. A man in a Starbucks apron is handing out samples of biscotti, wearing a charming Santa hat.

Christmas.

I'd completely forgotten. I haven't been in any stores blaring Christmas tunes. I haven't been in front of a television advertising a thousand commercials for what I should buy *this* holiday season. Even in Gloria's car, the radio is always tuned to an AM radio talk show.

I've seen the lights around town, and acknowledged the holiday in my mind, but it didn't hit me until now that I have no plans. I haven't sent my parents or brother or friends holiday cards. I haven't bought Jesse a gift. I haven't done a single thing to celebrate the Christmas season.

I don't even know what Jesse wants for Christmas.

I doubt she's thought about it either.

"What would you like, miss?"

I pull my wallet out of my pocket. "A grande white hot chocolate, please."

"Name?"

"Ally."

"$4.28."

I hand her my card and turn at the sound of the bell ringing. Gloria steps into the store with two people in tow. A very tall guy, maybe Egyptian, with dark hair, eyes, and skin. His beard is trimmed and as black as his glasses. A girl with a sleek, stylish bob comes to stop beside him. She wears a fuchsia coat that hits high on her thighs, an inch of lace petticoat exposed beneath. She's also wearing matching knee-high boots. If her legs are cold, she doesn't show it.

"Ma'am, your card?"

"Oh, thank you." I take the card from the cashier and slip it back into my wallet.

Instead of walking down the counter to the where the drinks are retrieved, I go to the threesome. I must say, this duo doesn't look like backup.

The girl isn't any bigger than me, and the guy is a little on the scrawny side.

"This is—"

"Ah, no names," the boy says, in a crisp English

accent. Not Egyptian then. And his voice is much more masculine than I imagined. So he isn't a boy at all. "Not here."

"You know me, don't you?" the girl asks, leaning forward and taking my hand. "By reputation if nothing else."

She stares hard into my eyes, a mischievous smile on her face. "Jessup and I have a past. I took a little vacation and *voila*. Here I am."

"Ray—"

"No names," the boy says again. "Honestly, if I have to black out another block in this city, someone is going to notice."

"Yes," the girl says with a smile. "I knew you'd heard of me."

Rachel. Oh I've heard of her, and I know how she came to be Brinkley's charge too. I don't think Rachel realizes how much I know about that. She might be embarrassed to know how much Brinkley revealed about her in his journal.

The image of Rachel tied to a bed while she's killed repeatedly for a snuff film burns the back of my eyes. Then Rachel, first becoming a partis, sitting in her living room floor, carving herself up.

Rachel holds up her wrist. "I kept the bracelet though."

She's wearing a hospital band, evidence of where she's spent the last couple of years.

The man grabs her wrist and shoves it down. "Low profile, darling. Do you know what that means?"

Rachel huffs. "Buy me a toffee latte, *Cariño*. Then I'll promise to be a good girl."

The guy slides past me to the counter where he does just that.

"He needs a bit of training," Rachel says with a grin. "But he is *awfully* cute."

I have nothing to say to that. I walk to the counter and retrieve my white hot chocolate instead.

Gloria's looking out the festive window, surveying the street. "We need somewhere we can talk."

"*Cariño* has a place picked out." Rachel turns her wrist over. "We'll go there in two minutes."

I blow on my hot chocolate. "Why two minutes?"

"Changing of the guard," she says, as if I'm supposed to know what that means.

"One toffee latte," the guy most certainly not named *Cariño* says. He slips a warm drink into Rachel's hands and then looks at his watch, just as Rachel did.

"Ninety seconds, ladies. Are you ready for a little stroll?"

Gloria adjusts her pack. "I'm ready."

"And you?" he asks, meeting my eyes.

I lift my hot chocolate. "I'm good for a stroll."

"Seventy seconds," he says.

"It's so sexy when you count down like that," Rachel giggles into her latte, playfully biting the plastic lid.

"Sixty seconds," he says, his voice even more sultry than before.

I look at Gloria and am relieved to see she is just as uncomfortable by this display of affection as I am.

"Fifty seconds," Rachel says, practically purring.

"Forty-*five*."

"Thirty-eight."

"Twenty-two."

I glance around the Starbucks to see if anyone is watching us, listening to this bizarre dialogue fit for a pornography film. Kids in the corner have big headphones on, typing furiously on the keypads in front of them. Another woman in a suit gesticulates wildly with someone on the phone while she scribbles notes.

The biscotti guy is shuffling our way.

"Ten. Nine. Eight..."

"No thank you," I say as he pushes the little silver tongs at me.

"Seven, Six, Five..."

He turns to Gloria next. "No, I'm fine."

"Three...Two..."

Rachel reaches forward and grabs a handful of the biscotti off the man's tray and with a wink is out the door at the same moment *Cariño* says, "*one.*"

I take the last biscotti off the stunned man's tray as an afterthought. "Thank you."

On the sidewalk, Rachel speaks to me around a mouthful of biscotti without turning around. "Stay close to us, all right? Don't walk in front of me. Stay just behind me and close, but not so freaking close you step on my heels. I hate it when people do that."

The man is holding a device in his hand, making some kind of fine tuning adjustments with a big knob as we walk. He doesn't look up, yet manages not to plow into anyone.

"Eleven o'clock, darling."

Rachel looks up and to the left. "I see it."

I follow her gaze, but I don't see anything. Then I

do. A small black camera is slowly turning our way. Then it stops and begins to turn the opposite direction.

"How did you—?" I can't finish my sentence.

The man smiles. "Trade secret, love. If I tell you, I'll most certainly have to kill you."

It goes on like this for ten city blocks. The man calls out a position to Rachel. Rachel finds the camera and no sooner than she finds it, it begins to turn away from us.

"Really, how *are* you doing that?" My chocolate sits cooling in my hand. For now the heat is still delicious.

"She's partis," Gloria reminds me, whispering almost directly into my ear.

"Careful what you say," the man says, glancing up from his device for the first time, scowling.

"If you're doing your job, Cariño, they can't hear us."

"Better safe than a dancing girl in Marrakesh, my love."

"Ooh, my love," she says, making a small motion with her hand to turn away a traffic camera on our right. "That's a new one."

"Are we almost there?" Gloria asks, her voice

pained.

"Two more blocks," the man says.

Two blocks later we are at the door of yet another apartment building. I've begun to feel as though I've taken a tour of Chicago's apartments and now have a great sense of what the city has to offer. Unlike Gloria's apartments, with their secret exits, this apartment is marvelous.

A grand high ceiling greets us in the lobby. A crystal chandelier worthy of the Titanic dangles from the center of the room above marble floors. Huge columns stand half-exposed from the walls where we push a button to call down the elevator.

"Whose place is this?" Gloria asks, clearly uncomfortable with the grandeur.

"We're using this flat while my friend is out of town," the man says. "I called in a favor."

"You stole it."

"Ms. Jackson, what a horrible accusation. I've never stolen anything in my life."

Rachel grins, twirling girlishly in her petticoat. "He borrowed it."

"He won't be back from Munich for another week. Trust me. It'll be like we were never here at all."

I glance at Gloria. *Who are these people?*

Gloria can't see me because she's too busy scowling at the man.

The elevator opens and we step out into a beautiful penthouse, not unlike the immaculate lobby below. I feel like I'm in a 16th century chateau rather than a Chicago apartment. A chaise stretches before a huge glass window. Dresses of every kind are strewn all over the room.

The man sees me eyeing them. "She's been shopping."

"How?" I blurt. As far as I know, she escaped an asylum not two months ago. Where did she get the money to go shopping? And these dresses do not look cheap.

"How have you been moving around the city undetected?" Gloria asks.

The man offers her the device he's been carrying. "This little guy. He's quite handy. He blacks out all recording devices within a twenty foot radius."

"And I take care of the ones that are a little farther away," Rachel adds.

"And she's fantastic at it." He grins. Something in my gut churns. "As long as we carry this little guy, we are effectively a blind spot."

"You and your gadgets," Gloria says, unamused. Now all of her attention turns to Rachel. "You look well."

"So much better," Rachel says. "I thought escaping the asylum was the worst idea ever, but how could I tell Brinkley no? I got lucky."

"I picked her up," the man says. "You should've seen her face when I pulled up in a Ferrari."

Gloria's face is so red it might explode. "A Ferrari is not low profile, Gideon."

"Life's little pleasures, Ms. Jackson. Who knows when we are going to die? Who would take the bus to hell when one can drive a beautiful car?"

Gideon. The name rings a bell. *Gideon.* A line from Brinkley's journal springs to mind. *Idolizing an Iranian smuggler should have been my first hint.*

"You're Gideon?" I ask. "Brinkley's Gideon?"

Gideon grins. "One and the same, my lady. And you're Alice Gallagher, are you not?"

"You wanted to be the most powerful man in the world," I say, recalling the entry from Brinkley's journal where Gideon—first taken from his family in Afghanistan—tells Brinkley what he wants to be when he grows up. So he can't be more than twenty now.

"Working on it, darling," he says with a mischievous grin. "This vixen is quite the accessory."

Rachel preens.

"So you all know each other," I say. "You're all tied to Brinkley."

A silence settles on the room. "May he rest in peace," Gideon says in a serious tone.

"I want to see his grave," Rachel adds, equally somber. "Once we leave the city."

"He's in Nashville," Gloria says.

"With all due respect," I begin, and both Gideon and Rachel bite back laughs. "What?"

"With all due respect," Rachel chides.

Gideon turns his eyes up at me. "Relax, darling. We are all friends here. Just say what's on your mind."

"I'm not your darling, for starters."

"I call every beautiful woman, darling," he says, with mock indignation. "Except Ms. Jackson, of course."

Rachel laughs. "Because she'll break your arm again."

"She broke my hand, actually," Gideon says, with a sideways glance. "But that's a story for another day."

I take a breath. "All right. You're Gloria's backup, I assume. I also assume you're here to help because Brinkley asked you to come after he was—gone."

"You're on fire," Gideon chides. "Don't stop now."

"But what do you *do*?" I ask. "You're probably not even old enough to buy alcohol, and last I heard, she was in an asylum half-insane."

Rachel grins. "Oh, I see why Jesse likes her. She's feisty."

Gideon frowns. "I didn't realize we were producing resumes for this little meeting, so you'll have to forgive me for not having anything prepared."

"I—" I begin an apology but he doesn't let me finish.

He pulls a device from his pocket and pushes a button. The walls begin to clink and clatter, and I worry that I'll regret chiding him. Panels flip. The ornate walls are false, revealing cabinets beneath. Some have weapons—a lot of weapons—almost as well stocked as Jeremiah's tenth floor armory, but other cases have devices. Strange electronic things that I've never laid eyes on. A few look extremely complicated, with buttons covering their faces. Others have only one, large, menacing button.

"I have well-equipped friends and many connections. I speak fourteen languages, know how to fly just about every aircraft ever designed. And I'm ridiculously rich."

Rachel snorts. "You shouldn't brag."

"Brinkley taught me quite a lot," Gideon says. "Far more than he ever taught his girls, I'm sure."

It takes me a second to realize he means Rachel and Jesse—they're Brinkley's girls.

Rachel folds her arms in mock petulance. "Sexist, if you ask me."

Gideon pouts his lip sympathetically, but continues on. "And what he didn't teach me, I either taught myself or learned through my connections."

"Some less than reputable," Gloria adds as she sets her sketchbook on a table and goes to inspect one of the rifles on the wall.

"I may have gone to one of the best boarding schools in the world, but I'm not *elitist*, Ms. Jackson," Gideon says, more mock indignation.

"Sometimes it's like you're the favorite child," Rachel says. "You got the fancy boarding school and the money, while I got the asylum."

"It was a very nice asylum, love."

His whole couch slides backwards across the floor, bumping against the wall. Gideon rocks forward, laughing.

"Careful," he says to Rachel. "You'll damage the furniture and this is very expensive to replace."

My heart hammers. "You're telekinetic."

Rachel grins. "That's one word for it."

Two guns lift off the wall and turn toward Gideon.

"Hey, now," he says, his voice losing its humor. "Never point a gun at someone, even in jest. It's dangerous."

The guns return to their places on the wall.

Gideon is red faced and breathing a little heavier than before. "No wonder Brinkley never gave you a gun. You're a little rash."

She gives him a warning look.

"In the most endearing and adorable way," he adds.

"Has Caldwell been hunting you too?" I ask her.

"Yes, which is why I've teamed up with Gideon. He's done a good job of keeping me hidden."

"I can't even find you," Gloria says.

"Good," Rachel says. "If he finds me, I'm sure

he'll kill me outright. I'm not Jesse."

"Why do you say that?" I ask.

Rachel wets her lips.

"You know about the angels, don't you? That they talk to us?"

"Yes," I tell her. "Jesse sees Gabriel."

She nods as if she already knows this. "Mine has tried to explain to me what's going on and what I'm supposed to do."

I wait for her to go on.

She bites her lip and sinks onto the couch that Gideon has pushed back into place. "It's hard to explain. When I say it out loud, it sounds crazy."

"It's okay," I tell her. "I'll believe you. Whatever you say."

I'll believe that she believes it anyway.

This seems to be the right answer. "The Earth's magnetic field comes at a price. It must be recharged every so often. It's the price we pay for life. That's where the partis come in. We have to choose whether or not we want to recharge the field, protecting the existing planet, or if we want to blow it up and create a new universe, starting all over. Does—does that make sense?"

I remember the television turning itself on in Gloria's apartment and the news story. "The ghost in your apartment," I say to Gloria. "Is that news story connected to this somehow?"

Gideon and Rachel burst out laughing as if I've made the funniest joke in the world.

"You have a ghost?" Rachel asks Gloria.

"Oh come on," Gideon says. "You have to tell her."

They laugh for a moment longer while I stand in the center of the room. Then Rachel takes pity on me. "It was me. I'm the ghost."

"You turned on the TV?"

"I pushed the button on the remote, yes, from a distance. It's how I check in with Gloria so she knows we are okay and that things are still on track. I also wanted her to see the science report. I thought it was very fascinating."

"She watches the discovery channel day and night, this one," Gideon says with an arched eyebrow. "The history channel. All that *Ancient Aliens* shit."

"The angels *could* be aliens. They could be beings from higher dimensions," Rachel says, stamping her foot. "We don't know. Have an open mind."

Gideon arches his eyebrows.

"What's wrong with watching educational TV? It's good for you."

My head spins. "A new universe?"

Rachel shakes her head. "Right. So the partis powers are the essential elements of the universe, and once one person has all of them they become the apex. Then the apex explodes, either with the intention of protecting the existing planet, or creating a new universe."

I collapse to my knees.

Gloria comes to my side. "Alice, are you okay?"

I breathe, in and out. "So either Jesse is murdered for her power or she explodes?"

I feel sick. I swallow several times against the threat of vomiting.

"*Or* we do *my* plan," Rachel says, straightening the lace of her petticoat over her knees. "We kill Caldwell and the other partis, then live long and boring lives until we're ready to die. I'll let Jesse kill me and explode, saving the world—you know, when we are like a hundred years old."

I can't breathe. A hand rubs my back.

"Through your nose," Gloria says. "In and out of

your nose."

"Is she freaking out?" Rachel asks.

"Most people find it difficult to accept their love is going to explode, darling," Gideon says.

"There's no rule that says we have to recharge the shield *now*," Rachel says. "We only have to stop Caldwell and the partis from trying to kill us *now*. After we survive that, we can take our sweet time."

"Breathe," Gloria says. I feel her hand on my back. "You're not breathing."

I finally suck in air. "I don't want her to explode." My voice sounds small, childish.

"Hel-*lo*," Rachel says. "Are you listening to me? We have like a hundred years. Trust me, by the time we're that old, we'll want to die. Who wants to live forever with cataracts and arthritis and all that crap? Not me."

"You don't age," I remind her.

"Uh, if I keep dying. But we'll stop one day, right?"

"It's a good plan," Gloria says, trying to bring my awareness back to the moment. "A long, happy life is the best one can hope for."

"Yes." I squeeze the word out. "Yes, I guess it is

our best option."

"And if you're worried I'm going to go all Dolores Claiborne on her when she's like ninety and decrepit, don't worry. I'll just, like, put a knife in Jesse's hand and fall on it or something. It won't be dramatic at all."

I give her a look. She says she'll defer to Jesse, let her be the apex, but I am not sure I believe her. It is easy to be magnanimous in theory. If Rachel were actually faced with her death, I wonder if she would change her mind. Then again, if it comes down to just the two of them, ancient crones as Rachel puts it, maybe it wouldn't matter. After all, both will die. It's just a matter of who will go first.

Rachel shrugs. "I'm trying to make you feel better."

My mind is swimming with this information. I take a breath and ask the only question I seem to be able to articulate. "You said something about forces of the universe?"

Rachel nods as if remembering. "Angel speak is pretty incoherent, let me tell you. Well, I should say, when he's trying to convey all this universal crap, it's gibberish."

"I have a theory on that, love," Gideon chimes in.

"I think they're simply doing their best to communicate a complex idea to a monkey."

"Uh, thanks," Rachel says. "I am not an idiot, you know."

"Oh, of course not, darling," he says with his sweetest smile yet. "Compared to your fellow monkeys. But if it were in fact a supreme being of some kind, I imagine it's much like a master trying to get its dog to do a very specific trick."

She smirks. "Like play dead?"

He gets her pun immediately. "Exactly."

"Anyway." Rachel turns to me again. "Yes, there are twelve forces. Jesse has one of the most volatile."

"Lucky her," Gideon says with a raised brow.

"What's her force?" I pull my knees into my chest.

"Fire," she says with a shrug. "Though I don't think that's a direct translation."

My confusion must show on my face.

"Humans have given all these things names: Life. Death. Force. Space. Light. Dark. Flesh. Mind. Water. Earth. Air. Fire—but I think these are oversimplifications. Our little monkey brains, as Gideon puts it, can only accept small concepts. I think on a universal scale, these forces are more elaborate.

Take my power for example. Force. Is it gravity? Not exactly. Is it kinetic or potential energy? Not exactly. But all of those things are connected to the same "source"—whatever it is that makes one object move to another place. That's what I'm channeling— whatever the angel-aliens are calling it."

Gideon gives me a patronizing smile. "She really is convinced the angels are ancient aliens."

"You don't know," she wails.

Gloria squeezes my shoulder, before crossing the room to inspect some of the guns on the wall.

Rachel keeps talking. "Jesse is fire. But is it the fire like what we make with a match, or is it like atomic bomb explosions or gamma ray bursts. Or all of it?" She shrugs. "Whatever the thing is that makes the *boom*. That's Jesse's thing."

"And Caldwell?" Gloria asks.

"Space," she says. "He steps in and out of dimensions, I think. I also think it's why he was one of the first called. He was probably closer to the angel- aliens."

Gideon snorts.

"I don't see you with an angel chattering into your ear," she chides him.

"Praise be to Allah," he says. "A conscience is the last thing I need."

"Are you a devout Muslim?" I ask, curious. I hope I don't sound judgmental. Both Gideon and Rachel burst out laughing. Even Gloria cracks a smile.

"Darling," Gideon says, with another upward glance. "The only god I serve is myself."

"He likes to talk about Allah the way I like to talk about being Mexican."

I did wonder about her complexion, the dark eyes and hair, the features of her face.

"We are a quite removed from our roots," Gideon says. "The infidels have ruined me."

He's smiling. Another joke. I try to relax.

The conversation lulls and after a stretch of silence, Rachel says, "Well, now that we're all acquainted, let's go get our girl."

"Yes," Gloria says, coming to life as if this were the cue she was waiting for. "We are going to have to attack The Needle."

She comes forward and lays her sketchbook on the floor in front of me. The three of them crowd around the drawing.

In the drawing, Rachel, Gloria, and I are in a boat

heading toward The Needle.

Gideon is nowhere to be seen.

The waters look choppy, and I'm holding the side of the little boat with white knuckles.

"Well," Rachel exhales, a great harrumph from her chest. "This will be *fun.*"

Chapter 40

Jesse

I'm going to lose my mind. I keep pacing the circular room looking for the door that doesn't exist. The crazy bastard really did build a needle in the middle of the lake with no entrance or exit.

The city taunts me. Sunlight reflects in the windows. Cars drive along the beach, a knot of people trying to get somewhere, completely unaware that Caldwell intends to kill them all.

I collapse on the sofa and my eyes take in the ceiling above. At some point, I begin to slip out of consciousness.

Gabriel appears, standing over me.

"Oh here we go," I say. "Initiate another lucid dream sequence. Any chance that I'll get some real sleep one of these days?"

He makes no reply. Instead, he reaches down and pulls me into his arms, holding me against his chest.

His wings extend and my stomach jolts at the feeling of being propelled up into space.

I seriously doubt he is actually flying or we are actually going anywhere. I get that my body is still on the sofa, asleep, even while he carries me up and away.

We land and we are at the beach house again.

I slip out of his arms and my feet sink in the sand.

"So what's for dinner tonight?" I ask. "Ally making spaghetti again?"

"We made progress. Let's try again."

I go into the beach house with the understanding that something must be different. I push open the front door, and immediately I know the vision has *really* changed.

A plastic tricycle and a floor full of colorful toys assaults me. A horrible whistling-whining comes from the corner, and I realize the racket is from a kid slamming a plastic, squeaky hammer down over and over onto a set of piano keys. The piano lights up and plays a tune with every whack.

"Uh, *no*," I say. "I think you're moving in the wrong direction."

When the hell did I give him the impression that I should have children?

Ally comes out of the room, wearing the same off the shoulder sweater as before and scoops the kid up.

"Are you making music?" she coos. "Are you my little musician?"

She falls onto the sofa and bounces the toddler in her lap. It laughs and laughs, and when she turns it over to blow raspberries on its belly, it squeals more.

"Jess?" Ally calls.

"Right here." How could she not see me standing in the middle of the room? It's true that I've gone stark still. I get that way around kids, sort of viewing them like dinosaurs. Maybe if I'm still enough, they can't sense me.

"Jess, can you come here a minute?"

"She cannot see you," Gabriel says.

"Why?" I ask. "I thought this was supposed to be my fantasy."

"This is one of many possibilities."

An older kid, maybe seven or eight, comes down the stairs two at a time. Jumping off the last step and landing on her hands and knees on the floor.

"*Careful,*" Ally calls out, annoyed. "You're going to hurt yourself."

"I did three this time." She brushes off her knees

proudly. "Last time I could only jump off two."

"Did you do your homework?" Ally asks the girl.

"Most of it," she says looking away.

"*Jess*," Ally says with a threatening tone. "We talked about this."

"Math is stupid," she says.

"Math *is* stupid," I grumble. "She's never going to use it."

"Bring it down here and I'll help you," Ally says.

"Mom—"

Whatever Jesse was going to say doesn't surface. With one look from Ally, the girl harrumphs and marches back up the stairs.

I shiver as someone walks right through me.

Nikki.

"Gee-*zus*," I say, shaking it off. "Watch where you're walking, Sasquatch."

She bends down and gives Ally a kiss. Then she takes the toddler and twirls it around. "How's my baby?"

"*Your* baby?" I whirl on Gabriel. "Ally had babies with Sasquatch?"

Ally sighs. "Natalie has been fed and changed, but Jesse—"

"Let me guess. Math?"

Ally gives a sweet smile.

"I'm on it," Nikki says, and after planting another kiss on Ally's lips, this one a little longer, Sasquatch starts to march upstairs with the toddler in tow.

Ally isn't quick to get up. She lies on the couch, clearly exhausted. Then she pulls herself up and starts gathering up the strewn toys and dumping them into the box in the corner.

She comes upon a collection of action figures, pirates, clearly too old for the toddler and smiles.

"She's just like you, Jess," she says. "What am I going to do with her?"

She looks right at me.

"I thought you said she can't see me?"

"She can't," Gabriel assures me.

Ally's gaze goes soft and she returns to dumping the toys into the box.

The house begins to fade, and I find myself on the beach with Gabriel. The house behind us in the distance.

"What the hell, man?" My temper flares, crashing against me like the waves. I jab a finger at the house. "What was that supposed to be?"

"Your choice," he says with all the calmness that I hate about him. "One of your choices."

"Uh, I liked the one with just us actually," I say, crossing my arms. "If you're needing me to verbally agree to something here."

"You desire her happiness. She desires children and a full life. You can give her that world."

"But that world is a world without me," I say. "Can you see me with kids? They'd be scarred for life."

"You can give her the world she wants. It is in your power."

"Are you asking me to be *selfless*?" I say, stunned.

"It is only my duty to show you all of your worlds. I cannot choose for you. It will be your choice."

"Thanks, Oprah."

Something rumbles in the distance. The sand beneath my feet shifts.

"What was that?"

Another rumbling roar and the sand shifts more. The sky darkens above us like a storm is rolling in.

Gabriel scoops me up. "I must take you back."

I blink my eyes open, the ceiling above coming into view. The Needle comes into focus around me, the feel of the couch solidifying beneath me.

"You're missing it," Maisie says.

I sit up and see Maisie at the big window—the side of The Needle that faces the city.

Black smoke is billowing into the sky.

"Shit." I jump off the sofa and go to the window. "What's happening?"

"Dad," she says. "It's started."

"He's blowing up the city?"

I don't need her to answer. Another explosion goes off and the vibration of the blast can be felt even here in The Needle. The glass windows tremble under my palm and the floor vibrates under my feet.

Ally. I see all the different Ally's out there. Ally in the beach house with me. Ally with kids. None of them will exist if she's blown up. *Please be safe.* At least I know Jeremiah wasn't lying about Caldwell's threat to the city, some ploy to get us to come to Chicago.

"Why is he doing this?" I ask Maisie. Beside me, her face is a mixture of regret, sadness, and resignation—way too serious a face for a kid of sixteen.

"Because everyone is here," she says.

"Everyone who?" I demand. Because she can't mean *everyone*, everyone. The whole world is not in Chicago.

"Everyone's here that needs to be."

Chapter 41

Ally

I'm not so sure about this.

The boat isn't much of a boat. More like a paddleboat, or even a little dinghy—but certainly no yacht, no ocean liner, which is what I feel like we would have to have in order to approach The Needle. From here I see no doors, only windows that circle the exterior of The Needle's head.

"What are we going to do?" I yell over the roar of the motor and the waves. The fierce wind rolling off of Lake Michigan tears at our coats and clothes as if trying to rip us from the metal cradle we're hunkered down in. I have both hands on top of my head, trying to hold my hair into place. "We can't shimmy up the side."

"Don't worry so much. I have a plan," Rachel says, from her place at the front of the boat. What is that called, the stern? The bow? I don't know boats. Gloria sits in the back, controlling the motor.

Rachel turns around and grins at me. "Think of it this way. If we don't die, hooray. If we do die, nothing matters. We're *dead*."

This isn't exactly how I would like to look at the world, but I force a smile. She is making the effort to rally my spirits. I can at least acknowledge and appreciate that, even if I might be pitched out of this boat and into the icy water at any moment.

I feel useless sandwiched between Rachel and Gloria, shivering. My coat isn't much protection on the mainland and, on the water, it's even less useful. It flaps around me wildly, and I clutch the fabric to my chest. My hair whips around my head too, sometimes falling into my face and blotting out the lake altogether, despite my efforts to hold it down.

The sound of a helicopter roars overhead. A nondescript black wasp with a propeller whizzes by, momentarily making the horrible wind worse.

"There's my boy," Rachel says, looking back at me and Gloria with a huge grin on her face. "He's good, right?"

I can't smile or speak because of my chattering teeth.

I peer over the edge of the boat at the gray water

sloshing against the sides. I feel sick.

"Okay, are we ready?" Rachel asks, holding her hand up to the helicopter.

"Ready for what?" I ask.

Her hand comes down and for a heartbeat, nothing happens. Then, what I am pretty sure is a missile, shoots out of the front of the helicopter and explodes into the side of The Needle.

"*That*," Rachel says, laughing wildly as if she is having the time of her life.

She really is crazy. The realization that I'm in a tiny boat on a huge turbulent lake with an escaped mental patient hits me all the harder. Fear, real fear, rakes across my skin. I scoot back so far I bump into Gloria's knees.

"Just keep breathing." Gloria cuts her eyes from Rachel to me. "It's all you can do."

"It's all I can do," I repeat, as another rocket slams into the side of The Needle, exploding on impact.

"Surely to god someone is going to notice this. What will we do when the authorities show up?"

"They will have their hands full," Gloria says.

"Get me a little closer." Rachel shouts over all the noise, pinning her own wild hair back away from her face. "Not so close that the debris falls on our heads though."

Gloria angles the boat a bit, veering off to the side of The Needle. A particularly horrible wave slaps the side of the boat, spilling over the side and soaking my leg. I gasp, sucking in icy air.

"It'll dry," Rachel says, after surveying my distress.

"Firing rockets at The Needle can't be the best plan, can it?" I ask. I hope I sound curious, diplomatic even, anything but miserably cold and terrified out of my mind.

"Jesse's got her shield and she can heal now, right?" Rachel asks. "She'll survive this. Our real concern is if Caldwell realizes what we're doing and comes running. We don't want *that*."

Jesse will survive this, I repeat. *God, I hope so.*

"What the hell did he make this building out of?" Rachel whines. "Steel?"

A third rocket slams into the small hole created by the second rocket and part of the glass is blown away, revealing the inside of The Needle. I stare into the jagged black mouth and wait.

Chapter 42

Jesse

Black smoke billows up into the sky above the skyscrapers. Another explosion goes off somewhere to the north—the Magnificent Mile maybe—and all I can do is picture all the stylish mannequins in storefront windows burning, their two hundred dollar scarves going up in flames.

Another explosion sounds and The Needle shakes. The plates in the cupboards of the little kitchen nook rattle and Winston howls the way he does at home if the UPS guy comes or it's trash day.

Maisie and I lock eyes.

"That sounded—" I begin.

"—like it was right on top of us," finishes Maisie.

"Caldwell wouldn't bomb The Needle, right?" I know I sound freaked out, even to me. "I mean, he put us here so we'd be out of the way. An I'll-deal-with-you-later kind of thing?"

This time I hear the whistle, followed by another explosion that rocks The Needle. A funnel of black smoke erupts from the other side of the room, the side facing the lake, not the city. I rush over to the other windows and see a giant helicopter hovering about two hundred feet away. I can't see who is driving it, but it's clear that it's packing and pointed at us.

"What the hell?" I ask.

"It must be one of the bad guys," Maisie squeals. "Winston!"

Winston comes running and she scoops him up into her arms. Then she looks at me. "What should we do?" she asks. "You've got the super powers."

"I can only shield myself or the people I've replaced," I tell her. "But maybe if I hug you hard enough I can get it to be big enough to cover all three of us."

Maisie's eyes are big and wet.

"Ah, don't cry," I tell her and I sound a little mean about it. I swallow and try to make my voice soft, the way Ally would do it.

"If one of those partis fuckers came to kill me, they won't be trying to get you," I tell her. "They'll be focused on me, okay? Just hold on to Winston and stay out of the way, and you should be okay."

She nods vigorously, her cheeks red.

A plume of smoke shoots out of the back of a third rocket and I yank Maisie away from the window before I hear the whistling whine of its release. I grab hold of Maisie and erect my shield. This time as the rocket hits, glass sprays into the room, raining down on us. But I do a decent job of protecting us from the blast.

If I grab on to her before I raise the shield, the shield covers her rather than repels her. Good to know.

A whirlwind of icy cold air bursts into the room through an 8-foot hole where the rocket blasted out the glass.

"Get your coat." I don't know why the hell that is the first thing I think of. But Maisie doesn't question me. She runs off in the direction of her bedroom, still clutching the fat pug to her chest, her blonde hair streaming out behind her.

I go to the hole and look out over the water. I don't see anything but the copter at first. And it occurs to me that by standing in the hole, I might be making myself a target.

Then I hear a noise, like a giant bee buzzing. It's

almost inaudible over the sound of the wind and waves.

I look down and see a boat. A small boat with three people in it. My heart floods with joy. Gloria, Ally, and…Rachel, of all people. Alive and here to get me.

Maisie comes skittering into the room. "Okay, I have my coat. And my computer. I messaged Dad."

"Shit." My happy feeling leeches away. "I wish you hadn't done that."

"Why? He'll save us."

"Only to kill me later." I point at the little boat down on the waves. "Those are my friends. They're here to rescue me."

"Oh." Confusion washes over her face. She suddenly doesn't look so ready to go with me.

The helicopter pulls back, giving me room, and I can see Rachel's hands out in front of her as she balances on the front of the boat. Ally waves and I realize what they want me to do.

"Come on," I tell Maisie. "We're going to jump."

"We can't," she says. "There are rocks down there."

"I jumped out of a skyscraper the other night.

That turned out okay. It can't be worse than that."

At least this time, if I die in the fall, they can get Maisie, Winston and my body into the boat. Ally was fine, so they'll probably be okay too. I hope.

She clutches Winston to her chest but doesn't come any closer to the broken window.

"Come on," I tell her again. "I can't leave you here with Caldwell. It's like child endangerment or something."

"He won't hurt me."

"You don't know that. He hurt me just fine. And yes, maybe he loves you more or whatever, but it isn't safe for you to stay here. Come on."

Maisie takes a step toward me, resolve in her eyes.

"I'm going to jump out first, holding Winston in the front," I explain. I want you to hold on to my back. If we hit the rocks, I think my shield will protect you from the worst of it."

"What about Winston?" she asks. "If you hit the rocks, he'll be crushed."

"No, the front of the shield will cover him," I say. "Okay? Ready."

I inch forward, my toes sticking out over the lips of the broken window. The water below thrashes against the side of The Needle's metal base, looking far more ravenous and sinister than the concrete below ever did. My heart lurches.

I hold Winston to my chest and try to situate him in such a way that he lies flat. I feel Maisie's arms around my waist.

"Hold on tight." I clamp one of my free hands over hers.

"I don't know about this," she screams into my ear over the roar of the wind and waves. She squeezes me tighter.

Neither do I, I think and jump.

Chapter 43

Ally

I watch Jesse ease her toes to the edge of the punched out glass, cradling Winston against her chest like a baby. Then I see two white hands wrap around her black hoodie.

"What the—" Rachel says, obviously seeing the hands too, but doing the math.

But I already know the answer. Maisie.

I look at the water beneath them, the jagged black rocks jutting up from the waves, and my heart hammers harder.

"No, no, no," I say and stand up. The boat rocks beneath me, almost pitching me out into the icy gray water.

"Sit down," Gloria barks. "You'll get hypothermia if you fall in."

"No, Jesse, don't. *Don't,*" I scream and wave my hands over my head. She doesn't look at me. She inches farther forward.

"You have to get closer." I sink into the boat. "Even if they survive the fall, we're going to have to pull them out of the water fast."

"I'm doing the best I can," Rachel hisses.

I give her a blank look.

"Oh, did you think we were just *sitting* here? Nope. We'd have been bashed against the rocks by now if it wasn't for me."

It takes me a second to catch up. She's been moving the boat, or counter moving it amongst the thrashing waves.

"Can lower them down?" I ask, unable to take my eyes off of Jess. "Or slow them down?"

The words are barely out of my mouth before Jesse jumps.

"Shit." Rachel screams and jolts to her feet, arms out in front of her as if she could catch them from here.

Gloria swears and tries to steady the boat from the back.

"Pull forward," Rachel shouts, chancing a half-glance over her shoulder at Gloria.

The motor sputters to life and we lurch forward.

The boat cuts through the waves more violently

than before, cold water sloshing over the edge and freezing my bare hands. Already my hands are chilled to the bone, a bluish-purple color settling into my fingers. I clutch the rim of the boat harder.

"Did they make it?" I scream, unable to see around Rachel.

She doesn't respond.

I try to look around her, but Gloria yanks me down into my seat by the back of my coat.

"Stay down," she barks. "I can barely see where we're going as it is."

"Okay, stop. Now, *stop*," Rachel cries.

Gloria cuts the engine and the boat bumps into something hard. I move my hand just in time, but not quite fast enough. My knuckles scrape across a rock and blood blooms from the torn flesh. Because my fingers are so cold, I barely feel it. I press the bloody knuckles into my red coat and find it damp from the spray coming off the waves.

I see Jesse. She is sitting on a big rock. Her hair is wet and Winston is shivering against her chest. Maisie too is soaked beside her, pushing damp hair out of her big blue eyes with a quivering hand. They're being pummeled by the waves assaulting the rocks.

"We've got to get them into the boat," I say.

"No shit," Rachel hisses.

"Why are we in such a small boat?" I ask.

"I needed something small enough that I could control," Rachel says. "Praise baby Jesus that we didn't have anything bigger."

The boat slams against the side of the rock a little hard, and I'm suddenly terrified that one more wave will crush the boat altogether.

"We have to get away from the rocks."

"I'm trying," Rachel says, clenching her fists. "Do something other than critique me."

"Pull forward," I tell Gloria. "And I'll get them into the boat."

After much difficulty, Gloria gets the boat to inch forward enough that Jesse is in arm's length. Her teeth are chattering.

"Come on." I stretch my arms out for her. "Get in the boat."

She hands me Winston first and I put him on the floor of the boat between my feet. He's never looked more pitiful, resembling a drowned shivering rat.

Then Jesse reaches behind her and pulls Maisie forward. Maisie is shaking almost as bad as Winston.

Her hands feel like ice even to my own frozen hands as I pull her into the boat. She curls up on the floor beside Winston, seemingly oblivious to the inch or so of water that has accumulated there.

I reach out for Jesse.

She grabs on to me and I yank her into the boat, almost crushing Winston and Maisie. But it feels so good to have her in my arms again, alive and breathing, and relatively unharmed.

"Fucking hell," she says through her chattering teeth. "Let's never do that again."

Chapter 44

Jesse

I can't feel my hands and my teeth are chattering so hard that I'm giving myself a headache. Winston looks like the saddest dog in the world, and I don't have anything remotely dry to wrap him in. My knee is skinned from where it scraped against the rock after I dropped my shield because Maisie had let go of me and I was afraid of knocking her into the water.

Maisie's soaked all the way through.

"Are you okay?" I'm looking her over for scrapes or any damage.

She nods her head but can't speak.

"We don't have anything dry." Ally reaches across the boat and places a hand on my wet knee. "I'm so sorry I didn't think to bring something dry."

I clasp her hand in mine. "I'm sorry that I made you come get me."

Gloria arches an eyebrow. Is it because I said I was

sorry? Is it that rare I actually apologize for something I do wrong? Okay, *maybe.*

I squeeze her hand. "I won't make you chase after me ever again."

A bizarre tingling in my knee makes me look down. I spread open the rip in my jeans to inspect the scrape. The skin is closing before my eyes.

"Weird."

Ally sees it too, her eyes widening. "How are you?"

I remember the four dead bodies in the hallway of the church. "I don't know."

"Once we get you dry, we should talk." Ally cuts her eyes to Maisie. "Are you okay, honey?"

Maisie nods for a second time. "Is Winston okay?"

"He'll live." I reach down and place a hand on the wet, shivering pug. "Can pugs die of hypothermia?"

"We'll get to shore soon, Jessup." Rachel lowers her hands from the Moses pose she's been holding this whole time.

I throw up my hands. "Where the hell have you been?"

"Oh, you know." She sinks down onto her little seat while Gloria starts the motor again and shoots off in the direction of the aquarium on the far bank. "I went to Bermuda and Tahiti for the sunshine. I had a scone in Bruges."

"Really?" I ask.

"No," she says with a snort. "I've been *working*."

She grins and I mirror it. It's good to see her. And it's especially good to see her in non-asylum clothes.

"After this we'll take a vacation," I tell her. "We deserve one."

"A little help," Gloria yells over the motor.

"Right." Rachel returns her attention to the water. The boat's horrible choppiness and zig-zag approach straightens out a bit. The helicopter overhead whizzes off, growing smaller.

"Who was that?" I ask, shielding my eyes so I can see the copter fly away.

"Gideon," Ally says. "Someone Brinkley sent to help."

"Brinkley is dead. How can he send help?"

"It's a long story." Ally tries to burrow into her coat.

"Is it part of the same story where you knew I had a sister before I did?" I ask.

Maisie looks up from her fetal position in the

floor, giving Ally a wary once-over.

"Yes." Ally forces a smile. "I'll catch you up after we get you dry and warm. I promise."

"Almost there," Rachel shouts, turning back to flash us a grin.

I want a latte. "After I dig my wet underwear out of my ass, can I have a coffee?"

Ally smiles. "I think a second hot chocolate would be good."

"I've been locked in a tower and you've been having hot chocolate?" I pretend to be angry. "You must've been *real* worried."

Her brow furrows, her mouth falling open in indignation.

"I'm kidding," I'm quick to add. "Relax. I'm so freaking happy to be away from the psycho."

Ally closes her mouth, swallowing whatever she intended to say.

"Shit." Rachel shifts her weight in the front of the boat. "We have a problem."

All of our heads snap forward. Caldwell stands on the shore. The planetarium's large golden dome behind him is a majestic backdrop.

"Can we drive the boat somewhere else?" Ally

asks.

"Wherever we go, he'll be there," Maisie says.

"We can't stay on the lake," Rachel adds. "I'm getting tired."

Unfortunately, they're both right.

"Grab on to me," I shout. "I'll try to make my shield big enough."

Rachel, Ally, and Maisie huddle close, Winston safe between our feet. My shield goes up and covers Ally and Maisie, but not Rachel. I can't make it any bigger.

"Get in here," I yell to Gloria.

"I won't fit," she says.

"Damnit, Gloria. I will climb in your lap if I have to," I yell.

"I have to drive the boat," she says. "Focus on the girls."

"Rachel—"

"I'm fine," she says. "I'd like to see the asshole try me today."

Gloria drives the boat right to shore, and Caldwell companionably reaches down and yanks the boat onto the embankment.

"Hello, Ms. Wright," Caldwell says with a grin.

"Where have you been hiding?"

"Up your ass," she hisses.

"Ah," he says, as if this is the most normal response ever. "I didn't think to look there."

"I'm surprised," she quips. "Your head is up there most of the time."

He regards her for a second longer, and Rachel holds his gaze.

"Get out of the boat, Maisie," he says.

"No," I say and grab onto her arm.

"Get out of the boat, *Maisie*," he says again.

Maisie starts to rise but I hold on to her tighter.

"No," I say. "You shouldn't be with a person who locks you in a tower."

Caldwell makes no defense. Instead, he says, "Your mother will be upset if you don't come home. Look at the city. It isn't safe out there for you."

He motions over his shoulder at the burning city. Pillars of black smoke funnel up into the sky. Too many to count. In the distance, sirens wail.

"You know why it isn't safe," he says, his gaze never leaving Maisie's. "Do you think it'll be safe for you with *them*? They'll kill you as soon as they know what you are."

Caldwell cuts his eyes to Rachel.

"I do not abuse children, you homicidal maniac." I think she's going to jump up and attack him. Every muscle in my body tenses. If she fights, I'll have to fight too and I can't firebomb with everyone here.

"What you are?" Ally asks Maisie.

In my momentary distraction, Maisie wrenches herself from my grip.

"Hey—" I lurch forward trying to grab hold of her. "Don't be stupid. We wouldn't hurt you."

Maisie slips right out of my shield. Caldwell reaches down and pulls her onto the sand.

"It's okay," Maisie says, as Caldwell wraps his arms around her. "My mom needs me."

Her words hang in the air as Caldwell takes a step back, and they are gone.

Chapter 45

Jesse

"**W**ell, you win some, you lose some," Rachel says, jumping out of the boat onto shore.

"Don't say that," Ally snaps. "She's a little girl. God knows what he'll do with her."

I give Rachel a harsh look. "He's hardly father of the year."

"Tell me something I don't know," Rachel says, rolling her eyes. "No, I'll tell you. She's partis."

"What?" Ally and I say in unison.

"She's partis."

"She's a kid," Ally argues. "She isn't some murderer seeking world domination."

She's partis. I try to absorb this information but I can't quite wrap my mind around it. *You have superpowers. Do something?* Was she just trying to trick me into thinking she was weak? Or does she have a power that isn't much good for jumping out of buildings?

"Did you see her do anything?" Ally asks.

"No. If she's partis, she didn't give any sign."

"Maybe you're wrong," I tell Rachel.

Rachel rolls her eyes. "You're smarter than that Jessup. Don't let the kid googly-eye you."

I remember Gabriel's warning about Maisie. *Be careful with that one. She's different than the others.*

"We need to get out of here," Rachel says, holding her hair back from her face and surveying the museum campus.

"How?" Ally stands on the shore, reaching out to help Gloria from the boat. Gloria takes her hand, more to pacify Ally than anything else, I'm sure. The shore is nearly empty in this freezing weather, but a couple of bundled onlookers stare at the city like we do. Many more stand in clusters on the steps of the museum, planetarium, and aquarium, as if waiting for the next explosion to come.

Rachel points at a helicopter landing in the distance. The black smudge lowers itself down slowly at the edge of the green field. "There's Gideon. Come on."

We run across the lawn toward the helicopter. People are now flowing out of the buildings as if a dam has broken. At first, I think they're going to try to steal our helicopter, but they aren't. Most are running for the parking lot. Others push themselves back inside the buildings as if they believe the massive structures will protect them

"People are starting to lose their shit." I grab Ally's hand and pull her closer. "It's going to get worse."

Gloria catches up to us, appearing on my right side. "Once the National Guard is mobilized, we won't be able to fly. They'll ground all planes trying to contain the perpetrators."

"It doesn't help that our helicopter pilot is Middle Eastern," Rachel says.

Ally makes a surprised clucking sound deep in her throat.

Rachel arches her eyebrows. "Sad but true, honey."

Gloria adjusts the pack on her back. "I'll fly if I must."

I whirl on her. "You can fly a helicopter?"

"It's been a long time."

The helicopter blades whirl to life as we close in.

"Hurry up," a man shouts from the cockpit of the plane. "We have seven minutes before the airspace over the city is shut down."

Rachel jumps in first and starts strapping herself in. I push Ally in ahead of me and let her have the next available seat. She cradles Winston in her lap.

I slide into the seat by the open door, and Gloria slips into the one next to Gideon up front. If he has any objections about her as copilot, he keeps them to himself. In fact, he looks relieved to see her.

She doesn't look as happy to have him.

Rachel makes gestures, trying to catch my attention. She mimes putting the headphones on and I do, lifting the heavy device from its hook on the wall.

Her voice is loud and clear in my ears.

"You missed a buckle, Jessup." Rachel points at a second seatbelt that goes over my lap, not just my shoulders.

"How do you know so much about helicopters?" I ask her.

She flashes a devilish smile. "Wouldn't you like to know?"

"I want to know a lot," I snort. "I want to know where the hell you've been. How the hell Ally knew about Maisie. Who the hell this dude is and when I'm going to get my damn coffee."

"I should've told you sooner," Ally says, adjusting the earphones on her head.

"Yes, you seem to say that a lot."

"Girls, don't fight," Rachel says, but she's grinning as if she's having the time of her life.

"Wipe that crazy grin off your face," I tell Rachel. "You're freaking me out."

"*Hello*, mental patient," she says with a wave of her hand.

"It's her face. She can't help it," Gideon's voice filters through the earphones.

"That's rude," Rachel says. "I have a lovely face."

"Prettier than a sunrise over the moors," he says.

Rachel falls against her seat grinning as if this is the best compliment she's ever heard. "Yes, let's go to England. Doesn't that sound fun?"

My phone pings in my hand and my heart leaps. I have service and a text message. Only it's not from Lane. It's from a fabric store that I went to *once*, ages ago, letting me know I have a 15% off coupon.

"I can't go to England. I have to check on my boyfriend," I say. "It's occurred to me that he may not be answering my texts because Caldwell killed him and buried him in a shallow grave."

And if he hasn't, I will.

"He's not your boyfriend. He dumped you," Ally says.

I shoot her a look. "Thank you for that reminder."

"We need to get out of the city," Gloria adds, more gently this time.

"We can make a pass by Wacker Drive, at least," Ally says. "We will fly over it won't we?"

"Yes, but we can't stop. *Minutes.* We have minutes before someone will shoot us out of the sky," Gideon says.

"They won't shoot us out of the sky," Gloria says. "Probably."

Rachel bounces in her seat. "Better practice making really big shields, Jessup."

"How far until we fly over Wacker?" I ask.

"About thirty seconds," Gloria says.

I turn on Ally who tries to look all sweet and innocent with Winston in her lap. At least his fur is starting to dry a little and he's starting to look somewhat snug, tucked into the side of her red coat.

"You have thirty seconds to tell me everything you know that I don't know," I tell her.

"That's not much time."

"Try," I insist.

She thinks for a moment, opens her mouth, closes it, and then spills her guts. "Brinkley left me some journals when he died. He said they were just for me. In them, he talked about how he met Gloria, their first case together, which is how I know about Maisie. She was born in the camp to Georgia and Caldwell. He smuggled her out, in that way of his, and then when he got out with Georgia about six years later, they reunited."

Reunited. Like a big fucking happy family. Without me.

"I'm sorry, Jess," Ally says, her eyes full of tears. "It seems like it was more of Georgia's idea than Caldwell's."

"Go on," I say. "What else?"

"It talks about how he met Gloria, their work together, how he became Rachel's handler and how Gideon came into his life."

"I'd like to read this journal," Rachel says with a cocked head.

"Me as well," Gideon says.

"Me three," I chime in. "Where are they?"

"A couple are the things we left at Gideon's. The

others are in a lockbox in Nashville."

"Anything else?"

"Not that I can think of right now," she says.

"Wacker Drive," Gloria calls into the headphones. "On your right."

Ally and I both crane our necks out to look down over the top of the skyscrapers below. Only, I don't really see the top of any skyscraper because of the smoke.

"It's gone," Ally says. "Tate Tower is *gone*."

"Not gone," Gloria says. "Burning."

Chapter 46

Ally

The smoke clears in the whirl of the helicopter blades and I see the tower, or what is left of it. Gloria is right. It isn't gone, not completely. What remains is half-eaten with black smoke, half-devoured by flames.

Nikki.

"We have to touch down. We have to check for survivors."

"Uh, no." Rachel says. "We need to get out of the city before Caldwell eats our brains like cereal."

Jesse snorts. "You weren't scared when you were mouthing off to him."

"Bravado, kid." Rachel crosses her arms over her chest. "Have I taught you nothing?"

"There could be survivors down there. We don't know if they were able to evacuate in time," I argue. "We can't just fly away."

Rachel shrugs. "Better them than us."

"Jeremiah is a jerk, but they fought by your side," I remind Jesse. "You have to see if they need our help. They put their lives in danger for you. More than once."

A strange look passes over Jesse's face. Her brow pinches and I have a feeling something is wrong.

Something happened, she had said.

"We have to go down," she says, her voice low in the microphone.

"We are not stopping," Gideon says.

"It isn't safe," Gloria adds.

Rachel folds her arms over her chest, content that she's won the majority vote.

"How far up are we?" Jesse asks and locks eyes with mine. Immediately, I know what she's thinking.

She is going to jump. She's ready to jump *now* without even thinking.

She'll become less stable the more power she has.

I could say no. I could refuse to jump from the helicopter because it is reckless, and hopefully that will slow her down. She looks almost excited by the idea of jumping. The alternative is to trust her and leap.

I take a deep breath and unbuckle the strap across my chest. I put Winston on the floor inside a box that

I'm sure was meant to hold parachutes or something useful. He looks up at me reproachfully.

"We're about 450 meters high," Gideon says. "Why?"

"No," Gloria yells into the headset, but she's too late.

Jesse snaps off her last buckle just as I undo mine and she grabs me. One yank and we're out of the helicopter.

Through the black smoke, we fall.

Chapter 47

Jesse

"This is going to hurt."

"Protect your head." Ally screams over the wind tearing at our hair and clothes.

Now that I'm far enough away from Rachel, another partis like me, Gabriel decides to show his pretty face. Well, not his face exactly.

Her or you, he says into my ears. I can't see much because of the smoke-thick air, but I get the distinct impression of wings extending, black feathers enveloping us.

Her. Always.

The shield glimmers around us, growing bigger and brighter than I've ever seen it. We hit something and I scream like a girl. Surprised. I also think I shake Ally a little, wrenching a yelp from her. But whatever we've hit, it only knocked us off course a little. I get the sense I'm in a giant hamster ball, tumbling into the ruins of Chicago below.

"You'll heal. You'll heal. It's okay, you'll heal." Ally keeps saying this over and over again and I'm pretty sure she is trying to reassure herself as much as me.

I just keep waiting for it. The hit, the moment when my body slams into the pavement and I feel the terrible explosion of pain like I felt before.

One breath. Two. My heart is pounding as loud as a marching band in my ears.

We hit—something. We shudder, the protective field rippling as a fresh pillar of smoke billows up around us, blocking out our view of everything else. The sound of rock and steel cascades down, clanking against the pavement.

We slam into the ground. I cry out, waiting for another bone-crushing impact, but I don't feel it. Instead, ash and pavement explodes around us.

I scream and scream as Ally runs her hands up and down my body looking for injuries.

"Stop screaming," she pleads. "You're fine. Oh my god, you're *fine*."

I gulp down the last of my scream and open both of my eyes. The purple field shimmers around us, giving us a good foot of clearance on all sides.

"It wasn't this big before, was it?" Ally asks.

"Caldwell said that all of my partis powers would get more awesome as I picked up other gifts."

Beyond us, a sheen of smoke and ash dances, blocking out our view of the city.

"Oh—" Ally says, frowning. She kneels down in front of me and wipes her thumb across my cheek. "You have a cut here."

Her eyes widen in surprise. "Uh, no you don't."

I grab her hand. It's soft in mine. A sudden desperate urge to hold her washes over me. To kiss her. I catch myself staring at her lips. I look away. "Is it weird seeing me heal?"

"No weirder than anything else," she grins. She brushes off her knees.

You missed your chance, I think. I can't tell Ally that I love her now. She's got a girlfriend and the world is falling apart. That's just stupid. I swallow everything I should've said ages ago and search the area.

The dust and dirt from our impact starts to clear, and I expect to see Wacker Drive come into view. It doesn't. Instead, I see only busted up black concrete everywhere.

We are in a giant hole. A crater. I place one hand over my chest and try to breathe.

"We're buried," I tell her. My throat goes tight.

"No, no, this is different." Ally pushes the hair away from my face. "We aren't buried alive. We're in a hole. We can climb out, okay? Jess? Take a breath."

I suck in a ragged breath. But I can't get the images of the coffin out of my head, of the dirt falling into my eyes and nose, while I lay there trapped several feet under the ground. *Caldwell did that to me—buried me alive. I jumped. This is different. It's different.*

I take another breath with Ally's hands on my back, rubbing it encouragingly.

"Good," she says. "Another big breath."

I take another.

She points up. "See. That's the sky. We just have to get out of this hole. We're not closed in at all."

We start climbing. At first, the shield surrounding us rubs away the busted up pavement and we can't get anywhere. I have to drop the shield so we can use our hands, knees, and feet to get ourselves out.

My palms are smooth and covered by a film of white chalk, by the time I pull myself out of the crater and reach down to pull Ally out after me.

An irritating cold sweat collects under my clothes. My hands and face are still freezing but my body is hot.

I glance around. My eyes fall on Tate Tower. It looks mostly unharmed, the building whole and windows unbroken, even if the glass is coated with ash.

"Come on," I tell her. "Let's go see if Sasquatch survived."

She doesn't complain about my nickname for Nikki. She doesn't even look annoyed.

"She's probably okay," I tell her. "She's…sturdy."

It's not a great compliment. I guess I can't really pretend to care about people that I don't care about. But I do care about Ally and I hate that she's so worried.

Gabriel appears beside me in all his winged glory. His suit looks like he just pulled it off the dry cleaner's rack, but I'm not fooled.

"What's wrong?" I ask him.

"Be careful." He starts to flicker as if he can't hold onto his form.

I jog to catch up to Ally, who is stepping through the busted entrance and into the half buried foyer.

"Don't get too far away from me," I tell her. "Something's up."

"What do you mean?"

"Gabriel is all glitchy like when a partis is around. It could be Caldwell or someone as charming as Jason. Just stay close to me, okay?"

"Okay." She searches the rubble. "Nikki?"

No answer.

Louder. "Nick?"

Her voice echoes in all that space.

"Hey, Sasquatch, can you hear me?"

Still no answer. Nothing moves.

Ally's face screws up with concern. "I never asked where the new location was. I don't see any bodies though. We should check the bunker downstairs and then we'll go. I can just run down alone?"

A little red flag goes off in my mind. I can't quite recall why, but something about this idea strikes me as *bad*. "No, we should stay together."

Relief washes over her face. Have I really been such an ass that she expects me to take off and leave her at every chance. My chest hurts.

"I'm sorry," I say, as she pushes open the door to the stairwell.

"For what?" She holds it open for me.

"That I went with Caldwell. It was dumb and

unproductive."

"He had Winston." She pushes her hair behind her ears. "I just wish you would've talked to me first."

My chest constricts again. "I'm sorry. I won't take off again without you knowing about it."

She snorts. "Don't make promises you can't keep."

"Really," I insist. "People are always going to go after you to get to me. Getting far away from you doesn't work. Instead of chasing me, they grab you and make me come back."

"Warfare for the lazy," Ally says, descending the steps. Emergency lights flood the stairwell, but after a certain point, it's only darkness. "Go for the easy target."

"You're not weak." I sound pissy even to me. "You're smarter than me. And prettier."

She spares me a smile. "All right, Casanova. Do you have your phone?"

"Yes, why?"

"I think I dropped mine in the helicopter or on the way down. And I need a flashlight."

I punch the correct application on my phone and a light shines from the camera's flash. "I've only got a little battery. Sorry."

Ally points it down into the void. There is a door, but it's blocked by debris. My phone dies. Ally frowns at it before handing it over.

"If they're in there, we aren't going to be able to get them out," I say. "Aren't there firefighters for that kind of thing?"

"If they are inside, they should be safe, assuming no one was hurt in the initial blast and they were able to get down to the bunker okay. If not, maybe they're safe in their new building. The lack of bodies is a good sign, right?"

"Right." I agree though I'm not sure we'd see a handful of bodies under all this debris.

I let her frown at the abyss for a moment longer before we trudge back up the stairwell. I'm about to ask her about Gideon, but I hear Ally's sharp intake of breath. I turn. "What?"

Caldwell has her from behind. His hand on the back of her neck.

The world stops. Caldwell's hands, on a neck. I can't think. All I can see is his hands wrapping around Brinkley's neck and *snap*.

"*Don't.*" My body ignites in blue flame. "Don't you

fucking *dare*."

His hold on her throat relaxes and I can't let go of the fact that one of his hands can almost entirely encircle her delicate throat. I try to run through my options. I can't actually explode now. Maybe if I can hold a shield around Ally at the same time I firebomb, but Caldwell already has ahold of her, so won't that protect him too?

"What do you want?" I hear the trembling fury in my own voice.

"We aren't finished and it's time we settle matters," he says. "Come to the cathedral on State Street, and we'll finish what we started."

My body ices at the mention of the cathedral. The last time I was there, I had to listen to Liza being murdered and I barely escaped with my life.

"No," Ally says. "Jesse, *no*."

"Don't take her. I'll come with you now."

Ally talks over me. "Don't be stupid."

"—I will if you leave her here."

Caldwell releases her and the second he does, I erect a shield around her, leaving myself unprotected. Ally jerks forward, trying to strike him but he disappears, only to reappear on the landing above.

"No, Jess, you promised. You said you'd never leave me alone again."

It's hard to look at the tears in her eyes. I'm an asshole, I know it. And an idiot. Have I really learned nothing? I was just here with Winston.

"I know. I'm sorry. But I don't want you in that cathedral."

I don't want you there when I die.

I feel Caldwell grab on to me, and Ally's eyes double, more desperate.

"I love you." I don't know if she heard it, because Caldwell chooses that moment to pull me through the nothing.

Chapter 48

Jesse

Caldwell pushes me away from him and I stumble into a large room. Columns run from the marble floor up to the cathedral ceiling. A huge mural of Mary hangs overhead, one hand over her heart, her other palm out as if in blessing. I remember the last time I was in this room—surrounded by the sound of Liza screaming like her skin was being sliced from her bones.

Caldwell grabs my arm, wrenching me around to face him.

"Hey," I say. I try to pull my arm away, but he doesn't let go. Instead, he spins me toward the center of the room: Cindy, Georgia, Jeremiah, a black man, an Asian woman, and Rachel, holding Winston, stand in a circle.

I lock eyes with Rachel. "What the hell are you doing here?"

"Oh you know, one minute I'm in a helicopter

trying to comfort a pug that just watched its mother jump, and the next, *that* asshole is kidnapping me." She nods at Caldwell.

I try to picture it—Rachel holding Winston, soothing him, and Caldwell popping in and out with both of them in tow.

Caldwell claps his hands together. "It was quite challenging getting you all here today. First I had to find you, discover who you were. Then I had to set a stage worthy of such an event. I had to blow up a whole city just to give us a little privacy."

Caldwell laughs, and Rachel and I exchange worried glances.

Cindy scoots over to my side. "What's going on here?"

Her Texas drawl is even thicker than usual, and it doesn't take a genius to know she's terrified out of her mind. There's too much color in her cheeks and her eyes are too wide.

"No idea." I tell her and take Winston from Rachel.

Caldwell can't seem to wipe that grin off his face. "With all the commotion, no one will notice if we get a little out of hand."

I search the faces in the circle. I know Cindy and Rachel have powers like me. And I've seen Georgia suck all the life out of a room. But I don't know what Jeremiah, the black man, or Asian woman can do.

I point an accusing finger at Jeremiah. "You said you weren't partis."

"Ah, you're right." Caldwell says. He crosses behind Jeremiah, speaking over his shoulder "Mr. Tate is our prophet. Every tale needs a teller, and he is ours. Not *my* choice, mind you. But we make do with what we are given."

Caldwell's giddiness is horrifying. He's practically prancing around the room. I'd rather he be trying to rip my head off.

"Like Matthew or Mark," Cindy says. Obviously, she isn't having as much trouble staying focused on the conversation as I am. "How's that possible?"

Jeremiah doesn't say anything.

"Don't be modest," Caldwell says.

"I have visions," Jeremiah says, as if he knows prolonging this will only make it worse. "I've seen each of you as you were chosen. I've seen what you're meant to become and what will happen to the world."

"Yes, now that we're all acquainted, let's not waste

time."

My shield goes up. Everyone but Rachel takes a step back. Georgia's black death ribbons reach up from behind her and strike Cindy, her eyes rolling up into her head as she collapses. Dead.

Blue flames erupt around Georgia and she starts screaming as if she's been lowered into boiling water.

Rachel and I exchange a glance.

And run.

Chapter 49

Ally

I walk four blocks in each direction, trying to get a sense of where State Street is in relation to the destroyed Tate Tower, but I can't. I don't think it's in this part of the city.

Firefighters and police flood the streets. I'm approached by three separate personnel.

"Ma'am, are you all right?"

"I'm fine," I say to the person hidden behind the mirrored visor. "Help someone else."

They never need to be told twice. They rush on to the next person without stopping. Cops break up groups of looters who are trying to carry TVs bigger than themselves out of busted store front windows.

"Al?"

It takes me a moment to process the sound of my name.

"Al!"

I turn toward the sound of the voice and see Nikki

in black tactical gear, gun slung over one shoulder. She is an imposing figure in the desolate landscape. Her high ponytail and taut face are severe.

She runs across the street and squeezes me hard, crushing me against the scratchy vest she wears. She kisses me just as hard, cupping my face in her hands and exhales a breath like she's been holding it for hours. "Thank god, you're all right."

"I'm glad you're okay too." I place my hands over hers. "I saw the tower. Did everyone get out?"

Her face pinches. "Caldwell took Jeremiah. We don't know where. We're checking each of Caldwell's properties one by one. We've been at it for a while."

"He took Jesse to the State Street Cathedral. Maybe Jeremiah is there as well."

Nikki reaches up and presses the snail-shaped device tucked into her ear. "Target 7: State Street Cathedral. Move in five." She gives me a once-over. "You're coming?"

"Yes."

"Thought so. Let's suit you up then." She takes my arm and leads me toward an armored truck parked on the curb ahead.

Chapter 50

Jesse

"God why did you have to bring Winston?" I ask. The pug snorts in my arms, growing heavy. Frankly, I'm tired of him being in danger.

"I was holding him when Caldwell took me," Rachel says. "Be grateful I carried his fat ass this long. I could've dropped him at any time."

My arms are killing me, and Winston makes it worse by squirming. We turn three corners and find ourselves in another large room much like the one we left. The ceiling stretches dome-like high overhead. Columns line the walls, but there's nothing to hide behind and no exit signs.

"Hey, stop. Ow. Come on." I have to set him down or I'll drop him. What happens is a mixture of both. Winston hits the ground running.

"What the hell?" I run after him.

"No Jessup, wait. Christ."

I can hear Rachel running after me, the heels of her boots slapping against the marble as I frantically try to catch up to Winston. His feet slide on the slick floor, yet he manages to stay in the lead.

The cathedral trembles, and again, I'm reminded of Liza being murdered in the other room. I see Cindy falling down dead and my chest aches. *What could you do? I tell myself. You can't shield her. You couldn't have carried her away.*

Excuses, excuses a voice says—a voice from somewhere deep inside me.

Winston whips around another corner and slides to stop at the feet of a girl, clutching her backpack.

"Hey," I say. "What the hell are you doing here?"

"Enjoying the last hour of my life," Maisie says, scooping up the dog and pulling him into her lap. Winston jumps all over her, licking her face wildly.

"You again, huh?" Rachel snorts. "I never properly introduced myself. I'm Rachel."

"Maisie," she replies.

"Have you seen a door around by chance, Maisie?" Rachel asks, saccharin sweet.

"There are no doors," Maisie says, matter-of-factly.

"No doors," Rachel and I cry in unison.

Maisie shrugs. "He renovated the church to have no doors. He doesn't want anyone coming in or out without his say so."

"Fucking control freak." Rachel crosses her arms over her chest.

I'm not surprised. After seeing his underground room and The Needle, I believe Caldwell would build a whole world without doors if he could. Of course, we'd all starve to death in such a world, and then who would he get to torture?

Georgia steps from the shadows behind Maisie and my breath hitches in my throat.

"Maisie," she says calmly. "Take the puppy and scoot, my love."

Maisie hesitates.

My shield is up again. "Get behind me," I tell Rachel.

Rachel doesn't have to be told twice. Maisie, on the other hand, still hasn't moved.

"You're up and running quick," I tell her. "Shouldn't you still be dead?"

"We can't waste time. We have to save the world," Georgia says. "It's our responsibility to make it a better place for our children. I might die, but Maisie and I will be together forever."

Maisie gets to her feet, holding Winston to her chest. She slides to the opposite wall, slightly behind her mother, farther away from me.

"We don't want to fight," I tell Georgia.

Georgia's black ribbons of death unfurl, stretching out into the room. "It's too late for that."

Chapter 51

Ally

"**O**ur intelligence says that he's collected all the partis," Nikki says. "We've been monitoring all of them, with the exception of Rachel, who we couldn't find. They've all disappeared within the last hour."

I fake surprise, as if I didn't know the partis were disappearing.

"Rachel is here too. She was with us when we saved Jesse." I don't mention Gideon or how they are able to move around the city undetected.

"If he's taken all of the partis to the church, he must be trying to finish this now," Nikki says.

"Finish what?" I ask. I think I know the answer, but I want Nikki to explain. Maybe she knows something I don't.

"I only know what Jeremiah has told me." She glances over to make sure I'm looking at her. "He has dreams. He calls them revelations."

"Like biblical revelations?"

"He's not religious," she's quick to add. "But he says the clarity and the way they repeat over and over again make them more than dreams."

I understand what she means. Dreams are vague and incoherent. Once I dreamt I was being chased by a spider through the house, and so I put a coat on the couch, knowing the spider would think I was the coat and fail to see me sneak out and take a plane to Lincoln, Nebraska, of all places, which in my dream was a place that spiders didn't go. Only the Lincoln in my dream was more like Hawaii, with fire dancers and pineapple drinks.

The cathedral comes into view at long last, and Nikki parks the armored truck on the curb. I hop out of the truck, scraping my back on the way down, it's so high up. Nikki opens the back and lets her people out.

"Once around for possible entrances, then report here," she says. "I want to know about every door, every window, every latch or keyhole. Move."

They disperse and Nikki gives me a heavy look. "Will you take a gun if I give it to you?"

"I don't need a gun."

She huffs. "Stay behind my left side."

I let her take the lead and follow her around the

church. We see the windows on the uppermost part of the dome, more decorative than functional.

She lowers her gun as we come around to the place where we started at the corner of State Street. "Shit. He did it to this church too."

I run my hands over the smooth façade. "No doors."

"All right," she says, slinging her gun over her shoulder. "Plan B."

Chapter 52

Jesse

Georgia steps forward. I step back.

"At first, I believed it was because you were his daughter," she says with a shrug. "Understandable. He may not be the most loving man, but he does care."

I snort. "About Me, Myself, and I."

"Then I saw the way he treated you. The way he seemed to delight in your misery. I thought perhaps it was because he still harbors a great deal of hate for your mother. Even killing her did not make him feel any better about her betrayal."

Her betrayal—which one? Calling the police on him? Having him carted off to the camps? Or marrying another man while he was locked away?

"I thought he saw her in you," she says quietly, taking another step forward as I take another step back. One of the black ribbons tries to squeeze past me and get at Rachel, but I shift and it hisses and crackles against my shield like oil on a hot pan.

"I'm sorry, ribbon dancer, but where are you going with this?"

Her cheeks burn red and the black ribbons darken more.

"Uh, that can't be good," Rachel murmurs in my ear.

"He does see your mother when he looks at you, but it's more than that."

Another snap of the black ribbon reminds me a great deal of a large black snake, head reared and striking. My shield shimmers, deflecting a second and third blow.

"You remind him that he was once human," she says. "When he sees you, he sees his own flaws. The imperfections. He begins to doubt his cause."

"It would be hard not to doubt yourself in the face of such awesomeness," I say, and gesture to myself. "I mean, just look at me."

Rachel swallows a giggle behind me.

Georgia doesn't laugh. No surprise. Few people get me.

"I don't know what kind of weird thing you've got going on with Caldwell. Clearly you guys made some kind of emotional connection while being tortured, but what I don't get is why you're with him now."

"I love him."

"Weird," Rachel and I say in unison.

"He wants to kill you, and your kid. Isn't that a good enough reason to leave his ass?" I hope she can hear my super judgy tone.

"I am grateful for every minute of every hour that I was allowed to be Maisie's mother," she says. "But our lives are not our own. This cause—our purpose—is so much bigger than us."

Georgia looks at Maisie, and something is exchanged between them. Some kind of sad acceptance.

"Dumb," I say. "You sound like cult victims."

Georgia is about to whirl around and lay into me, no doubt, but Rachel steps around me and shoves Georgia against the wall. Not with her hands but with her telekinetic thing. She shoves Georgia up into the ceiling, and Georgia is howling.

Maisie charges us. My only warning is Winston's yelp and the sound of his nails scuttling on the marble.

I get between Maisie and Rachel before Maisie can tackle her.

"No," Maisie wails. "Stop. You're hurting her."

"You realize she's going to drown you in a tub like an unwanted kitten, right?" I say, knocking her back easily.

Tears stream down her face. "I don't care. She's my mom. Stop. *Stop*, you're hurting her."

Her desperate screams tear me in half. Dammit.

"Rach," I say. "You can't kill her mom in front of her."

"We're doing her a favor. She just doesn't know it."

"Nor will she," Caldwell says, appearing behind Rachel.

In one fluid movement, he grabs her and hurls her across the great antechamber.

Rachel's body slams against a massive column and a sickening crack rings off the walls. A second *thwap* resounds as Georgia hits the ground, screaming out as her leg juts bizarrely from underneath her. The angle is all wrong.

My stomach turns.

After inspecting Georgia, Caldwell turns on me with wild eyes. "You'll pay for that."

Chapter 53

Jesse

Rachel's body lies motionless at the foot of the column.

I'm on fire.

The rage rolls along my skin again and again, and all I want to do is see Caldwell bleed. I can't think or consider my next move. I just want to put my hands on him.

"Oh you're so upset about her fucking leg, but I can be murdered and you're all, *meh*." I shrug. "*Meh*."

I see red and lunge, but Caldwell disappears and I'm left connecting with the marble. The impact jars my knees and wrists, sharp pains shooting up my arms and into my neck. I realize my shield is down, and I'm about to erect it, but a foot connects with my ribs.

Blinding white pain erupts through me. I swear I feel one of my ribs crack. Every breath hurts. Every inhale is sharp and murderous.

"You don't know how hard I worked for this," Caldwell says, laughing. "I kept pushing you, threatening you, but no matter what, you would never fully rise to the occasion. I showed you my new family, my *better* family, and still you didn't hate me. I tried to complicate the bitterness with mock affection. I killed your handler and turned your boyfriend against you. None of it filled your heart with the hate I so desperately needed. I thought I was going to have to kill your little bitch," Caldwell sneers.

"You're never going to lay another finger on her," I say. "By the end of the day, you won't fucking have fingers."

I shoot a fire bomb. It bursts forth from me, and I consider my actions afterward, as I see Maisie clutching Winston, peeking her head out from behind a column.

"Stay back there," I tell her. "And what do you mean you turned my boyfriend against me?"

"Oh, did you think he actually loved you for you?" he asks with a snort of derision. "The moment I knew where Brinkley intended to house you, from whom he intended to rent the office space, I capitalized on that opportunity. I saw the way you looked at him. Waste not, want not. And since I've stopped whispering orders in his ear, he's stopped calling, hasn't he?"

I scream and erupt in the brightest flames yet. My shield shimmers and fades, leaving me exposed. Caldwell grabs me again, and I clamp my arms on his, pinning him against me.

I fully ignite, the blue white fire engulfing us both.

I swallow my pain, refusing to let him go. "You want to burn? Let's burn."

Chapter 54

Ally

Blue fire erupts on one side of the cathedral. At first, I think it's a trick of the light. Some cop car has cut down a side street or a helicopter beam was momentarily reflected in the glass. Then I see it again. A bright blue explosion.

"There," I say and squeeze Nikki's arm. "They're in that part of the church."

Just as I say it, windows blow out the other side and glass rains down onto the pavement.

"Jesse is on this side," I insist. "Unless someone else is shooting blue fire. Unless someone was just murdered."

I have to believe she's alive. After all, everything in me tells me that if Jesse were to die, I would know it. But everyone believes that, don't they? They think their love and connection is so strong that if one were to die, the other would surely know, instantly.

I take a breath, but it's hard. It feels as though there is very little air in my lungs.

"You have to at least put on the vest," Nikki says.

She's trying to strap thick black material over my body, and I'm resisting, shrugging her off like the dark water of my thoughts.

"Wear it, Nat, or I'm going to lock you in the back of the truck," she says, angry with me.

I freeze.

Nikki's face blanches. "Sorry. Shit. I'm sorry. I don't know why I said that."

"Who's Nat?" I ask as members of her team come up and lay explosives against the side of the cathedral. So that's the plan—blast our way in. Jesse would certainly approve.

"Natalie," Nikki says. "She was my wife."

I feel like she's punched me in the gut. The little air in my lungs goes whooshing out again. "*Wife?*"

"For all of four months," Nikki says. "Before she was shot and killed."

Another eruption of blue fire shines through the windows.

"You're going to tell me all about it later." For now, I have to stay focused on rescuing Jesse.

The layer of demolition bricks is finished. "We're ready," someone says.

"Okay, move back," Nikki calls out, and we all move away from the cathedral, back across the street, back behind the armored trucks. When everyone is safe behind the trucks, Nikki gives the order. "Demolition in 3...2...1..."

Chapter 55

Jesse

Caldwell is screaming.

The more he screams, the more invigorated I feel. A powerful pleasure as intense as the flames burning around me, rolls through my body.

Yes, I think. *Yes, I want to see you hurt for what you've done.*

An explosion rips apart the wall on my right but I don't let go of Caldwell. Someone is going to have to rip my arms off to make me let go of him.

"Jesse?" Ally's voice is carried into the room by the wind blowing in from the giant hole they made.

"She's going to kill him," Nikki says, her voice surprised.

Yeah. I'm going to kill Caldwell. Right here and now and I've never wanted anything more in my life.

"No!" Ally rushes forward and throws her coat over me. It disintegrates in the flames, the remnants of the fabric burn to ash and float up and away. "No, Jesse, stop! You can't absorb all his powers at once, it'll make you crazy!"

Still I don't let go. That is, until a huge chunk of what-the-fuck sends me flying across the room. I slam into the wall, breathless. A stabbing pain racks my spine, causing me to scream out.

I'm still screaming as a shadowy shape climbs over the debris, an assault of gray light filtering in behind her. Then the form solidifies and I see Ally's face, her eyes fixing on me as she clamors over chunks of marble.

"Can you hear me?"

I can't answer her. All I can do is scream and squirm against the pain.

"Be still," she commands. "Be still, I can see you healing. Just give it a minute."

"Caldwell—"

Ally looks around the room. "He's gone."

"What about Georgia and Maisie?"

"Maisie I see. No Georgia."

"Rachel?"

Ally turns away from me for a third time and has an exchange with someone I can't see.

"She's dead," Ally says, voice low.

"*Dead* dead, or like just-for-the-weekend dead?" I speak through gritted teeth, but at least I can speak. Ally is right. I am healing.

"We're not sure," Ally says at long last. "Let's get you out of here."

My skin and flesh tingle. I can feel tendons tightening around bones and the strange feeling of those bones shifting back into place. It feels like an army of ants have swarmed my body, doing these repairs with their tiny ant hands.

"What the hell hit me?"

"Marble," Nikki says, kneeling down in front of me. "How's your head? How many fingers am I holding up?"

I flip her the bird. "This many."

Nikki groans and wanders away from me.

"Close your eyes! Close your eyes!"

Ally is screaming her head off. I crane my neck in time to see an Asian woman standing in the middle of the room. A burst of bright white light floods the room.

"Shit." I cover my face. "What the hell?"

Gun fire goes off, the rat-tat-tat-tat of bullets

flying ricochet off the walls. The sound is deafening, making my ears ring horribly. Then the light stops.

I blink open my eyes and squint against the dots floating there. It's a full minute before the room comes into focus.

Nikki and Ally are staring down at the corpse of the Asian woman. Her brains are spread all over the floor.

"So what happens now that she's dead, but no one absorbs her power?"

Another is called.

"Just great," I groan, pulling myself to standing. Ally rushes forward and slips her arms under mine. "Now we'll have one partis out there that we don't know about."

Chapter 56

Jesse

"Come on, buddy." I call for Winston. I see him lying against the wall where Rachel had slammed Georgia into the ceiling. I call his name again.

Winston doesn't move. A chill runs down my spine and a knot forms in my chest.

"Get up, buddy, we've got to go."

Winston still doesn't move after I cross the room and kneel down in front of him. I pull him into my lap. He falls into my hands, heavy and a little cold.

"Winston?"

Dead.

Winston's dead. I roll him over and see blood coming out of the corner of his mouth.

"No, no, no, no, no," I scream, my hands igniting in blue flames. His fur singes under my touch, blackening like a plague. I fall back, scooting away, terrified I'm going to ignite his little body.

Tears stream out of my eyes.

"Jesse?" Ally asks.

"He's dead," I say to no one in particular, wiping away the tears with the back of my hand. "Winston's dead. He laid there and bled out with no one to hold him or tell him he's okay or fucking save him."

My flames die. I can't sustain them without anger. And I'm not angry now. I'm crushed. Totally crushed.

I blink back tears and see Maisie coming onto her knees beside Winston.

"No, Maisie, don't." I get up. "Leave him alone."

She turns him over in her hands, her palms slicking red with blood.

"Stop it."

She bends down, and I think she's going to kiss his little nose. But she doesn't kiss him. She puckers her lips and blows a thin, steady stream of air up into his nostrils.

She does this three times, and on the third time, Winston's eyes come open. He rolls over and pushes himself on to his feet, shaking off like he does when I pull him from the bath. The blood is still stuck to his side, but he's alive. He's breathing.

I snatch him up and squeeze him. I kiss his nose a

hundred thousand times and cry into his fur. He wheezes. I'm probably choking him to death.

"Oh god, sorry. Sorry."

Maisie places a hand on his fur, meeting my eyes.

"You're really partis," I tell her. "I thought maybe Caldwell was just fucking with my head."

"Life," she says. "Mom's Death, and I'm Life. Death gave birth to Life." She half laughs.

"That's why he locked you up." I'm putting all the pieces together.

"He didn't want any of the partis finding me."

"You have to come with us," I tell her. "You can't stay with him, especially not if you're partis. He'll kill you, you know that right? He's probably murdering your mom right now."

"No," Maisie says. "He can't kill his human heart until last."

Winston licks my face and I'm so happy his little snot face is breathing, I don't give two shits that he's snotting in my ear. I search his fur for injuries but I don't see any.

"The human heart can't die until right before the apex ascends." Maisie looks at Ally. "Haven't you wondered why he hasn't killed her yet?"

I follow her gaze to Ally.

"She's my human heart?" I ask. "I'm assuming this is some kind of weird metaphor, right? Because I've totally got a muscle beating in my chest right now, and I'm pretty sure it's human—unless someone slipped some pig's heart in there when I was dead and didn't tell me."

"That's why he planted Lane," she says. "He was trying to make a new human heart for you, one he could control."

My chest aches. "I hoped he was lying about that."

"No," Maisie says, she looks away as if ashamed. "He brought him to Chicago once. He was wearing this smiley face button."

I know the button she pulls out of her bag.

"How do you know about the heart?" I ask her.

"Because Mom is his human heart," Maisie says, scratching Winston behind the ear. "And I'm hers. We're all sort of stuck together, the three of us."

She looks around the room and a darkness fills her eyes. She's too young for all this. She should be reading comic books and eating chocolate. She shouldn't be breathing dead dogs back to life in a room full of bodies.

"It's like one of those cubes," she says. "Where you have to move it right so all the colors line up. He needs you to be mad so you fight, but not too mad, or you'll win. He can kill everyone but me and mom. Then he'll have to decide who he wants to challenge. If he kills me first, mom will be stronger. If he kills mom, we will be evenly matched, both heartless."

"But he'll have more powers," I say, kindly overlooking the fact that she just ran an entire scenario where I'm clearly dead and have failed at life.

"If Mom dies, I won't want to live anyway."

"Are you *sure* he brainwashed Lane?" I ask her. "I mean, you were locked in a tower when we met. I'm not sure I believe you're his confidant."

"I listen," she says. "I know things."

Unfortunately, I believe her.

Her face softens. "Maybe he did really like you. Before dad talked to him, I mean. Maybe the feelings are real."

Maybe.

"We need to go," Ally says, pulling on my arm. "Nikki has a truck."

Nikki and more men in black vests file into the room. They got a couple of body bags between them, but Rachel gets a stretcher. Jeremiah and the black man are left standing.

I point an accusatory finger at the black man. "He's partis. He can't come. He's going to slit my throat when I'm not looking."

He holds his palms out. "I ain't got no problem with nobody."

"This is Monroe. We found him hiding in a closet," Nikki says. "He wasn't fighting. Cindy was dead on the floor, but it doesn't look like he touched them. Not a drop of blood on his hands or person."

"Would there have been blood?" Ally asks.

Nikki arches her eyebrows. "Yes. Definitely, the bodies—"

"No details, please," Ally begs.

"Georgia killed Cindy." My heart aches.

Nikki sees my face. "I'm sorry for your loss. I know she worked with you."

I see Cindy in my mind the day she came to tell me she'd started seeing her angel, Raphael. I can see her huge wet eyes and the way she held herself protectively, looking for answers I didn't have. I told her we were going to be okay.

And now she's dead.

Ally squeezes my arm, and I see Nikki stiffen. Normally, I'd enjoy it. I'd lean into Ally, let her hold me, really play it up. But right now I feel numb. The only feeling I can manage is relief that Winston dodged a bullet. My mind doubles back and I turn to Maisie holding Winston. "Your power doesn't have a time limit or anything does it? I mean, he's not going to be alive for a day or something?"

"Not that I know of," Maisie says. "But this is only the third time I've used it. And the first time I used it twice in one day."

"You brought your mom back," I say, realizing just how smart it was for Caldwell to bring the kid here and keep her close, but out of the way. They probably intended to split the powers between them, using Maisie to make them revive faster than ever before.

"You have to come with us," Ally says to her. "We can't leave you here."

Maisie looks like she might object, but after her eyes circle the destroyed room once, she agrees. "But he's going to come and get me again."

"We'll see about that," I say. "I'll carry Winston." She obediently hands the dog over. "Go get your backpack."

Nikki looks to Jeremiah to give the order.

Jeremiah nods, looking half-dazed himself. "We're done here."

Chapter 57

Ally

We find a second armored truck waiting on the curb behind the first. They begin with the business of loading up the bodies—Cindy, Minli, and Rachel.

Our attempt to load up is interrupted by a siren and the shadow of a massive truck blocking the road.

"I'll talk to them," Jeremiah says, stepping off the sidewalk, heading toward the vehicle. Before he reaches it, two familiar faces emerge from the smoke.

"Gloria," I call out, relieved to see her alive.

"It took us a minute to find another ride," Gideon says, companionably. "But we found this beauty, unattended and waiting for us." He pats the driver side door of the fire truck.

"How's Jesse?" Gloria asks.

"Alive," Jesse says, stepping out from behind me.

Gloria grabs each of Jesse's shoulders and inspects her. Then she nods as if reaching a conclusion.

"Where's Rachel?" Gideon asks.

"Dead," I say.

The smile falls off his face.

"They think she'll wake up," Jesse says. "Her body was sort of crushed against the column, but her head is okay. No reason to think she won't wake up."

Gideon doesn't look any happier despite this news. "Put her in the truck."

"We're happy to transport her to our facility," Jeremiah begins, pushing the glasses up on his nose and moving toward us.

"No, thank you. Please put her in *my* truck," Gideon says again, his gaze heavy on Jeremiah.

Nikki makes some motion beside me, and the two men holding Rachel's stretcher behind the armored truck, carry Rachel toward the fire truck.

"We need to get out of the city," Gloria says.

"You're leaving?" Nikki asks, her hand soft on my arm.

"There's no need," Jeremiah says. "We have a medical facility, state of the art, in the south of the city for this exact situation. The danger has passed."

"The danger has not passed," Gloria tells them, heading to the truck herself.

"Fighting is inevitable," Jeremiah says. "You cannot simply decide you won't."

Gideon laughs. "Oh sir, that is exactly what we can do."

With Rachel in the truck, Maisie and Jesse hoist themselves up into the main cabin, pug in tow. Gideon and Gloria climb in after, leaving me alone on the sidewalk with Nikki and Jeremiah. Their own men wait in the armored trucks for their next orders.

Jeremiah stops in front of me, his hands on his hips. "You can't go off alone, not with so few of you."

"You say it like I make the decisions," I say, with a short laugh.

"You influence Jesse."

I laugh harder. "Do I?"

It's not true. I can no more to control Jesse than I can control the sun in the sky.

"You don't understand," Jeremiah says, nostrils flaring as he shoves his glasses up on his nose with a finger.

"Explain it to me," I say. "Please explain why you feel like you should manage Jesse. Have you seen something horrible in these visions of yours?"

Jeremiah shoves his glasses up on his nose. "The

very first vision I had was of Caldwell, eleven years ago."

This certainly gains my attention.

"I saw him take Henry Chaplain's gift. I've seen him take every gift he has, and I saw Jesse take Jason's gift too."

"How is that possible?" I ask. He's not talking about remote viewing.

"Caldwell called me the observer. The prophet. It is a good enough name for my role in this. I am meant to *see*."

"So what did you see that makes Jesse seem like such a liability?"

"She kills us all."

My breath catches in my throat. "Excuse me?"

"She becomes the apex and instead of saving the world and recasting a new shield, she destroys it. She can choose anything, but she chooses to destroy us."

"I don't understand. How can Jesse decide the fate of the whole world? She's one girl."

"I thought if she worked with us, understood that there were good people here, people worth saving, I could change that."

I don't know what to say. I open and close my

mouth more than once.

Jeremiah doesn't wait for me to process what he's said. He climbs into the armored truck and turns the key. He pulls away from the curb, driving off into the half-destroyed city.

"He's just angry," Nikki says. "He doesn't actually believe you're responsible for Jesse's actions."

"But he does believe she's going to destroy the world?"

Nikki reaches out and takes my hand.

"And you knew?"

"I didn't want you to worry. He thinks we can change it. He's changed a vision before."

Jesse is already walking toward the fire truck, Maisie in tow. Maisie likes her. Jesse will never believe it. She believes everyone hates her as a rule. But Maisie has the same look on her face that I often give my brother.

Nikki grabs on to me and pulls me into a hug. Her lips are soft on my neck and for a moment, I think I won't be able to leave her.

"Natalie?" I ask.

Her hold falters. "She had NRD and was killed. A bullet to the stomach and she bled out. Jeremiah recruited me at the height of my depression. He gave me a purpose again."

"I'm sorry."

"You knew about Minli. If you hadn't warned us about the light, we would all be blind."

I nod, not sure what to say. "Jeremiah has visions?"

She looks away, her eyes falling on the fire truck. "It looks like we've both been keeping secrets."

I take her hands in mine. "We can't do this right now."

She searches my face for meaning.

"We're both trying to work right now. I have Jesse. You have Jeremiah and Natalie's memory. We can't build a loving commitment under conditions like this."

Jesse stands in front of the truck, waiting.

Nikki gives my hands a squeeze. "I'm still holding out for our happily ever after."

"We should focus on what needs to be done and if someday things change—"

Nikki kisses me, cutting off my words.

A little embarrassed that everyone in the fire truck is surely watching, I break the kiss.

Nikki gives me a sad little smile. "Don't let Jesse talk you into anything reckless. Be the voice of reason."

"I'll try. And don't let Jeremiah take your loyalty for granted."

Nikki pushes my hair back behind my ears, her expression heartbroken. "If you need me, call. You know I'll come running."

Chapter 58

Jesse

"Sweet Gee-*zus*." I'm going to throw up in my mouth if I have to watch Sasquatch slobber on Ally for a second longer. "How long is this going to take?"

"Don't enjoy a bit of snogging?" Gideon says. "I do."

"I don't know what snogging is, but it sounds way dirtier than what they're doing."

"It's British for kissing," Maisie says, feeding Winston bits of beef jerky.

"How the hell do you know that?" I ask.

"Harry Potter, *duh*," she says. "Haven't you read them? I have. Twice."

I snort. "Do I look like I have time to read books?"

"My boy Kevin loves 'dem books," a man says.

I jump in my seat, whirling toward the sound. "Holy shit, where did you come from?"

Monroe blinks wide eyes at me. "I didn't mean to scare you, miss."

"He's coming with us." Gloria's face and tone definitely have an I-dare-you-to-say-otherwise fierceness about them.

I shrug. "Whatever. If he stabs me in the brain with an ice pick, it's your ass I'll be haunting."

"Do you really think we should swear so much in front of a child?" Gideon asks.

Maisie gives him a drop-dead stare. "I'm not a child. I'm *sixteen*."

Gideon gives her a devilish grin. "My apologies, madam."

I glare at him. He looks away.

"How old is your kid?" Maisie asks, shoveling a piece of the jerky into her mouth, despite Winston's whining.

"Thirteen," Monroe says. "He loves books and airplanes. They's his two favorite things."

At long last, Ally climbs into the truck, leaving Sasquatch on the sidewalk like a lost puppy.

I snort.

"What's so funny?" Maisie asks.

I consider making a Sasquatch joke, but Ally

doesn't look too happy herself.

I frown at her. "Are you okay?"

"I'm fine," Ally says.

I don't believe her, but with Monroe breathing over my shoulder and Maisie staring at me with half a piece of jerky hanging from her mouth, it's hardly the time to talk.

I turn to Gideon, waiting for him to fire this truck up. "Do you think we can fit this thing through a drive-thru?"

We do not find a drive-through. Most of Chicago is either shut down or in complete chaos. Also, it turns out that taking a fire truck through a drive-thru is a bad idea, since this truck is stolen.

Instead, we drive the truck an hour southeast to Gary, Indiana. I have to say, this place looks more apocalyptic than Chicago did, and Chicago was in flames. We pull off the interstate into a desolate town with run-down, not-at-all-white houses and crappy roads.

Gideon stops the truck at a junkyard. A high fence topped with barbed wire runs along the perimeter. Behind the fence, cars in various conditions stretch as far as the eye can see.

"Wait here." Gideon slides off the driver's seat, hopping down to the gravel road. A man a little darker than Gideon comes out of a squat brick building and meets him halfway. They are laughing and talking in a language I don't understand.

"This is shady," Ally says from her seat behind me. Maisie and Winston are sleeping upright on the end of Rachel's cot. I have to give the kid props. I'm not sure I could have taken a nap by a dead body when I was sixteen. I don't think I was that desensitized to crazy by then.

It makes me wonder if my childhood would've been worse if my father had come back for me. Or maybe not worse, but just as bad in a different way.

We wait in the truck as Gideon and his friend pull two cars up front and begin affixing license plates to the back.

"Really shady," Ally says.

"I don't care if there's a body in that trunk as long as someone buys me a freaking pizza. Or a veggie burger," I beg. "I'm so hungry. I've never been so hungry in my life."

Gideon finally returns. "Okay, get your things. We're leaving the truck here."

Gloria helps Maisie and Winston climb down, and then Ally and I follow. Monroe and Gideon carry Rachel out of the back of the truck to the larger of the two cars. Apparently we're taking this rust-colored clunker to Nashville. It's a boat, as wide as it is long. A faded name brand is scrawled in silver script above the bumper. They prop Rachel up in the backseat and lean her against the door like she's a sleeping person.

"I'll sit beside her," Gideon says.

"I'll sit in the back too," Maisie says and gives Gideon a sheepish sideways glance.

Oh, you like him. I almost say it, but I don't want to embarrass the kid.

"Why two cars?" Ally asks.

"I'm going to take Monroe home," Gloria says. "I'll catch up with you later."

"You're leaving?" I whine. "Why?"

"You'll be able to find us?" Ally says.

Gloria smiles. "Yes. I won't be long. I promise."

Ally hugs her. Then it's my turn.

"Don't push yourself," I say.

Gideon gives her a polite nod.

Maisie grabs Gloria and hugs her though. Gloria's face breaks open with a surprised smile. "It's good to see you again, Maisie. Take care of yourself."

"You too."

We watch Gloria and Monroe get into a car and drive away.

"He better not kill her," I say.

"Jackson could fillet him three ways," Gideon says. "Now, shall we be off?"

"I'll drive," Ally volunteers.

"What about the fire truck?" I ask.

"Ahmed will take care of it." Gideon gestures to the man wiping his hands with an oil rag.

We all climb into the car. Gideon slides in next to Rachel and Maisie climbs into the back, pulling the door closed behind her. I take shotgun up front by Ally.

"She's breathing," Maisie says, and points at the window where Rachel's breath is fogging the glass.

"Thank god," Ally says, adjusting the mirrors. "Now I don't have to worry about being pulled over with a dead body in the car."

Chapter 59

Jesse

Seven hours later, we make the first of three stops in Nashville, my office. Rachel, Gideon, and Maisie wait in the car while Ally and I go in. We do a walkthrough and take everything important. The petty cash, the address book and so on. Ally digs a couple of file folders out of a cabinet and stuffs them into her canvas bag.

"I'm going to bring these granola bars and cookies too. Hopefully they're not stale," Ally says. "Jesse? Are you okay?"

Am I okay? I don't know. I'm standing in the office as if I've never been here before. In my mind I can see myself at the desk, two years ago, giving potential clients pre-death advice. And now—how did I get here? What happened to me?

A man's voice echoes down the hall and my heart lurches. Lane. Lane must be in his comic book store.

A flood of anxiety washes over me. My skin itches and my heart pounds.

"Jesse?"

"I'm okay," I answer. "I'll be right back."

She tucks her hair behind her left ear, her canvas bag hanging loosely in her right grip. "Make it quick."

I open the door to the little hallway that connects the comic book store and my office, passing by the two little bathrooms, their doors partially ajar and rooms dark.

I hesitate at the thought that his door might be locked, another rejection. But the cold handle turns in my grip easily and the door swings inward.

A couple of kids sit on the huge couches playing a video game. Four more are at a table in the corner, laying down cards in turn and laughing riotously. Lane is up at the counter, selling a girl an energy drink from a Coca-Cola cooler behind the desk. I'm surprised by the volume of people. It must be Friday. I can't even keep track of days anymore.

He sees me.

Halfway between giving the girl her change and drink, our eyes meet. The coins clatter on the glass countertop. The drink slips from his grip to hers.

"Sorry," he mumbles.

She shrugs it off, scoops up the money and goes back to her friends on the couch.

I cross the room, hyperaware of how my heart is pounding in my ears. *Did you only love me because Caldwell made you?* "Hey," I say.

"Hey," he says, matching my reserve. "You look great."

"Well, you know, I killed someone and now I can heal on the spot. It's better than makeup."

His brow furrows.

"You never called me."

He looks down. "I know. I was going to, about a hundred times but—"

"How do you feel about me now?" I ask him. *When Caldwell's not in your head making you love me.*

He meets my eyes.

My heart lurches.

"I miss you," he says. "I miss walking into your office and seeing you there. I must have driven past your house a hundred times in the last two months. I cut your yard once in October. We had a warm spell."

I don't know what to say. I squeeze the edge of the counter, trying to steady my weak knees.

"But something's changed," he goes on. "I'm not sure what, but something's changed."

Caldwell hasn't been around whispering into your ear.

"Maybe you're over me." I try to sound casual, but it feels like a giant hand is in my chest, squeezing my heart and lungs to a pulp. "It happens."

"But I'm happy to see you," he says.

"I'm leaving tonight. I'd tell you where I'm going but—" *Caldwell will pluck it from your brain.*

"You're leaving?" he frowns. "Already?"

Maybe what he felt was real. Before Dad talked to him, Maisie had said. But did it matter? Am I here because I want Lane back? No, I don't think so.

"Caldwell's not dead," I tell him. "Until he's dead, I'll always be leaving."

He wraps his arms around me. I startle then soften into his embrace. It *feels* real. I see the shadow of a wing in my periphery, and turn my head ever so slightly. Gabriel stands there in all his glory, his green eyes bright.

I remember Ally in the beach house. Ally with her cute high ponytail and brilliant smile.

I showed you your heart's desire.

I pull out of Lane's embrace. No, it doesn't matter

how Lane really feels. I know what I want.

"Take care of yourself," Lane says, sensing my departure. "Maybe I'll see you around?"

I force a smile. "Anything is possible."

Chapter 60

Ally

Jesse is quiet in the passenger seat on the short ride from her office to her house. I really hope that Lane didn't say anything cold or cruel. It's possible, given her silence. I couldn't discourage her from seeing him though. My parting with Nikki is fresh in my mind. I understand firsthand that if we hadn't said our goodbyes, a sense of unfinished business would pervade, and we need to focus, regroup.

"We're going to grab some important documents, clothes, and food, then we're off," I say, turning my mind to business. I use the rearview mirror to look into the backseat at Maisie, Gideon, and Rachel. "Maisie, you're almost as tall as Jesse. She'll have something for you to wear."

"We have to hurry. I want to get to the cemetery before dark." Rachel tilts her neck from one side to the other.

I imagine she must be as stiff and uncomfortable as Jesse is after a death replacement. But Rachel refused the ibuprofen I took from Jesse's office. I sigh. Having a second, equally stubborn, headstrong, smartass woman around won't be easy.

Gideon keeps close watch on the device in his hand. "We should still be invisible to cameras, but given Caldwell's familiarity with Jesse's home, we should get in and out as quickly as possible. No doubt he's watching the place."

We pull up outside Jesse's house not five minutes later and everyone files out.

"Gideon and I will get the food," Rachel volunteers.

"I'll get Winston's stuff," Maisie says.

"It's in the kitchen pantry. Can you take him out to the backyard to pee too? That'd be a big help," I tell her. Once we're alone, I turn to Jesse. "While I'm getting our papers, can you pack a suitcase? Clothes, toiletries, anything that'll keep us out of the stores for a couple of days. Gideon's device seems to work well, but I don't want to press our luck."

She nods and trudges up the stairs to her bedroom. I hear the closet door creak open and the soft thud of the suitcase hitting the bed.

It takes me a few minutes to tuck all the important files into a small box and tape it shut. Rachel and Gideon dump four canvas grocery sacks of food on the foyer floor. Rachel holds up a bottle of tequila and smiles.

"The drink of my people," she says with a sultry stare. "We will *definitely* break this open later."

"I know how to salsa," Gideon coos, handing her several shot glasses.

"Great. You can teach me," Rachel says.

I'm not sure how to respond to this banter, so I start picking up bags and boxes and carrying them out to the car. I come in the third time and know something is wrong.

The energy of the house has changed.

"Jesse?" I ask.

"He's here," Rachel says, her voice venomous.

I follow her voice into the living room.

Caldwell stands in the middle of the room holding Maisie in a loose headlock. Gideon is in a corner, his back protected on all sides, which is very smart given Caldwell's inclination to pop in and out. Rachel stands beside him, her fingers twitching in expectation. Jesse stands in front of the half-bath where she must have tucked Winston, given the howling and scratching radiating from the shut door.

"We aren't finished," Caldwell says. "Come with me. Both of you." His eyes flick from Jesse to Rachel.

"No," I say.

He glares at me. "You're welcome to join us, Alice. But the dog and the desert brat, I've no use for."

"Let go of her and maybe we won't kill you," Rachel says.

"So we come with you and you let her go?" Jesse asks.

"Don't," Maisie says, her face red. "I'm not worth it."

"You are worth it," Jesse says. "Do you hear me? You *are*."

"Maisie understands her place," Caldwell says. "She knows her mother needs her."

"That's bullshit," I say. "No good mother wants her daughter to die."

I think he'll disappear and reappear in front of me. Maybe he'll snap my neck. Maybe he'll crush my throat. I'm not the only one who senses Caldwell's intentions. The shield goes up, shimmering around me.

"Protect yourself," I tell Jesse.

Jesse gives no sign that she heard me. All of her attention is on Maisie.

"It's okay," Maisie says again. "Really. It's okay. Don't get hurt because of me."

Rachel's hands twitch and Maisie is tugged from Caldwell's arms. His grip loosens, surprised. Jesse runs forward and grabs hold of Caldwell. As soon as she has her hands on him, her body erupts in flames. Caldwell wrenches himself away but he's on fire.

Screaming, he disappears.

I yank the door to the bathroom open and grab Winston. Rachel and Gideon grab the remaining bags off the foyer floor, and the four of us flee the house. Jesse is the only one still inside.

My heart aches. Everything Jesse worked so hard for, this life she built for herself after Eddie, it's all burning. Burning to the ground.

Chapter 61

Jesse

For a minute, I stand in the burning house and watch what's left of my old life go up in flames. If I stay here, I will die, and I'll put everyone else at risk. Ally will insist on staying here until they can recover my body, and it isn't safe for her.

I'm still on fire when I walk out of the house. I have enough sense not to get into the car until I've managed to extinguish my flames though. I take a deep breath and the flames go out.

Maisie runs up to me in the yard. For a second, I think she's going to hit me, but she doesn't. "You're stupid! You should've let me go with him."

"You're stupid if you want to be with him."

"This is what he wants!" She throws up her hands. "When he had me he was talking in my head. He told me I have to watch you, learn all about you and your friends. He said that if I don't tell him everything, he's going to hurt my mom."

I grab hold of her and squeeze hard. She tries to pull away.

"He's going to hurt my mom. I can't stay with you."

I squeeze her a little harder and she goes soft. Her soft sobs vibrate against my chest.

"It's okay," I tell her, placing a hand on her head. "Let the bastard spy if he wants. But you're staying with us."

"I'm going to get you killed," she sobs. "You have to let me go."

"No," I tell her. "We need you. Who's going to take care of Winston while I'm fighting assholes?"

Ally comes up on the other side of us and wraps her arms around us both, sandwiching Maisie between us.

Maisie's sobs quiet. "You really want me here?"

"Of course. Don't be stupid."

She wiggles free of us and wipes her snotty nose on her sleeve. "I don't mind looking out for Winston."

"Good. Now let's get out of here before we're all arrested."

I slide into the backseat next to Rachel, and she immediately wraps her arms around me.

"You're doing so much better than me," she says.

I cast a last look at the burning house. "You're kidding."

"I tried to stab you," she says. "You're just blowing up a few houses. It's fine."

Her earnestness makes me smile if only for a minute. Then the reality that everything I own is burning to the ground hits my chest like a cold stone again.

"We have insurance," Ally says from the passenger seat. "Possessions can be replaced."

But not a life, I think. This life is dead.

Chapter 62

Ally

We pull into the cemetery just as the sun dips behind the horizon. It gives the early winter night a red glow. Now that we're wearing proper coats, I feel warmer than I ever did in Chicago. A thin layer of frost tints the grass between the paved drive and the gravestone.

Maisie wants to wait in the car with Winston, the heater running.

"Will you be okay?" I ask her. "They just need a little time with an old friend."

"I'm okay," Maisie says and snuggles up to Winston.

I bring a thick fleece blanket from the car and lay it down on the grave before the marker.

Rachel is the first to put her hand on the stone, tears in her eyes. "Oh B. You stubborn bastard."

Gideon snorts. "He was that."

"Don't talk about him that way," Jesse says. "He's

dead."

Rachel takes Jesse's hand and squeezes it. Jesse lets her. Then Rachel grabs Gideon's hand and does the same.

I scoot back a little, giving them their moment.

"He'd like this," Rachel says, placing her head on Jesse's shoulder. "The three of us, together."

"Not that we're fighting," Gideon says. "But otherwise, yes, I believe you're right."

"It's my fault he's dead," Jesse says, tears forming in her eyes. "If I could've just killed Caldwell —"

"Hey." I place a hand on her back. "You didn't break Brinkley's neck."

"He didn't want you to fight," Rachel says.

"You don't know that," Jesse says through the snot.

"Uh, actually I do. He asked me to kill Caldwell so that you wouldn't have to."

Gideon is the only one of us who doesn't look surprised.

Rachel shrugs at our expressions. "Everyone is allowed to have their favorites."

Gideon squeezes her hand. "You're mine."

She gives him a placating smile before turning to

Jesse. "And you're mine too, Jessup. Not one person here believes you're to blame for any of this."

Jesse pulls away from her and scoots closer to me. I open my coat and tuck her inside. Her cold hands clasp behind my back.

We fall silent. Jesse grows warm in my arms and Rachel leans against Gideon. We stay there until the last of the light dies and night creeps up on us.

I replay everything that Nikki, Gloria, and Jeremiah told me. *She's going to become less stable as she acquires power. She will be the apex. She will destroy the world. Be her voice of reason.*

I'm the first to break the silence. "At least we figured out who the partis are. We've seen their faces." I give Jesse a brief recap of Brinkley's list and Gloria's belief that there were eight partis left.

"But Cindy and Minli are dead, so that's six," I say.

"Seven," Jesse says. "Because no one absorbed it, Minli's power will transfer to someone else. So there's a partis out there that we don't know about."

Caldwell. Georgia. Maisie. Jesse. Rachel. Monroe...and someone new. "I guess I'll have to go through the list again—but it didn't have Georgia or Maisie on it, so maybe I need a better method."

"Jeremiah said he saw everyone get 'called'." Jesse uses air quotes. "We'll make him tell us who the seventh partis is."

"Should we do that first?" Rachel asks with a mischievous grin.

"No, now we disappear," Gideon says, his eyes still on the gravestone.

"We can't disappear and pretend none of this is happening." Even as Jesse says it, I get a sense that it's exactly what she wants to do. Hope tinges her words.

"We won't be gone forever," Gideon adds, standing and brushing off his knees.

Rachel stands and wraps her coat around herself tighter. "We need some time. We are always reacting to Caldwell. He makes a plan, sets it in motion, and we jump."

It's true. And it was worse when we tried to act under Jeremiah's guidance. I'm glad to be away from Tate Tower and on our own again.

Gideon grins. "We're going to change that. With your lovely talents, tenacious bodies, and my copious amounts of money, favors, and technology, *we* are going to make the plans."

Gideon and Rachel go back to the car, fingers still

laced together. I pull Jesse to her feet and pick up the blanket. Jesse holds the other end, helping me fold it in half, then quarter it.

"What happened with Nikki?" she asks me.

I exhale, searching for the right words. "I like her, but now just isn't the right time."

She nods. "We *do* have a lot going on."

"What happened with Gabriel?" I ask her. I'm hoping she opens up about the apex stuff soon. I can't be her voice of reason if I don't know what he's telling her.

She looks out over the cemetery and then meets my eyes. "He said I can have whatever I want."

She's going to become less stable as she acquires power. She will be the apex. She will destroy the world. I drown out all the voices who want to decide Jesse's fate for her. I push back the fear and find my love. I bring it to the surface of my mind and hold onto the warmth of it until my voice finds me again.

"And what do you want?" I ask.

She smiles, coming closer. She wraps her arms around me, her face nearly touching mine. "I want you."

I smile, drop the blanket, and take her face in my

hands. "You have me."

Keep reading for an exclusive peek at the fifth novel in the Jesse Sullivan series, *Worth Dying For,* coming May 2016.

All this screaming is killing my ears.

"Nine, Eight, Seven—"

I turn to Ally to find that she's counting down with the crowd as well. "I never understood the countdown. Are they trying to build tension?"

She smiles bigger, squeezing my hands in hers. "Six, Five, Four—"

"I mean, it's not like we don't know what's happening." I gesture at the swarm of bodies clustered on the balcony with us and even more pressed against each other in the streets of New York below.

"Three, Two, One—"

"Oh look, the New Year. What a surprise! I had no idea what was going to happen when we reached one!"

Ally grabs ahold of me. "Shut up and kiss me."

I wrap my arms around her waist and pull her

against me. Her hair smells like some kind fruity shampoo and her lips taste like the wine she drank earlier. I kiss her deeper, my hands twining up in her hair. I don't care who sees or what they'll think.

Tonight is all about us. Me and Ally. And Gideon, Rachel, and Maisie. We're celebrating. After weeks and weeks, we finally have a plan for taking down Caldwell. And it's a *good* plan.

Ally pulls back, laughing. "I can't breathe."

"Sorry," I say, without the least bit of sincerity. "I just can't stop."

I pull her close again, kissing her. Then her cheeks, her neck. She devolves into laughter, hanging heavy and drunk in my arms.

"Stop, stop," she begs, trying to pull away.

"I can't. I'll die." But I stop long enough for her to catch her breath and because I know firsthand that if I torment a drunk girl for too long, my chances of getting vomited on increases tenfold.

Gideon and Rachel stumble forward from the crowd around us, arms around each other. Their faces are just as relieved and relaxed as my own. We've done well and we know it. And starting tomorrow, Caldwell is going to regret ever hurting us.

"We should head back," Gideon says. "Or risk being crushed by the crowd."

"Where's Maisie?" Rachel asks, leaning against Gideon. She buries her chin in the neck of her jacket.

"Here," Maisie shouts over the roar. "I'm freezing. So if everyone is done making out, I'd like to go home and check on Winnie pug."

Ally frowns. "We weren't making out. It's good luck to kiss on New Year."

"It is," Gideon adds. "Do you want a little kiss for yourself?" He smiles at her devilishly.

"I will cut you," I tell him.

"I don't need your charity slobber," Maisie says. "I kissed that guy."

We all turn and see a kid not much older than Maisie, also sporting the double black X marks of underage on his hands. He's grinning, goofy but cute. His black hair hangs in his eyes. Black eyeliner encircles his lids. Totally Maisie's type.

I shrug. "Good for you."

"Call me, Michelle!" The boy yells as the five of us start to push our way off the balcony into the dark club.

"Michelle?" I ask, holding the door open for everyone.

"I couldn't give him my real name, could I?" Maisie says.

Good point. We'd been on the run for almost a month. No one knew where we were and we had to keep it that way. I knew that Gideon's fancy gadgets, money and stealth skills wouldn't hide up from my murderous father for too long. We needed to be careful until we *wanted* him to come to us.

I grab Ally's hand and pull her into the club after Maisie. Rachel and Gideon take up the rear. For the few minutes it takes us to squeeze past the bodies toward the street, we're warm. The collected body heat of a hundred revelers is welcome despite the sour smell of beer and sweat.

I reach forward and grab Maisie's hand so we don't get separated. She twines her cool fingers in mine and pulls all of us out toward the street. We regroup on the sidewalk as bodies push past us on all sides. Cold wind frosts my cheeks and I wrap my blood red scarf tighter around my head.

My mouth is covered so I can't speak. I point at my sister's unzipped coat and she looks down.

"Duh." Maisie yanks the zipper all the way up to her chin. "That might help."

Ally wraps around arms around my waist and I tuck her cold hands into my pockets. Then our little group proceeds to march the five blocks back to our hotel.

I see more drunk people than I've ever seen in my life. Of course, if I was also drunk, maybe I wouldn't notice, but I don't drink. Earlier in the night, I'd had two Shirley temples which left a sloshy feeling in my stomach that I'd tried to soak up with super greasy cheese sticks.

A dumb idea.

I probably felt just as nauseated as the drunk people around me.

Maisie shivers in the fierce cold, her hair blowing back as she bends forward, bracing herself against the cold. I pull her in beside me and the three of us cluster behind Gideon and Rachel. Let his behemoth ass block the wind.

As soon as I see the neon sign of our hotel glowing overhead, I rush into the warm lobby. I yank my scarf off my head, pulling the fabric damp with my breath off of my face.

"I'm sick of being cold," I groan. "I'm so glad we're heading somewhere warm."

Gideon gives me a look that I've memorized at this point. *Don't say anything until we're in the suite.*

I roll my eyes and pile into the elevator with them. Rachel is so drunk she mashes the buttons for floors 14 and 16 before managing to hit the correct 15 button.

I look up at Gideon. "She's going to need water or Gatorade or something before she goes to sleep."

He scowls at me. "Really, you act as though I don't know how to treat a hangover. You're the one who doesn't drink."

I shrug. "I'm just saying be sure she drinks some fluids before she goes to sleep or we'll all regret it tomorrow. I've met Hungover Rachel. She's a bitch."

We reach the suite at the end of a beige hallway with red carpet.

Maisie is the first one in. "Winnie Pug? Winnie Pug where are you?"

The pug leaps off the white Victoria chaise in the corner and runs toward her. He presents his belly for a scratch in three seconds flat.

The rest of us squeeze past them into the foyer of the suite. Gideon throws his keycard on the lacquered table by the door. Ally and I kick off our shoes. Rachel pulls off just about every layer of clothing she'd swaddled herself in.

"Such a good boy," Maisie coos, scratching Winston's fur and ears, then patting his fat belly. "You wanna go for a walk? Let's go for a walk."

She finds his leash on a table by the door and slips it over his head.

"It's freezing out there," Ally reminds her, still hanging on to me. "So don't be too long."

"Yes, Mother," Maisie says, but she's smiling. I think she likes the way Ally babies her, even though Ally can't be more than nine years older.

Gideon disappears into the dark bedroom with Rachel and softly closes the door behind them. I plop the buzzed Ally on the couch.

"So what'll it be?" I ask her. "Water? Juice? I don't think we actually have Gatorade but I can walk down to the convenience store."

"Water's fine," she says, grinning up at me. A light pink blush spreads over her cheeks. She finger combs her hair. "My hair is so pretty. I love my hair."

I snort. "I love your hair too."

"What else about me is cute?" she asks.

"Just about everything," I say.

If I wasn't worried about destroying her liver, I

might be tempted to get Ally drunk all the time.

Gideon steps out of the dark bedroom and passes me to the mini fridge, grabbing one of the wrapped water glasses over the top.

"Grab us one too," I tell him. I have zero problems designating tasks to other people. Sometimes I wonder if it was a mistake going into death-replacing. Dying for other people is cool, but I'm really good at bossing people around instead. It's like a calling.

Gideon fills two water glasses with some fancy bottled water from the fridge and handed me a glass. I don't dare remind him that Ally vowed not to drink the water yesterday. She ranted about the effect of plastic on the environment. I didn't want to remind her that the planet is about to explode anyway. That's means Gideon would've won the argument and I'm team Ally all the way.

I put the glass of water in her hand. What she doesn't know won't hurt her. "Here you go. Drink up."

She waves her water around. "I just feel so *good*, you know?"

I smile. "I can tell."

She grins, running a hand through her hair. "It's a new year. A new beginning. And we have a great plan for kicking Caldwell's butt."

"We do."

"And you're so cute," she says. "Life is good."

With arched eyebrows, Gideon closes the bedroom behind him. Thankfully, the sound of the television comes on, drowning out any sex sounds that might come next.

I plop down on the couch beside Ally and help her sit up. I want her to drink this water. I tilt the glass toward her lips, encouraging her.

"This is good," she says and frowns at the water. "Is this tap water?"

"Yep," I lie.

"Because I'm not drinking that $8 water Gideon bought."

"It's tap," I say again. "You're just too drunk to taste it."

Ally shrugs and finishes the glass. Then she hands me her empty cup.

"You want more?" I ask.

"No," she grins. "I want something else."

"Food? I think we've got chips, but that's about it."

She shakes her head, grinning.

Then I realize what she's saying.

"Oh," I smile. "Okay."

She crawls over the pillow between us and pulls herself into my lap. She straddles me, wrapping her arms around my neck. She kisses me once on the cheek, probably a missed target rather than sweet and then manages to get my mouth.

She pulls back. "God, it is you or is it really hot in here?"

"We're still wearing our coats."

She laughs and looks down at herself. "Oh. Right."

I reach up behind her and pull her jacket down. "Better?"

She snuggles up to me. "You're still hot."

"Thanks for noticing."

"Let me help you take your coat off."

"Okay." I let her attempt to pull off the jacket but it's not really going anywhere and she accidentally pulls my hair twice. So I help her get my jacket off and throw it over the arm of the couch.

Ally doesn't stop there. She slips her hands under my shirt, giving me a curious look. "Is this okay?"

It's more than okay. She would have been naked

an hour ago, in the grubby bathroom of some bar if I didn't have a conscious. But Ally and I haven't had sex in a couple of years and doing it while she's drunk seems a little sleazy.

"What's wrong?" she asks. "Don't you think I'm pretty?"

"Don't be stupid."

I reach up and pull her down into my arms. I kiss her, even more deeply than I did on the bar's balcony. I slip my hand under her shirt and unsnap her bra with one twist of my fingers. So much for moral withstanding.

She gasps in my mouth and the sound of it makes my whole body shudder. I stand, still holding on to her and drop her on the sofa. She laughs, surprised, but her voice goes all deep and breathy when I climb on top of her, positioning myself between her legs. I kiss her neck and she squirms, bucking her hips up against mine.

"Do you love me?" she asks.

"More than anyone."

"Are you sure?"

I cover her mouth with mine. "Please stop talking." I pull back. "Unless you want me to stop."

"No, no." She forces me down on top of her.

I have the button of her jeans between my forefinger and thumb when a voice calls behind me.

"I'm so sorry to interrupt, but you need to see something."

I turn and see Gideon standing in the living room, his back to the bedroom he shares with Rachel.

"Worse timing," I groan. "Can it wait?"

"No," Gideon frowns.

"Ugh." I pull myself off of Ally.

"You too," Gideon says to Ally. "If you're feeling all right."

She frowns. "I'm fine."

"I'm not," I grumble as I pass him.

"The news program ends in a few minutes. Then you can go back to doing whatever you like, if you can stomach it." Gideon's voice is grave.

I stop and look up at him, frowning. He just points to the dark bedroom, where the blue light of the TV dances along the walls.

I creep inside, trying to be quiet when I realize Rachel is storing louder than a train. Gideon put her in her PJs, but the glass of water sits untouched on the nightstand beside her.

Gideon lifts the remote from the bedside table and turns up the volume. But I don't need to hear to know I'm not going to like this.

Caldwell, my homicidal father stands behind a podium, his face a mask of grief. Tears that I'm certain are fake as hell, stream down his face. Even in his beautifully tailored suit and nice haircut, he looks like shit. The woman beside him, Maisie's mother Georgia, doesn't look any better.

"We just want our daughter back," Caldwell says to the sympathetic crowd. The camera pans to the crowd and there isn't a dry cheek in the house.

"We want the people responsible for this to be brought to justice. We'll give a reward to anyone who knows something."

The camera cuts to the reporter, who also has tears in her eyes. "The following suspects are wanted for questioning: Jesse Sullivan—"

My mugshot from last year flashes up on the screen. Not the most flattering picture, I must say.

"Rachel Wright—"

Rachel wearing her mental hospital gown flashes up on the screen. At least she looks a little worse than I did.

"Alice Gallagher—" Ally's driver's license photo fills the top right of the screen, making our square ¾ complete.

"Captain Gloria Jackson—" An old photo of Gloria from her days in the military flashes up on the screen. She looks sharp in her uniform.

"And an unknown man who is believed to be helping the trio. He's of Middle Eastern descent and believed to be a radical Islamist, and the man responsible for the bombings in Chicago that took so many lives."

"What racist bullshit," I say, half-choking on the words. "Caldwell blew up the city himself!"

"Any information leading to the capture of these criminals or the return of Maisie Caldwell will be justly rewarded."

Gideon turned off the screen. "My devices can't hide us from the public, only technology. It is only a matter of time before someone spots us on the streets."

"I'm not hiding!" I tell him.

"Jesse," Ally goes on. "We will all have to hide. If we go to jail, there's no way we can stop Caldwell."

She's right. Dammit.

I look up at Gideon. "But what about our plan?"

"It can still work. We will just have to be more cautious with our movements."

I accept his answer with a sense of unease. I wish I could ask Gabriel what he thought, but I haven't seen him except for once or twice since we left Chicago. I know he's still there. I can *feel* him so to speak. But he can't materialize as long as Rachel and I are together.

"Just don't tell Maisie," I tell them, looking from Ally's face to Gideon's. "If she knows, she'll do something stupid and heroic like turn herself in, trying to save us. And we need to stick to the plan."

Gideon clears his throat and cuts his eyes over my shoulder.

I turn and find Maisie standing in the doorway, her expression dark. Winston sits at her feet, his collar and leash still around his neck.

I can tell by her face that she heard every word.

Acknowledgments

I would like to gratefully acknowledge all of the proofreaders and editors that helped me bring Jesse's story fully formed into the world: Angela Roquet, Monica La Porta, Kathrine Pendleton, Karen Sahagian, Katrina Pitts, Juliann Krute, Colleen McGuire, Andrea Cook, Joe Thomas, Rachel Menzies, Ashley Ferguson, Wendy Nelson, and CC Ryburn. A special shout-out goes to Michelle Pike for her keen eye and take-no-prisoners approach to editing. Without you guys, the story wouldn't be nearly as good.

Many thanks to those who first showed love for *Dying for a Living* and no less enthusiasm for this fourth book. There are too many to name, but I adore every single one of you. Your encouragement makes the hard days easier.

Thanks to John K. Addis for his help with the cover and author photo. If you haven't read his awesome book The Eaton, you're missing out.

And thank you, Kimberly Benedicto, for your unending support and encouragement. You've given me five beautiful and happy years. Life wouldn't be the same without you.

About the Author

Kory M. Shrum lives in Michigan with her partner Kim and a ferocious guard pug, Josephine. She'd love to hear from you on Facebook, Twitter, or her website.

And if you like her work, she asks that you please support her by reviewing it, wherever possible.

Made in the USA
San Bernardino, CA
16 July 2017